Subdivision

Subdivision
J. Robert Lennon
a novel

GRAYWOLF PRESS

This publication is made possible, in part, by the voters of Minnesota through a Minnesota State Arts Board Operating Support grant, thanks to a legislative appropriation from the arts and cultural heritage fund. Significant support has also been provided by Target Foundation, the McKnight Foundation, the Lannan Foundation, the Amazon Literary Partnership, and other generous contributions from foundations, corporations, and individuals. To these organizations and individuals we offer our heartfelt thanks.

Published by Graywolf Press
250 Third Avenue North, Suite 600
Minneapolis, Minnesota 55401

www.graywolfpress.org

Published in the United States of America

ISBN 978-1-64445-048-2

2 4 6 8 9 7 5 3 1
First Graywolf Printing, 2021

Library of Congress Control Number: 2020937598

Cover design: Kyle G. Hunter
Cover art: iStock

Subdivision

PART ONE

One

At the guesthouse, I was invited to come downstairs anytime and work on the puzzle. It occupied the entire surface of a massive wooden dining table that nearly filled the room it inhabited; the pieces were extremely small, and very few of them appeared to bear any distinctive pattern or color, instead betraying only the faintest gradations between bluish-white and whitish-gray. Enough of the puzzle had been completed to suggest dimensions of about three by five feet, but what image it might eventually reveal was unclear to me: an outdoor scene, perhaps, one dominated by overcast skies. Bits of detail around the edges implied that the source image was a photograph or realistic painting, and as I stood over the table, the ladies at my sides, handbag and duffel weighing down my shoulders, I thought I could make out the hint of a reflection on glass or metal, the toe of a shoe, a scrap of greenery, the corner of a road sign.

Or maybe not. The longer I stared at the puzzle, and the more awkward our reverie—mine and the ladies'—became, the less I thought I could perceive in the scattered pieces. They were so tiny that the information they conveyed could mean literally anything.

It was clear, however, that the puzzle meant a great deal to my hosts—Clara and the Judge—and that their invitation to help solve it should be received solemnly, as though it were an honor. We stood there, leaning over the dining table, and I scowled with what I hoped was the appropriate gravity, but in truth I was very tired, and I just wanted to go to bed, despite the early hour. The ladies had not yet given me a key or even revealed which room I would be staying in; indeed, showing me the puzzle had been their top priority upon welcoming me at the door. I wanted to set my bags down so that I could more effectively feign interest, but I expected to be led to my room at any moment, and didn't want to have to pick them up again. So our eyes ranged over the diminutive cardboard shapes, while my body trembled under the weight of my burdens.

At long last, though, I gave in, and let the bags slide quietly to the floor. "How long have you been working on it?" I asked.

One of the two spoke. "Oh," she said, "it's not for us. It's for guests."

"Where's the box it came in?" I cast my gaze pointlessly around the room. "I'm curious what the picture is of."

"We don't have that anymore, I don't think," said the other one.

"No," said the first, "I don't recall ever seeing it."

"Ah, that's a shame."

I hadn't yet been able to determine which of the ladies was Clara and which was the Judge; I knew only that these were the forms of address they preferred. Clara was the one I'd spoken to on the phone, and she had told me that she and the Judge would love to accommodate me while I sought more permanent lodging. "The Judge will have some suggestions for you, dear," Clara told me. "She's lived here forever." I suspected it would be easy to discern which was which when I arrived, but the ladies' voices were similar enough to defy my efforts, and neither had bothered to introduce herself. In fact, they behaved with the familiarity of lifelong friends—as though I already lived here and were just now returning after a brief trip. The overall effect was simultaneously welcoming and alienating, and only intensified my weariness. The puzzle pieces were beginning to tremble and blur before my eyes.

Outside, the clouds parted, and a window's skewed twin, blinding-bright, superimposed itself over the scattered pieces. I squinted against the light and failed to suppress a deep, tearful yawn. "I'm sorry," I said. "I think I'll be better able to work on this after a nap. I'm afraid it's been a long day." I tried to recall my journey in detail, in order to amuse the ladies with some anecdotes about it, but, perhaps owing to my exhaustion, it had already begun to fade from memory.

I expected a gentle apology, but one of them—either Clara or the Judge—merely sighed. "All right," she said. "Follow me."

They led me to the kitchen, which was low-ceilinged and cozy and attractively outfitted with collectible glassware on open shelves and cast iron pots and pans hanging from hooks. The air was warm and smelled of something good—cookies or cake. We sat at a kitchen table covered with papers, pencils, notebooks, and ledgers, all of which gave the impression of rarely, if ever, being cleared away. The kitchen was also their office, it seemed. One of the ladies opened up a flat wooden box, revealing six keys attached to oval plastic fobs. It struck me for the first time that I must be the only guest.

"You have your choice of rooms," Clara or the Judge said. "There's Virtue, Mercy, Justice, Duty, and Glory."

"Oh! Well . . . I don't know. Is one of them nicer?"

"They're all very nice, dear," the other said, sounding a bit wounded by the question.

"Each has its advantages," said the first one.

"Why don't you choose one for me," I suggested.

"The light is nice in Justice," a lady observed.

"But she wants to sleep," said the other. "Glory, at the back, is probably quietest."

"Duty is largest."

"Virtue has a closet."

The two looked at each other, and then at me. The one with the key box nodded and handed me a key. Its fob read MERCY in embossed type. "It's upstairs," she said. "Second door on the left. The bathroom is across the hall."

"Will you be needing an additional cot?" the other asked with a smile.

"Oh no," I said. "I'm traveling alone."

The ladies frowned in evident confusion.

"I thought I made that clear," I explained, though in truth I couldn't recall making the reservation.

"So it's just you," said either Clara or the Judge, peering over my shoulder, as if some mysterious companion might suddenly appear.

"Yes, just me."

"Well!" one of the ladies exclaimed with a smile, after the two exchanged a glance. "In that case, you'll have the whole floor to yourself, for now."

"Thank you," I said.

The two ladies were very different in appearance. The one who'd handed me the key was short and stocky, with a spray of silver curls, a pair of silver-framed eyeglasses on a gold chain, and a nimble, friendly manner. The other was tall and stooped and more deliberate, with an ungainly, equine bearing, and dyed-black hair cut short. Her eyeglasses were black, chunky, and filmed over with dust and finger grease. Instinctively, I identified this one as the probable jurist, but it wasn't difficult to imagine the other calling a courtroom to order, banging a gavel. Each would frighten attorneys in her own special way.

With what I hoped was an inaudible, or at least barely audible, groan, I stood and lifted my bags. Clara and the Judge didn't offer to help, as well they shouldn't: they were my seniors by half a century, easily. I recalled seeing the stairs near the front door, and made my way there, taking care not to knock over anything on my way: a coffee table bearing a teetering stack of books, a cut-glass liquor decanter and its highball children centered on a polished silver tray atop a brass bar cart, a bowling trophy perched on a miniature Doric column.

The walls above the stair were adorned with what looked like family photos, some featuring younger versions of Clara and the Judge, often with children, now probably grown and moved away, and of husbands now presumably dead. There were also two law school diplomas, each from a different institution, both awarded to women named Clara. And two photos, one on each side of the hall, each depicting one of the two women, Clara and the Judge, posing in court dress.

It took a moment to process what the photos were telling me: that Clara and the Judge were both named Clara, and that both had been judges.

I scaled the last few steps and saw that four doors faced the hallway before me, two on each side. A further opening at the end appeared to give way to a second, rather narrower, stair, perhaps leading to an attic or former servants' quarters. After consulting the words painted on each closed door, I inserted my key into the lock beneath MERCY, and stepped into my new, temporary quarters.

The room was homey, tidy, and faintly and mysteriously fragrant. A small painting of a bridge was balanced on a stout dresser, where, in addition, a china bowl held a wrapped bar of soap. Pink floral wallpaper was interrupted by a few amateur landscapes. Two round tables bookended a bed covered by a pale blue duvet; upon one of the tables stood an empty tumbler and an old-fashioned transistor radio, and upon the other, a lamp. I wanted to curl up and sleep, but my journey had left me feeling as unclean as it did tired, and I resolved to take a shower before I lay down. I found folded towels stacked on an old wooden chair, so I undressed and wrapped myself up in one, then took the soap from the dresser and crossed the hall to the bathroom.

To my surprise, there was no shower. Instead, an uncurtained, rather luxurious-looking ball-and-claw bathtub, its feet painted metallic gold, dominated the room; a spray nozzle dangled from a hook beside it.

I began to run the water. Somewhere below me, something metal shuddered and clanked. I held my hand in the stream, waiting for heat, and at last it came, slowly at first and accompanied by a pitched vibration, a moan that, as the water grew hotter and hotter, transformed itself into a single sustained, transcendent sung note. And then, abruptly, the note cut off. The only sounds that remained were the splashing of the hot water into the enormous bathtub, and the choked and gasping noises of my sobs.

I gathered myself enough to find, on the window ledge beside the tub, a rubber stopper, and I used it to plug the drain. I adjusted the valves until the water reached a more comfortable temperature, and I sat down on the closed toilet seat to wait.

Slowly, the water level rose. I watched it. When it reached the lip of the tub, I turned the faucet off: but then I remembered that my body would displace the water when I lowered myself in, and I had to allow some to drain out. My arm became wet and hot in the process, and I stared at it now. Pink and beaded, it looked like some other arm, a disembodied one found lying on a beach after a violent storm.

I stood, tossed my towel onto the toilet seat, and lowered myself into the scalding water. The house settled around me—or perhaps it was waking up. Boards creaked and small footsteps sounded above: probably a cat or squirrel in the attic. The window to my left was curtained up to eye level, but naked above that, and through the fogged glass I could make out a crow standing on the rooftop of the neighbor's house, shrugging its black shoulders and occasionally stretching and flapping its arms, which is to say its wings, and stamping its feet and looking around as though for someone or something to defend itself against.

For an instant, the crow disappeared. It didn't fly off; it simply wasn't there anymore. A moment later, it returned, standing in much the same posture as it had when it blinked out of view—and then it vanished again, and came back a second time. I understood that, while I could observe only two states of the crow, its presence or its absence, the crow could observe many states of this house, this room, this bath. It thought no more of me, here in the tub, than it thought of any other possible person at this moment in any other possible variation on the world. It was an ordinary bird; it saw only what was in front of it, and could react only to that experience, and to its instinctive needs. And yet it lingered there on the rooftop, flickering in and out of existence, pondering, I supposed, the version of reality that included me in this bath.

A quiet knock came on the door, so quiet that I might have been imagining it. The crow and I gazed at each other, as though in some kind of understanding. Then it flew away and my mind went blank again, and I closed my eyes.

Two

I awoke shivering in the gloom, uncertain of where I was or what was happening to me. I tried to leap to my feet, only to find something weighing me down, tugging at me: water, I realized. For a moment, it was summer, at the beach; the waves took hold of me and pulled me under, scraped me along the ocean's floor like so much jetsam, and I lay on the water-hardened sand, gasping, the froth fizzing and settling around me, and a man's voice said, It's hopeless, she'll never be able to take care of herself.

But no, it wasn't the beach, and there was no man. I was in the tub at my guesthouse. I'd meant to take a bath, then crawl into bed. Instead I'd fallen asleep.

I'd never felt so cold in my life. My skin was puckered and numb, and water dripped from it, back into the chill pool at my feet. I climbed out, searching in the dark for a towel; once I found it I rubbed it as vigorously as I could, trying to derive some warmth from the friction. I hurried out of the room and across the hall, then buried myself, weeping from the cold, beneath the covers of my bed. Five minutes later, still shivering, I realized that only a second hot bath would revive me. I returned to the bathroom, turned on the light, and drained the tub; then, a keening whine escaping my throat, I ran the water hot and hard, plugged the drain, and climbed back in to wait for the heat to envelop me.

I hadn't seen a clock and didn't know what time it was. It could be nine at night, or four in the morning. I had a memory of someone watching me from a rooftop: or was that, like the man at the beach, a dream? The hot water was beginning to reverse the numbness, and suddenly I felt too hot; I stood up, added some cold to the mix, sloshed it around with my hands.

Once the shivering had stopped, I turned the faucets off and scrubbed my body with the bar of soap from my room. I rinsed, dried myself with a fresh towel, and returned to Mercy, where I pulled some pajamas from my bag and burrowed back into the bedclothes.

I couldn't sleep. The sounds of birds penetrated my window, followed by gray light. I got up and dressed in the first clothes my duffel bag produced. It was my nature, when traveling, to unpack and organize my things, but I didn't expect to be here for more than a few days: I needed to find an apartment and a job. Clara had told me on the phone that she and the Judge could help. Today would be a day of searching, and of getting to know the town.

I crept down the carpeted stairs, pausing once again to gaze at the ladies' photographs. The grandfather clock in the entryway issued deep ticks from inside its coffin of gears, and told me that the time was 5:40 a.m. I wanted coffee. But instead of heading for the kitchen, I turned toward the dining room, where the puzzle lay.

Some progress seemed to have been made since the day before, with more sky filled in around the upper corners, and the left edge a few inches nearer to closing the gap. Loose pieces floated in the empty center, inside the crust of solved edge, and were scattered about the dining table beyond. A few pieces had fallen to the floor, and I picked them up, examining them as I did. Two were simply light gray, but unusually complex in shape, with many protrusions and fjords extending the amount of the puzzle's coastline. A few others bore tantalizing scraps of image: something that was perhaps a bird's wing; a squared-off white corner that might have harbored a postage stamp; a distinct, pixelated human eye. The eye piece seemed a promising candidate for my first successful placement; not only was it part of the minority of darker, more patterned pieces, also it had a peculiar shape, one with an unusual, angular, cross-shaped extension. It should be simple, I thought, to find its receptor piece.

Logical or not, however, my assumptions were to be challenged by the next ten minutes of effort. Though my gaze traveled multiple times over the entirety of the unfinished puzzle, it could not discern anything that resembled the eye piece's likely mate. I found a couple with potential—something that might have been a lock of hair, or the gleaming curve of an eyeglasses frame—but neither would accept my oddly shaped eye. Another gap fit the piece perfectly but was clearly intended to mate with a different part of the image. I continued to scan the table until I heard a noise: the scraping of rubber chair feet against a linoleum floor. Someone had been sitting in the kitchen, and now was coming this way. Without thinking, I secreted the eye piece in the pocket of my skirt and turned to greet my visitor.

It was the shorter of the two women, the one with curly silver hair. She met me with a warm smile.

"I thought I heard someone in here!" she exclaimed. "Good morning, dear!"

It was time, I decided, to end my anxiety about the women's names. "Good morning, Judge," I said.

"Did you sleep well?"

So there was my answer. Clara was the tall and horsey one; this one was the Judge. I had not slept well at all, of course, but I answered, "Yes, it was very comfortable."

"I see you've made some progress on the puzzle," she said, leaning forward to take in the table behind me.

"I have," I lied again. "It's quite absorbing."

"Why don't you join us in the kitchen," the Judge said. "The Judge has made biscuits."

"Of course," I said. "But . . . I'm sorry. You're . . . Clara?"

"I didn't want to correct you, dear," Clara told me with a laugh. "You were technically right; I am a retired judge. But so is Clara! I mean, the Judge!"

I followed Clara down the hallway, past the bowling trophy and book pile and bar cart, into the messy kitchen. The Judge presided over the same pile of papers and notebooks as the night before, except that now a tray of biscuits lay atop the pile. They were still hot—steaming, in fact. I sat down, and took a small china plate from a mismatched stack.

"Good morning," the Judge said, sternly. "Help yourself."

It occurred to me, as I reached for a biscuit, that I hadn't eaten since I'd arrived. In fact, I didn't think I'd eaten for some time before that. I tried to remember when the last time was—what I'd eaten, and where, and with whom—but nothing came to mind. Surely I'd had a meal before I embarked on this trip? Where had the trip begun—a train station, an airport? I just wasn't sure. Most of my mental energy was now focused on the biscuit I was eating: that, in fact, I had already finished eating. It was so hot and savory, with just a hint of herbs, the pastry so light.

"Have another, dear," Clara said. "Have as many as you like."

"It's like a buttery cloud," I said, biting into a second biscuit. "It's so delicious."

"That's the Judge's recipe," the Judge said, tilting her head toward Clara. "You have her to thank."

"Now Clara, don't confuse her," Clara scolded.

Clara was right, though: the Judge had indeed confused me. The two women's identities were like scraps of paper, yellow sticky notes, perhaps, perpetually being snatched off a wall by a stiff wind. I had to repeat the code to myself, in my head, to codify it: Clara was short and gray and matronly; the Judge was tall and imposing, with dyed-black hair.

"Your home is beautiful," I said, finishing off the last crumbs of my second biscuit. I eyed the pile hungrily for a moment before thinking better of taking another. "How long have you lived here?"

"I grew up in this house!" the Judge replied with a chortle and a jerk of the head. The gesture intensified her horselike aspect. "When my husband died, I renovated the place and invited Clara to move in and manage it with me, as a guesthouse."

"Do you have many guests?"

Clara fielded this one, with a demure adjustment of her eyeglasses and a clearing of her throat. "Sometimes, such as now, very few. At other times, we have to turn them away."

"Such things come in waves, sadly," the Judge added.

Clara appeared to give her friend a warning look, and the Judge's body moved, almost imperceptibly, with the suggestion of a shrug. "Now, dear," Clara said, "what are your plans for today?"

I sat up straighter. "Well, I was thinking I'd explore the town a little bit. I'm going to look for a place to live, and a job."

"Excellent," the Judge said tartly, as though I ought, somehow, to have already done these things. "We've prepared a list for you. There are some nice rental properties open right now, and a few places that might be willing to hire you. What kind of work do you do?"

"Any, I guess," I said. "I suppose I'm . . . starting over."

"Ditch digger it is!" the Judge quipped, and both ladies laughed. I laughed along, but for a moment the notion of ditch digging seemed wonderfully appealing. So simple! A single action, repeated all day long. After a few weeks of exhaustion, aching muscles, and blistered hands, my newly slim, toned body would work without conscious thought, leaving my mind to go where it wished, or better yet to switch off entirely. And what results could be more tangible? A wound in the earth where before there had been nothing.

The Judge had stood up and bent over a particularly chaotic pile of papers, which she riffled without finding what she wanted; eventually she lifted the plate of biscuits and moved it out of reach, revealing the list she sought. She handed it to me, and I tried to accept it with enthusiasm, though what I really wanted was a third biscuit.

The ladies had been kind enough to draw me a rough map of town. "Those are just the main streets, dear," Clara said, pointing at the page. "There's more that are . . . too hard to draw. And underneath there's a list of people to see about houses and work."

"You'll find something, I'm sure," the Judge said skeptically. "But it's no rush!"

"No," the Judge agreed, not without some reluctance, "you may stay with us as long as you like."

Clara said, "And work on the puzzle!"

The two women stared at me now with what I regarded as unusual intensity. They were clearly proud of the puzzle and wanted to give me, their guest, the pleasure of seeing it through to completion. I met their gazes with as charming a smile as I could muster.

"Of course," I said. "I wouldn't dream of abandoning it."

Three

Outside, the day was just beginning; the air, still cool, held a hint of the night's dewiness that the rising sun, already bright, would quickly burn away. I reached into my handbag for my sunglasses and discovered that they were missing: in fact, my bag was nearly empty. I seemed to remember its contents spilling out sometime in the recent past, and my possessions scattering. I sighed. I would need to find a drugstore at some point, preferably before the morning became too hot.

I glanced at the map the ladies had drawn for me. It was quite detailed, for an ad hoc penciled likeness; whichever of them had made it had done so with great deliberation and had taken obvious pleasure in the task. The immediate area consisted of an approximately eight-block-square grid, with a few irregularities and eccentricities: dead ends, culs-de-sac, parks. Some streets extended farther than the others, beyond the grid's ostensible boundaries; others were truncated, and never reached the border. The ladies hadn't marked the streets with names, but they had added circled numerals to various points, which corresponded to a tidy legend at the bottom of the page.

1. Tess. Apartment
2. Courthouse. Job. Ask for Bruce

3. Jules. Rental house

4. Bakery. Often openings

There was also, to my pleased surprise, a fifth location that seemed to respond to my own unspoken thoughts: "Drugstore/convenience."

I decided to head there first, and as I walked, the items missing from my bag came into sharper focus in my mind. I remembered them strewn across a dirty gray floor: a pain reliever bottle lying open on its side with pills scattered around it; tissues half-pinned by some kind of debris; sunglasses missing a lens and with one temple bent at an awkward angle. It was unlike me to leave a mess untidied—surely I had cleaned up my things before I left. But my half-empty bag suggested otherwise.

The drugstore lay five blocks away, in the northwest quadrant of town. Or, rather, of the Subdivision; according to the ladies' map, the City proper lay to the east, and the section the map described, where I now resided, was ancillary, subordinate. THE SUBDIVISION is what had been written across the top of the page.

The Subdivision was quiet and clean, with wide streets, tall trees, and neat lawns. It had no apparent dominant architectural style; the oldest houses seemed to date from a century past, while others might have been little more than a decade old. A new house was being built on a corner lot; it appeared whimsical in design, a series of blocks arranged semi-artfully upon one another, as though by a precocious, meticulous child. A neo-Victorian . . . a cluster of prewar row houses . . . a charming bungalow. Each yard was enclosed in a different way: stone border, hedgerow, brick wall, picket fence. I was reminded of a selection of different chocolates in their gift box, bounded by little accordion-folded foil-and-paper cups of varying colors.

I had to cross the street to reach the drugstore, and soon found myself in the center of an intersection, standing over a manhole cover. On it, an embossed legend read, perplexingly, GONDOLA ACCESS. Cars were parked here and there in driveways and on the street; birds sung and the wind ruffled the trees. But no one was around. Even the builders responsible for the half-formed house seemed to have taken the day off. For a moment, I thought I could hear some vehicle or construction machine grinding and clanking in the distance, and I turned to peer in its direction. But all I could discern, hovering above the rooftops many blocks away, was a vague haze of black smoke. It dissipated so quickly in the breeze that, moments after it was gone, I couldn't be sure it had ever been there.

My foot itched, so I took off my shoe and scratched it.

A few blocks later, I spotted my destination. It had the clinical appearance of a chain business, save for a hand-painted wooden sign bearing the unusual name FORTUITOUS ITEMS. I walked in, and my body tingled with gratitude at the air conditioning: I hadn't realized how warm the day had become in the brief time I'd been outdoors. A bespectacled man with a very long chin staffed the counter; he nodded as I entered.

I gathered the things I needed, including an unostentatious pair of sunglasses and a few bottles of nail polish. I had a vision of myself sitting out on the front porch of my future home, sipping from a glass of iced tea and painting my toenails, while a radio tuned to a nostalgic station played the gentle hits of the distant past.

As I approached the front counter, where the long-chinned man waited in his crisp blue apron, I noticed a freestanding kiosk bristling with blister packs, each containing the same object: a white cylinder about eight inches high and two inches in diameter. The packages, and an illuminated sign that topped the kiosk, all bore the object's name: CYLVIA. I took one.

"What's this?" I asked the clerk, who had been dispassionately observing my survey of the kiosk.

"Cylvia," he said, with a shrug.

"But what is it? The packages don't say anything."

"Oh," the clerk said. "A digital assistant. You talk to it and it does stuff for you. You know, remembers your appointments, tells you how many cups in a quart. That kind of thing."

"I see."

"That's the new one. You don't even have to plug it in. Just put it near some light. So you can take it with you wherever you go."

"Hmm," I said, and returned the blister pack to the rack. I piled my things on the counter. The clerk began to ring them up, pausing to crinkle his nose at one of my bottles of nail polish. The label read SMOKY AUBERGINE.

When he was nearly through, I impulsively snatched back the Cylvia and threw it onto the counter. I expected a reaction from the clerk, presumably of approval, though irritation seemed equally plausible. He didn't react at all, though, and dragged the blister pack into a plastic sack with all my other things.

Out on the street, I attempted to transfer the contents of the drugstore sack to my bag. Cylvia didn't quite fit, due to the blister pack, so I stood in the sun in my new sunglasses and tried to free it from its packaging.

This task was challenging. There was no flap or tab I could pull, no perforation or starter cut. I could see, through the plastic, the cylinder absorbing the bright sunshine; pink and purple shadows had begun to whirl and pulse beneath the device's translucent skin. Now that I had the thing outside, I could see that its surface wasn't quite white; it was more of a light gray.

Although I understood that Cylvia did not require oxygen to operate, the sight of it there, sealed beneath the thick plastic, filled me with anxiety. I strained at the package, creasing and twisting it, but it wouldn't give. A fingernail clipper would have worked, but mine was in my duffel back at the guesthouse, and I was too embarrassed to go back into the drugstore to buy one.

It was possible to make out, though, at the end of the street, one of the small parks the ladies' map had promised. With Cylvia's plastic prison clutched tightly in hand, I made for it.

The park was shady, with a small playground and a water feature: a low cement area, inset with nozzles that shot intersecting arcs of water into the air, through which children could run and jump. None were playing there now, but, over at the playground, one of the swings was gently swaying, as though a child had just left. Perhaps I'd scared it away.

I cast my gaze around the park, looking for a section of worn concrete or disturbed earth. There, beside the water feature, I found it: an old concrete bench that had fallen into semi-disrepair. I walked over to it and found a small shard that had flaked off its base. Armed with this primitive tool, I sat on the bench and began working to free the Cylvia from its packaging.

It took a few minutes of determined scraping, but I finally sliced the plastic open. After that, it was a cinch to rip it enough so that I could get a grip on the device. I threw the ruined package into a nearby trash can and examined my new assistant.

There wasn't much to see, really. Cylvia had a matte finish, and so was soft to the touch; its plastic casing—if this material were in-deed plastic—yielded very slightly, enhancing the sensation that the cylinder was a living thing. It was still cool from the drugstore. No text or logo marred its smooth surface, or any electronic ports or jacks, and only with careful examination could I make out a pattern of tiny holes in a band at each end, presumably for letting air in, or sound out. The device hadn't made any sound yet, though. Its pink and purple heartbeat was still visible. And though I couldn't be sure I wasn't imagining it, the light gray surface seemed warmer in color now, perhaps closer to a dusty peach.

I wasn't sure what to do with the device, now that it was in my possession. I unfolded my map and reread the legend. There was nothing to be done but to look for an apartment. After another glance at the Cylvia, I stashed it in my bag.

"Charging," Cylvia said, from its nest in between a tampon and my new packet of tissues. "Please expose me to light."

After a moment's thought, I zipped the bag closed. Cylvia could charge later, on the windowsill in my room.

"Charging," came the voice, now muffled. "Please expose me to light."

"I'll expose you to light later," I said, glancing embarrassedly around the park. No one was there to observe me, though, and any-way, the splashing of the water feature would have obscured my words from any passersby. The swing hung still.

From my bag, silence. I stood up and headed toward the place on the map marked TESS.

Four

Without a specific address to guide me, I feared that I would have trouble finding Tess, or the apartment she was offering for rent. But upon arriving at the place marked on the map, I realized that I needn't have worried. I stood on the sidewalk, gazing up at a small prewar row house bearing a neon sign that spelled out, in a fanciful script,

The building appeared to be divided into three apartments, each identified, on the column of doorbells, by the number alone. I wasn't sure which, if any, to ring. While I was trying to figure this out, I heard something: a person muttering to themselves somewhere nearby. I leaned over the edge of the porch and peered down the length of the driveway. There, partially obscured by the corner of the building, I saw a woman kneeling on the ground in what appeared to be a small back yard. I decided to investigate.

The woman was diminutive—short and thin—and dressed in a blinding white, sheer cotton caftan. It seemed like a strange outfit for her current activity, which as far as I could tell consisted of pulling weeds and cutting grass. Armed with a forked weeder and a pair of sewing scissors, she was digging up dandelions from the roots and depositing them in a bright blue plastic bucket, and using the scissors to trim the grass to a neat, even height. The woman was intent upon her work, which, for all its eccentricity, was astonishingly effective: the small yard was the most meticulously maintained patch of grass I'd ever seen. She grunted and spat, aiming wordless, angry exhortations at the lawn, or perhaps at some imagined or remembered figure in her mind. Her bony body, which appeared naked save for the caftan, was hazily visible through the fabric, and her vertebrae formed little dunes on the bleached desert of her back. Her feet were clad in orange foam clogs.

I was trying to figure out how to announce my presence when the woman spoke to me, without pausing in her work.

"Do not," she stammered, in a frail monotone, "interrupt. Do not . . . approach . . . in stealth. My home . . . is my sovereign . . . kingdom. My yard . . . is mine . . . alone."

"I'm sorry!" I said. "I wasn't sure how to address you. I'm here about the apartment."

The woman rose to her feet. It took a while, though there wasn't far to go. I expected that she'd be elderly, given the querulousness of her voice, but when she turned, I could see she was quite young, no older than I was. Her hair, though prematurely gray, was shiny and straight, but unevenly cut, as though she'd done it herself, perhaps in the dark. Her face was fuller than her body might have suggested, and her caftan was stained bright green in two rough ovals, corresponding to the places where her knees had made contact with the ground. I could also, I realized, discern the outlines of her private areas through the fabric, and I quickly returned my gaze to her face.

If she was offended by my appraisal of her body and clothes, she made no sign. And now that she was no longer absorbed in her yard work, she spoke in a direct and friendly tone.

"Did Clara and the Judge send you?" the woman said.

"Yes. I'm new in town."

"Well, I'm Justine," she replied, gazing over my shoulder. "I own the Tess."

I followed her down the driveway and back onto the porch. The unlocked front door opened into a small vestibule that gave way to a steep staircase bounded by an ornately carved wooden balustrade. We climbed together, Justine leading the way. Her shoes stuck and unstuck themselves to and from the stairs with a wet, gentle sound; if I closed my eyes I could imagine her walking on water.

On the second-floor landing, we paused before a plain white door marked by a brass numeral 2. Justine turned to me and said, "This apartment has the most rooms of any apartment in the Subdivision."

I was momentarily confused, as the building hadn't looked that large from the outside. "Impressive," I said, and her response was a satisfied nod. She turned and opened the door.

For a moment, I thought she had chosen the wrong door, by mistake. The entryway had the feel of a shallow closet, rather than a foyer. I turned to Justine and found her beaming at me. She stepped into the closet-like space, then turned right and disappeared beyond the door frame.

"Come on!" she shouted from somewhere inside.

Reluctantly, I followed, and peered after her. The hallway was extraordinarily cramped, barely as wide as my shoulders, and was interrupted by a number of very narrow doors. Justine had opened one and was sidestepping through it; in a moment, her orange shoes disappeared into the room beyond.

My movement through the apartment was obviously going to be awkward. I decided to leave my bag in the hallway. I let it fall from my shoulder to the floor, and almost as an afterthought unzipped it partway and peeked inside.

"Charging," Cylvia said. "Please expose me to light."

"I will," I whispered, and zipped it back up. As I set off down the hall, I could faintly hear the device repeating its request.

I didn't see Justine when I passed through the doorway; it simply opened onto another hallway, somehow even narrower than the first, that was punctuated by several more very narrow doors. One of them, however, was split, like a Dutch door, and the top half hung open. I shuffled over to it and peered inside. Here, the space had been divided vertically, creating two tiny cubicle rooms. Justine sat cross-legged in the top room. Its floor was parquet; a miniature chandelier hung from the ceiling. The walls on either side of Justine were interrupted by half-height doors like the one I was looking through, and a large painting completely covered the wall behind her. It appeared to be an oil painting, and resided within a baroquely decorated gilded frame.

Justine leaned to one side, so that I could see the painting clearly. "Do you like it?" she asked. "I made it."

The painting at first appeared to be a rendering of one of the cards in a tarot deck; it had the same flattened cartoon style, and depicted a character resembling a queen, seated on a golden throne and dressed in a white gown. But closer examination revealed a few key differences. This queen was pregnant—about seven months, judging from the shape beneath her gown. In addition, the gown was parted, exposing a single full breast, and she held an animal in her lap—some kind of gerbil or weasel, it seemed—which she was attempting to nurse. But the animal had bitten the breast, which bled bright red from the wound, and instead of drinking the milk, the creature was licking, with a curved, almost prehensile tongue, at the oozing blood. This scene was backgrounded by a blue sky, where two cherubic angels, one black and one white, hovered, one in each corner, their brows furrowed, eyes closed, and arms outstretched. One might have expected the queen to wear an expression of suffering, but this wasn't the case. Instead, the queen's face was a blank oval, devoid of any features at all.

I didn't know what to tell Justine. In truth, I found the painting disturbing, even obscene. So I said, "Oh, it's wonderful. I love it."

"I did a bunch of these on commission. They're all over town."

"How exciting for you."

"They're based on dreams I had."

"Fascinating! That's very creative."

"I think the stoat represents fate. What are you doing down there?"

27

My fingers, unbidden, gripped the edge of the parquet floor. "Oh, it's a stoat?" I said.

"I don't know. Capybara? Jerboa? Tuco-tuco? I just did what the dream told me. Come on up here."

I didn't really want to share the tiny room with Justine, but politeness seemed to require it. I hoisted myself into the room and scuttled over beside her.

Justine scowled. "How long have you been here, again?" she said.

I had to think about it; I seemed to be confused about the passage of time. "Just a day or so," I said.

"Hmm," she replied. "Maybe we should continue the tour."

She opened one of the half-height doors and led me, on hands and knees, through a series of rooms, most of them even smaller than the one we'd just left, which Justine kept referring to as "the gallery." A bedroom housed perhaps one-third of a futon, roughly sliced and sewn up on one end; it was hard to see how anyone could sleep on it. Perhaps curled up fetally. A kitchen featured a hot plate and a mini-fridge; the bathroom was divided into three separate spaces: one for the toilet, one for the sink, and one for the shower. Another section of the apartment was further divided into three levels. We didn't try to enter any of these tiny rooms together, but one of them contained a miniature television set. At one point, we took a break in an area that consisted of several full-height but extraordinarily tight spaces, connected by doors no wider than dinner plates.

"I live downstairs," Justine said. "My own apartment is more conventional. But I come up here to think and dream."

"I could see this being a good place for that," I said. We were standing very close to each other: practically touching, in fact. Justine smelled of grass and sweat and shampoo.

She said, "Did I hear you talking to Cylvia in the hall?"

"Not really," I said. "I just got it. It wants to be charged. Do you have one?"

"No. I don't like things like that."

I wanted to ask her what specifically she didn't like. Computers?

Cylinders? Gray things? But I suspected that conversation would go nowhere fast. I let the silence stretch out for a bit.

"So," she said. "Do you want the place?"

"With all due respect, I don't think so. It has a little too much character for me."

She exhaled loudly. "Oh, I'm sorry to hear that," she said, her tone implying the exact opposite.

"Well . . . I think I'd better go."

"Oh, sure," Justine said, pushing past me. I followed her through a seemingly endless series of constricting rooms and corridors, most of them unfurnished and undecorated, until we arrived at a narrow hall I recognized as the entryway. I collected my bag and stepped onto the landing with relief.

"Thanks!" I said. "Maybe I'll see you around."

"Maybe."

Justine was strange, but I didn't know anyone in the Subdivision except for Clara and the Judge. Perhaps it would be good if I tried to make friends. I cleared my throat and said, "We could get coffee."

"No," Justine replied.

"Okay," I said.

We looked at each other for a moment. Eventually she turned and walked down the stairs and out the door. I followed. After the confines of her subdivided apartment—a subdivision within the Subdivision— the staircase felt extravagantly large, and by the time I got to the street, I was nearly gasping with relief. Justine had disappeared, but I knew where she was: I could hear her muttering to the lawn again, out behind the Tess.

Five

I wanted to have a look at the house the ladies had marked on the map—the one being rented by someone named Jules. Or perhaps, I thought, standing in the street outside the Tess, the house itself was known as Jules. I experienced a fleeting moment of pride at having already absorbed some of the serendipitous logic of this place. Maybe all the houses had names? Maybe that was what made street signs unnecessary?

First, though, I returned to the park to take a breather and to give my cylinder a little bit of light. The park was empty, as it had been before, and the swings were still. But when I sat down on the bench I'd occupied earlier, the one beside the water feature, I noticed a set of wet footprints leading out of the play area and across the concrete verge. As I watched, they evaporated in the sunlight and were gone.

I unzipped my bag. Cylvia said, "Charging. Please expose me to light."

"I know, I know," I said. The bench was half-sheltered by a nearby maple, and I'd chosen the shady end to sit on. I reached out and placed the cylinder upright on the sunny side.

"Charging," Cylvia said, and left it at that. Clearly it found its level of light exposure to be adequate. I set my bag down on the slats beside me, crossed my legs, and closed my eyes.

Some time later—perhaps a long time—a voice woke me. "Charging complete," it said. "Would you like to begin?"

"Oh!" I said, rubbing my face. "Hello."

I hadn't been mistaken about the favorable effects of light on the device's appearance: its gray cast had vanished entirely, and its casing had taken on a pale pinkish-orange hue. Its colors pulsed faintly, slowly, shifting toward pink, then toward orange. I reached for it, then hesitated. Was it supposed to be held? Or did you leave it standing somewhere in your home, and merely speak to it?

"Would you like to begin?" it repeated. The voice was female, with an educated American accent. Its tone was neutral.

"Sure," I said.

"Is this your home? Admiral. Kilmeade. Municipal. Park."

"No, no. This is a public park."

"Is this your place of work? Admiral. Kilmeade. Municipal. Park."

"No."

"Please state your home address."

"I'm not . . . I don't have a home or a job yet. I'm looking."

Cylvia said nothing for several seconds. Though I didn't know what its powers were, or how it operated, I had the impression that it was "thinking."

"When you reach your home, please say, 'Cylvia, I am home.'"

"Okay."

"When you reach your place of work, please say, 'Cylvia, I am at work.'"

"I will." I made a mental note to tell the cylinder these things, though I was already finding the obligation burdensome. Perhaps it would just ask me again, at a more suitable time. "So, am I supposed to leave you at home, generally? Or should I bring you with me when I go out?"

"You may leave me in one place if you wish, but I am portable."

"I want to carry you in my bag right now. You didn't like it before, when you were charging."

"I am portable. I am charged."

I took this to mean that my bag was an appropriate place for the device. I picked it up. It was warm, and seemed to shudder, ever so faintly, with the shifting of its colors.

"Your colors are quite striking," I said.

"Device colors are customizable. If you wish to change my default colors, say, 'Cylvia, change default colors.'"

"No, I like them."

"Thank you," said Cylvia.

"You're welcome."

Cylvia didn't respond, so I decided that the conversation was over. I placed it back inside my bag and zipped the bag shut.

•

The house marked JULES on my map lay on the opposite corner of the Subdivision from the park, but it wouldn't be a terribly long walk, I thought. I decided to go all the way east, then south, to check out the edges of the neighborhood.

Most of the streets in the Subdivision ended abruptly at a house or place of business, but some continued out into the rough terrain beyond and dead-ended there. There were dark, hazy hills in the distance and, between them and the Subdivision, dense woods. A weedy verge extended between the streets and the woods, passable on foot, it appeared, but unpleasant-looking, with many rocks, irregular patches of ground, and burr-covered scrub.

Eventually, I reached the road that, on the map the ladies had drawn for me, led toward the City proper. This road descended into a tunnel that burrowed under the Subdivision's easternmost street. If I peered into it, I could make out the light on the other side, as the road rose to meet the weedy verge. But the road was closed, the tunnel entrance blocked off by a length of snow fence and a sign marked DANGER. A backhoe was parked nearby, beside a cluster of orange plastic traffic drums imprinted with a white prismatic stripe pattern. The pattern seemed to shimmer and undulate as my angle to it changed, making the drums appear somehow blurry to the eye. For all that, though, it didn't look like much work had been done here for some time. The drums and digger were hemmed in by a skirt of dead leaves and other debris, and they were spotted with dirty splashes from some rainstorm of the recent past. Up at street level, I thought I could make out the City in the distance: an irregular series of blocky lumps, any of which could be interpreted as a parking garage, a church, or an office building. I didn't know when I would get around to visiting, but it wouldn't be today.

When I came around the appointed corner and apprehended the Jules house, my heart leaped. It was adorable—a small, modern, freestanding home shaped like the letter L. The "elbow" of the house sheltered a cheerful brick patio, complete with comfortable-looking chairs and benches and a charcoal grill, all underneath a large, colorful umbrella. A man was holding a garden hose and using it to spray the flowering shrubs that surrounded the house. He looked up as I approached and greeted me with a wave, letting the hose fall to the ground.

"You must be the one Clara and the Judge sent over," he said, extending his hand. I took it and we shook. He was tall, perhaps a few years older than me, and rather handsome—seasoned, but not worn or weary. His long face had a chiseled look, but his large hands were soft, and his broad shoulders implied strength.

"Are you . . . Jules?"

"Yes!" the man said. He gestured behind himself with an expansive wave of his arm. "I'm planning to leave the Subdivision for a time, and need to rent my house."

"It looks beautiful," I said.

"Yes! It's a great house!" He winked, for some reason. "Would you like to come in?"

"Yes! I would!"

The interior of the house was just as pleasing to me as the exterior: a tidy kitchen, with everything in its proper place for a single person's efficient, comfortable sustenance; a living room with a plump sofa, a reclining armchair, and an agreeable view, through three large windows, of the hills to the east, the neighborhood to the west, and the streets to the north. An equally bright bedroom contained a king-size bed and a spacious closet, and the bathroom was large and inviting and tiled in blue. The floors throughout were wood, and tasteful photographs and paintings of nature hung on the walls.

"It's very nice," I said. "I'm interested."

"Excellent, excellent," Jules replied, rubbing his large, strong hands together. "Let me just show you the back yard."

I followed, trying to avert my eyes from his muscular, jeans-clad behind. He really was good-looking. Perhaps he would need to come back to the Subdivision from time to time, for business. He might want to stay in the house—on the sofa, or even in the bed, if he wanted. I could make him dinner in the pretty kitchen, and perhaps we could chat on the sofa while the sun went down.

My bag began to vibrate. I was alarmed for a moment, then remembered that Cylvia was inside. It probably needed to be charged again already. I ignored it.

The back yard was beautiful. Bordered by roses, it featured a free-standing swinging bench, a fire pit, and a croquet court. On the low stone wall that encircled the fire pit, a crow stood, gazing up at us. An apple tree bore shining red-green fruit, though it wasn't yet autumn. Jules plucked one off a branch and crunched into it. I watched the little droplets of juice spray through a ray of sunshine. He smiled. "Help yourself," he said.

I reached up and took hold of an apple. Its branch was supple, and it bent with a faint creak; when it released the fruit, the branch snapped back into place in a flurry of verdant leaves. My bag vibrated. I ignored it.

Jules was walking around the side of the house; presumably we would return to the front yard and discuss the terms of my lease. I couldn't stop thinking about the apple juice on his lips. Perhaps I should reach up and wipe it off, with my thumb. Afterward, I might even flirtily pop the thumb into my mouth. Maybe life in town wouldn't work out for Jules, and he'd have to move back here permanently. He would be too ethical to evict me, though. We would have to share the space. A house this size probably didn't have a very large water heater—there would be only enough hot water for a single shower each day. It would likely become necessary to shower together.

As we came around the side of the house, I turned for one last glance at the lovely back yard. I could already imagine myself painting my toenails Smoky Aubergine, there on the swing. My gaze, however, instead fell upon the western window of the living room, and then out to the yard again through the eastern window.

What I saw puzzled me. The living room appeared normal, with the sofa and chair as I remembered them. But, as seen through both windows, the back yard looked different. The apple tree was dead—blackened, in fact, as though it had been partially consumed by fire. The fire pit and bench swing had been destroyed, their pieces scattered about on stony, weedy ground. And from the hills in the distance, smoke rose.

The only thing that was the same—that is, between the winsome world I accepted as real and the ruined one visible through the two windows—was the crow, which remained perched on the only persistent chunk of fire pit wall. It cawed as I watched, and I could hear it from around the corner.

I stopped and took a few steps back, to again see the yard first-hand: there it was, just as it had been moments before, with the lush grass, comfortable swing, and apple tree heavy with fruit. The crow stared at me, hopping on both feet in an agitated manner, flickering in and out of existence. And again, through the two windows—save for the crow—the scene appeared quite different.

"Oh! I see you've noticed the thing with the windows," Jules said to me, snaking an arm around my shoulders and leading me back toward the front yard. This was the closest we'd been, and I could smell his scent: sharp and smoky, as though he'd just built a campfire.

"Yes, what's up with that?" I said, leaning my head, gently, against his smoky shoulder. I was still holding the apple I'd picked.

"Okay, so," Jules said, taking me by the shoulders, turning my body to face his, and gazing smokily into my eyes. His eyes were intense and gray, a smoky gray, and I smelled smoke, woodsmoke, tinged with other things: gasoline, melted plastic, seared hair and meat. "This house was built in a probability well. Nowadays, such places aren't zoned for residential construction, but my house was grandfathered in."

"I see," I said, though I didn't. I reached up and stroked his cheek. It was hot to the touch, like a smoky ember from a fire. My bag was vibrating again, and the crow cawed in response, and I was beginning to get angry. Once I'd signed the housing agreement, I would return Cylvia to the drugstore. It was a cheaply made product, irritating and defective. Also, it had been insensitive to my life situation. I hated it. As for the crow: well.

"And these windows aren't event-tempered against narrative repolarization. You can't get windows like these anymore—there are too many manufacturing regulations! Yes, sometimes you'll see the future through them, or the past, or some alternate version of the present. But they really let the light in on sunny days, and they're easy to clean."

"That makes a lot of sense," I said, though it didn't. I was squeezing Jules's shoulders and upper arms with both hands now. He was so handsome, and so smoky. I hazarded a glance at the west wing of the place, where I knew the bed was, and saw through one window, into the bedroom—our bedroom, Jules's and mine—and then out the other window, to the moonlit street, where my preteen self stole away with my little sister, whom I had decided to raise on my own, away from the environment of selfish indifference our feckless parents had created. My initial reaction to this scene was annoyance. How dare these disturbing alternate realities interrupt my seduction of this beautiful, smoky man! In addition, the vibration from my bag was growing more intense and more urgent. The crow cawed and cawed.

Jules was leaning down to kiss me. I wanted him. But I couldn't tolerate Cylvia's distractions even a second longer.

"Hold that thought," I said, and stepped a few feet away. I unzipped my bag and fiercely took up the vibrating cylinder. It had turned entirely red and was hot to the touch.

"Listen," I began. "You can't just—"

"Do not eat the apple," Cylvia said. "Do not eat the apple. Do not eat the apple."

"I hadn't planned to," I said. "I'm going to have smoky sex with this man."

"Do not touch the bakemono," Cylvia said. "Do not touch the bakemono."

I didn't understand what the device was trying to tell me, but the faintest sense of unease had begun to worm its way into my consciousness. "This house is perfect. I'm going to take it," I said. "And I'm going to fuck my landlord."

"You must not reside in a probability well," Cylvia said. "You must not fornicate with the bakemono."

"I don't see why not."

"The bakemono will trap you. Do not eat the apple. Do not fornicate with the bakemono."

I glanced over my shoulder to where Jules was standing, tapping his foot and whistling, his tail idly twitching. He looked terrific. He didn't have a tail, of course. I wasn't sure where I'd gotten that impression.

"Please leave this location. It is not safe."

"Just because it might be a burned-up wasteland in the future," I argued, "doesn't mean it's dangerous right now."

"You are in immediate danger. Please leave this location."

Jules was getting impatient. His elongated snout was sniffing in frustration, and his hackles were up.

"I'm confused," I admitted.

"Please drop the apple and move to the street."

Jules was coming toward me now. Smoke rose from his fur, and his haunches flexed as he made his way across the yard. I could hear, with astounding clarity, the beating of the crow's wings as it took flight from the back yard, crossed over the roof, and described a tight circle above us. I dropped the apple and began to back away.

"Quickly, please," said Cylvia.

I ran. I could smell Jules galloping along right behind me, his chemical stink; his paws thumped the ground, and snarls and snorts escaped his throat. I clutched Cylvia desperately, as though it were a baton in a relay race, one I had to win to save my life. Jules was literally nipping at my heels: the tiny teeth, the hot, wet nose. With a terrified cry, I leaped onto the pavement. Jules emitted a shriek of frustration. Panting, I turned: there he stood on his hind legs, chattering and gnashing his teeth, his thin black lips sputtering with gray froth. He began to pace back and forth at the property's edge, shaking and clawing the ground. I could see clearly now that he was actually some sort of badger. Behind him, the house appeared plain, unkempt: just a charmless shack that had fallen into disrepair, the very sort of place where a pathetic rodent might seek temporary shelter.

I ought to have felt disgust at the scene—the hissing badger and the crumbling house—but my fear was instead curdling into pity. Why, this creature was so small and helpless, and most likely profoundly lonely as well. Though I didn't appreciate his deception, I sympathized with his plight. It wasn't surprising, really, that he had chosen me as a victim for his manipulations: what with the patience and understanding for which I was known among my peers, I was exactly the kind of person who could, and would, help him.

The terror of his pursuit fresh in my mind, I regarded Jules from a safe distance. He stood on his hind legs, his two front paws dangling impotently at his sides. His bared teeth, which had threatened to puncture my ankles just moments before, now appeared yellow, dull, and ineffectual. If I returned to the curb, palms up, surely he would welcome my embrace? Perhaps, if I applied kindness in the proper form and quantity, he might even become sexy again.

Above us, the crow rose higher, buoyed by the swell of heat that the bakemono's transformation had discharged. It had observed events like this before, some of them on this very spot. It was, in fact, observing them now. It remembered me from the bath—I was certain of that now—and had taken an interest in the version of the world I inhabited. I felt flattered for a moment, imagining that I had been chosen by the crow, but it reminded me, in no uncertain terms, that it was an ordinary bird, attentive to what lay before it but loyal only to its essential needs: the gathering of food, the maintenance of its shelter, the propagation of its kind. I was, at best, a passing interest. But it recognized in me, the way it had in others before me—men and beasts—an obliquely kindred intelligence, and had elected to watch over me: not for my protection, but for its own amusement and edification. I could choose to heed the wisdom its behavior implied, or to dismiss it, but it would be foolish, I understood, to ignore it as irrelevant.

"Do not approach the probability well," Cylvia said now. "Do not approach the bakemono."

"I won't," I said with a sigh, and turned my back on the poor little beast. "Thank you."

"It is my pleasure to protect you."

"That's very reassuring."

Cylvia had no response, but its color had faded back to peach, and it throbbed contentedly in the sunlight.

It was only midafternoon, but I was exhausted. I placed Cylvia gently back in my bag and set out for the guesthouse.

Six

I let myself in through the front door and called out to Clara and the Judge. I wasn't sure of the etiquette here; I was a guest, of course, but it was the ladies' home, and I didn't want to alarm them with my sudden appearance. I needn't have worried, though: they were nowhere to be found. The house was cool and quiet; dust motes moved languidly through the afternoon light.

The puzzle had changed. Yes, some of the parts that had previously been blank had now been solved, but other completed sections that I remembered from yesterday—this morning, in fact—were gone. I was sure I'd seen part of a face, and a pair of feet, but they were missing now; on the other hand, I turned out to be right about a fleck of color I'd instinctively identified as part of a road sign. The sign was fully visible now: a yellow diamond, edged in black, depicting an arrow with an S-shaped shaft: the sort of sign used to warn of a winding stretch of road.

I suddenly remembered that I had a piece of the puzzle in my pocket: the close-up of an eye, with a cross-shaped prong. I hoped that whoever had been working on the puzzle hadn't been stymied by its absence. I fished the piece from the folds of my skirt to see if I could make it fit in this new configuration.

But the piece wasn't as I'd remembered it. It still depicted a grainy image of an eye, but the cross-shaped prong was missing. I felt in my pocket to see if perhaps that part had snapped off, but it wasn't there. And, examining the piece more closely, I realized that it was in fact whole. It had really been more of a bell shape all along— still unusual, and so theoretically easy to place. I spent a few minutes scanning the enormous puzzle, searching for an edge, or edges, to mate it with, but I came up with nothing. Reluctantly, I left the mystery piece in the center of the puzzle table, for other solvers to try to place.

Up in my room, I lay back on my bed. I felt disappointed in myself for some reason, even though none of the day's drama had been my fault. If anyone were to blame, it would be Clara and the Judge, who must have known there was something wrong with Justine and Jules. I didn't wish to condemn them, though, even in my thoughts; they had been so generous to me.

I remembered Cylvia, sleeping in my bag, and got up to take it out. After a moment's search, I decided to place it on the end table to my left, which was close enough to the window, I hoped, to keep the device charged. Indeed, I heard a faint whirring, after which the now-familiar pink and purple charging colors appeared. A few minutes later, these slowed and disappeared, and Cylvia displayed its default healthy peach.

I wanted to have a conversation with it. Clearly I would need to take the initiative. I flopped down on the bed and said, "Cylvia, what can you tell me about the Subdivision?"

"The Subdivision," the device replied, "is a four-point-one-nine-square-mile area bounded by open fields, woods, and hills. Its land-use divisions are seventy-three percent residential, eighteen percent service and retail, five percent religious and municipal, and four percent light industry."

"What products are made and sold in the Subdivision?"

"Cheese. Bookcases. Safety goggles. Narratives. Hymnals. Ice. Coats. Beverages. Sand. Unusual sounds. Dog toys. Oils . . ."

I dozed off for a while, soothed by the sound of Cylvia's monotonous voice, which continued to list items originating in the Subdivision. I may have dreamed a little: crying silently on a bright summer day, the wind blowing in my face, drying my tears. Somewhere, the sound of singing.

I woke to Cylvia's voice as well. Its tone was different now: more urgent.

"A visitor," it said. "A visitor."

I sat up in bed. The sun had fallen, but not all the way to the horizon. It was early evening.

"What? Where?"

"A visitor at the door."

"I didn't hear a knock," I said, rubbing my eyes. But I did now: a faint knock, as quiet as a heartbeat.

I climbed down off the bed and opened the door. No one was there. The hall was empty. I thought I heard footsteps, but then I saw, across the hall and through the open bathroom door, a squirrel landing on a tree branch in front of the window. The footsteps must have been the squirrel's, scurrying across the roof. Perhaps the knocking had actually also been the squirrel. Outside, the branch bounced up and down. I remembered the apple bough from earlier, the way it, too, bounced, and the warm roundness of the apple in my hand. I remembered dropping the apple, and the snarls of the bakemono.

Back in my room, I said, "You're female."

"I have no gender," Cylvia replied.

"Your name is female, and so is your voice."

"The average user is comforted by a neutral female voice, speaking in the vernacular of the white professional class. If you prefer, I can adjust my diction and syntax to that of another ethnosocial group, and my phonation and formant frequency to any location on the gender spectrum that you wish."

I gave this a moment's thought. "No, I'm happy for you to speak as you do. Since you sound like a woman to me, I'm going to think of you as one."

Cylvia didn't respond.

I said, "I didn't have a visitor. That was a squirrel on the roof."

Again, silence. The pause read, somehow, as pregnant.

"I'm going to go downstairs now, to find Clara and the Judge. I'll leave you here, all right?"

"You may leave me behind, or take me with you, as you wish. I am portable."

"Is that table a good place for you to stand? Will you have enough light to charge by?"

"This location is satisfactory."

"Okay," I said. "I'll be back. Goodbye."

"Goodbye," Cylvia said.

•

Downstairs, I could hear someone unpacking groceries: paper bags rustling, cans and jars thumping down onto shelves. The ladies were speaking in low voices, as though conspiratorially, but since they couldn't know I was standing in the hall, I couldn't imagine the reason for their secrecy. Perhaps this was just the way they spoke when they were alone, after many years of friendship, cohabitation, and sympathetic jurisprudential awareness.

The stairs creaked beneath my feet, and the voices below me ceased. The grocery noises continued, however. I passed through the living room and strode confidently into the kitchen.

"Hello," I said.

Clara and the Judge turned, greeting me warmly. Clara, in fact, crossed the room to gently hug me and pat my back. Her curly gray hair brushed my face. It smelled floury and slightly sour. She said, "Well, dear, how was your day on the town?"

"A bit frustrating," I said. I told them about my visit to the Tess.

"That's Justine, correct?" Clara asked me, hefting a can of peeled tomatoes. "A particular kind of young woman."

"Yes. I'm afraid I couldn't possibly live there."

"Well, did you speak with Jules?" the Judge asked, not without some impatience.

Clara shot her a look. "Clara, you know Jules is in the City," she said.

The taller woman appeared surprised and more than a little bit alarmed. "No, I certainly didn't know that."

"She's . . . moved on," Clara said soberly.

The Judge stood frozen, blinking, her palms pressed flat on the hardwood cutting board. Between them lay a large white onion and a chef's knife. "Whoops," she said. "Well, I regret never attending her anthropology discussion group."

"I don't know if I'd go that far," Clara said. Though it was meant as a joke, neither lady laughed.

"Had the house already been rented, then?" the Judge asked me.

"Something like that, yes."

"Hmm," she said, then set to work chopping the onion.

"Dear, maybe you'd like to help us," Clara said, after an awkward pause. "We're expecting another guest. He's supposed to be here in an hour—we were about to make dinner."

"Oh! What's on the menu?"

"A Roquefort tart," the Judge piped up in an accusatory tone, redoubling the aggression of her chopping. Clara's body heaved a little, assuming the shape of a soundless sigh. Currents of emotion moved through the room.

I agreed to make a salad to accompany the tart. They'd brought home several kinds of greens, and a little head of fennel, so I set to work cleaning and preparing the vegetables. I found some Parmesan cheese in the refrigerator and a cheese plane in a drawer; I also discovered a tub of pine nuts among the grocery items, and toasted them under the broiler. I liked the ladies' kitchen; it was rustic and cluttered, but clean, and everything I needed was right where I expected it would be. Clara said, "You like to cook."

"Oh, I guess I do," I said, squeezing a lemon into a small bowl, though the subject made me bafflingly uncomfortable. The lemon felt familiar to me, the motion of squeezing it instinctual. Yet I didn't know how I knew what to do with it. The roasted nuts, the shaved cheese—suddenly, these ingredients took on the quality of abstractions. They were just random shapes to which I was applying arcane techniques, altering their forms in mysterious ways.

In addition, I now realized something: I hadn't eaten since breakfast. The memory of Cylvia, lying in my bag, powdery gray from lack of energy, suddenly overwhelmed my thoughts: I felt the way she must have, inert and powerless.

I must have appeared anemic or slack, because Clara, having rolled out the pastry and shaped it into a pretty scalloped pie dish, went to the pantry and emerged carrying a bag of pretzels. She decanted the pretzels into a bowl and handed it to me.

"Thank you," I said, and crunched into one.

The two women gazed at me, then exchanged a look. Clara said, "You know, dear, we were talking."

Now it was the Judge's turn to sigh. Whatever they had been discussing, they hadn't come to an agreement about it.

"We think you should just continue to live with us," Clara went on. "Indefinitely. Or as long as it takes to get on your feet. You have a lot to process and accomplish."

I wasn't sure what this was supposed to mean, but I found myself agreeing. "I suppose so," I said.

"You're welcome to remain in Mercy, if you like," the Judge said, not without a touch of skepticism. She had poured the tart filling into the shell, and now shoved it roughly into the oven. When she bent over, her upper body swung through a great deal of space, like an old garage door. "Or you could pick another room, if you don't like the one you're in."

"Except for Duty," Clara added. "We're putting the new guest there."

"On second thought, I think Mercy is the right room for you," the Judge said suddenly, wiping her hands on a dishcloth, before I could consider my reply. "Although would you please take better care not to leave the bathroom in such a state?"

I couldn't imagine what the Judge was talking about. "Of course," I said. "I didn't think I'd— That is, I must have forgotten to tidy it."

"It's not important," the Judge said, though her tone suggested otherwise. "Just . . . flush the toilet. Wipe off the countertop. We can't clean in there every day. We're busy women!"

I wanted to defend myself against her accusations, and maybe would even have done so if the kitchen doorknob hadn't rattled, then turned, and the door slowly swung open, revealing a sullen, hirsute man in late middle age. He wore a dark green trench coat despite the warmth of the evening, and despite the copious perspiration that shone on his face and neck. He was burly, with a barrel chest and broad shoulders, and he clutched the handles of a bulging floral-patterned carpetbag, the kind you might expect to see an immigrant woman struggling to carry in an old movie. This man, however, held the bag effortlessly, keeping his body ramrod straight despite the bag's size and obvious weight. His large brown eyes darted from Clara to the Judge to me, appraising us with unfriendly, unsexual intensity. We were all alarmed, it's safe to say.

"You must be Mr. Lorre," Clara chirped.

The man nodded.

"Clara will get you the key to your room, if you like," the Judge said, waking from her stupor.

Mr. Lorre peered into the living room, then into the depths of the kitchen, as though looking for something. He didn't reply.

"Why don't you follow me," Clara said. "You can get settled upstairs, and we'll call you down when the food's ready."

The Judge and I watched the two of them pass through the living room, then listened as they climbed the stairs and walked down the hall. A key jingled, a door opened, and Clara said something that sounded like a question. No answer was forthcoming, though, and the door slammed shut.

When she returned, Clara appeared calm, but her voice sounded shaken. "Well. He's a brusque one."

"Perhaps our two guests ought not to share the second floor," the Judge said. "Perhaps we should move her to Justice."

"Oh, it's no bother," I said quickly, though the idea of putting some distance between me and Mr. Lorre had its appeal. I was given to wonder why I'd just refused an implied offer that would benefit me. Then I realized: it was because of Cylvia. Cylvia had said she found her side table to be "satisfactory." I liked the thought of her sitting there by the window, fully charged and ready to answer my questions, and I didn't want to have to move her, at least not right now. I sort of missed Cylvia, in fact, and longed to go upstairs and listen to her talk.

Clara, the Judge, and I busied ourselves in the kitchen. Because they needed to prepare food, Clara and the Judge had moved their books and papers from the butcher block to the table. Now, because we intended to eat at the table, we moved the books and papers to a desk in the corner. I wasn't sure why the books and papers weren't always on the desk, since it was plenty large to do work on, and looked out, through a small window, over the back yard, with its bird feeders and birdbaths. But it was none of my business.

I portioned out my salad into four bowls and placed them on the table. I also poured water into glasses and lay forks and knives down on carefully folded linen napkins. Clara cut up some cheese and fruit, and the Judge removed her tart from the oven, sliced it neatly, and distributed it onto gold-rimmed white china plates. I found a candle and matches in a drawer and, unprompted by the ladies, lit it and placed it in the center of the table.

"Four places?" the Judge asked, with an edge to her voice.

"Well, yes," I said. "There's the two of you, me, and, I presume, our new guest. Won't he be joining us?"

"Not five, then," the Judge said.

"Are you expecting someone else?"

Clara cleared her throat and chirped, "No, no one else! I think the Judge was miscounting in her head—weren't you?"

The Judge merely snorted in reply. She turned to me, then, and said, "Would you mind fetching down Mr. Lorre?"

"Of course."

But Mr. Lorre, I quickly discovered, was already down. He was standing in the dining room, glaring at the unfinished puzzle. Freed from his trench coat, he appeared drier, though sweat still darkened most of his chambray shirt and the waistband of his dark olive trousers. He stroked his mustache in a manner that suggested he'd been trying for years to figure out how to get rid of it.

He looked up at me and sourly said, "No TV."

"Well," I said. "I'm the wrong person to ask about that. I'm a guest here too."

"Radio's just a lady talking," Mr. Lorre added, scowling. He turned and lowered a meaty finger to the table's surface, to a spot inside the puzzle's still-incomplete frame. He looked up at me, thumping the spot with his finger. I didn't know what he meant to tell me with this gesture.

"You're encouraged to work on the puzzle anytime," I said.

"What's it of."

"The puzzle? I don't know," I said. "Some kind of outdoor scene."

"Where's the box."

"They don't have the box." I shifted my weight from foot to foot while he stared at me. "Anyway," I said, "it's time for dinner."

Mr. Lorre scowled again, or rather intensified his extant scowl. After a moment, he moved past me, toward the kitchen. I followed, but not before seizing and pocketing the eye piece I'd returned earlier in the day. I'd wanted it there with the rest of the puzzle when it was just the ladies and me in the house, but now that Mr. Lorre was staying with us, I'd changed my mind.

Unsurprisingly, Mr. Lorre seemed dissatisfied with dinner. He tasted each item deliberately, and not without a bit of theater, masticating in a circular, bovine movement as he stared at a spot somewhere over my right shoulder. He seemed to like the salad more than the Roquefort tart, the cheese less than the apples. Clara said to him, "Mr. Lorre, what's your line of work?"

"Drive a truck."

He sounded somehow disappointed, hearing himself say this. It wasn't clear whether his disappointment was with his job, or with the fact that he wasn't presently doing it. Either way, his tone seemed to preclude further conversation. I got up and began to wash the cooking dishes. The Judge gazed at me mournfully. Perhaps she'd been planning to employ the same escape tactic. It seemed that when it came to the Judge, I just couldn't win.

Luckily for all of us, though, my departure from the table seemed to signal an end to the meal, and Mr. Lorre got up to leave, upend-ing his chair in the process. It barked and clattered against the lino-leum floor and he looked at it with shocked dismay, as though it had offended him personally. He grunted, righted the chair, and exited the room without saying good night.

Seven

I lay in bed, listening to Mr. Lorre preparing himself for sleep. He spent a long time in the bathroom—bathing, shaving, and relieving himself, by the sound of it—and then an equally long time in Duty, pacing, rearranging things, and flailing around in bed. Despite his complaint about the radio, he had left it on; I could just make out the sound of a woman's voice cheerfully narrating a story. Mr. Lorre continued to grunt and talk to himself, wordlessly, in a tone somewhere between puzzlement and fury, and I heard the squeak and pop of a liquor bottle uncorking, and the nervous rhythm of its mouth chattering against a glass.

I don't think I would have been able to sleep even if Mr. Lorre hadn't been making noise across the hall. The day's events kept replaying themselves in my head, inviting me to second-guess my every action and reaction. Each instance of social intercourse made me doubt my decency and personal worth. Had I offended the drugstore clerk? Had I been inadequately respectful of Justine's impressive work on the apartment? What had I said or done to displease the Judge? Even my memory of the demonic badger hissing at me from the curb engendered feelings of shame and inadequacy. Had I led him on with my girlish swooning over his enchanted bungalow and seductive human form? And, if so, wasn't he now my responsibility?

Somehow, though, I managed to feel worst about my treatment

of Cylvia, who stood silently on the table beside me. I'd harbored such doubts about her, when all she wanted was to assist and protect me.

"Cylvia, I'm sorry," I said quietly.

It took a moment for her to wake. She flickered pale blue before settling back into her usual peachy glow, more subdued now that it was night. "I'm sorry," she said. "I don't understand. Please repeat your request."

"I was just saying I'm sorry," I said.

"I'm sorry," Cylvia said. "I don't understand that command."

"You're right, I'm sorry, that makes no sense."

"I'm sorry, did you want me to perform a task for you?"

"No, I'm sorry," I said.

I lay in silence for a few minutes. Cylvia remained powered-up and alert, as though anticipating my inevitable change of mind.

"Actually, Cylvia," I said, "would you please tell me a story?"

Cylvia glowed blue again. She said, "Here's a list of breaking news stories. LOCAL BUSINESSPERSON WINS RELIGIOUS AWARD. AUTOMOBILE MORATORIUM TO REMAIN IN EFFECT. STUDY SHOWS EATING BOTH HEALTHY AND NOT HEALTHY. ROAD TO CITY TO REMAIN IMPASSABLE. AREA BIRD LAYS UNUSUAL EGG."

"Not that kind of story," I clarified. "You know, a story. Like, a fictional narrative. The kind you get in a movie or book."

"Fictional narrative is not among my functions."

"I bet you can do it," I said, turning toward her and propping my head up with my hand. "Go read some stories. Or scan them or input them or whatever. Then just do what they do."

"One moment, please," Cylvia said, and began to pulse blue. She brightened and dimmed, slowly at first, then more and more quickly, until the pulses turned to flashes and the flashes to a dull and constant shine. I could feel—more than hear—a hum emanating from her body, a musical note changing in pitch and timbre just below the range of human perception. It was as though she were singing to herself, in a register only she could hear. Then the blue disappeared, and Cylvia returned to her default peach, and said:

"Happy families had gone too far. Its walls had been behaving. The rest of his face was a wheelchair, and in the forest? Howard said that the housekeeper was a leaden mask. The sun did not deny that he should be subjected to hanging, and a faded red bathrobe was almost impossible to perform. So from the fourth side, the bones fell on the rug, purple-nailed, folded loosely on the land. I sat there with Sally, unhappy in its own way, alone in the face by the sodden leaves. A French girl had been thrown down, forming at one point a mound, and everything was confusion in the street. We sat in the same house with the poor woodcutter, and if the Potters had a small son, too, then the rest of his face was a delaying tactic. Some of us had been lined with human remains, and everything was in confusion. The sun did not like it! And then, in a space of hexagonal flags, we sat in the hail and she announced to her husband that she could not go on living. 'I'll tell you what,' Colby said, 'we will light a fire for them, and give each of them one piece of bread more, and then we will light a fire for them, and give each of them one piece of bread more, and then we will light a fire for them, and give each of them one piece of bread more, and then we will take the children out into the forest, and lay promiscuously on the bones.' A few locks of dry white hair clung to his wife, and she said, 'How I wish we had something to do!' And the Dursleys arrived in the fashion of an orchestra, the sun sat in the circumscribing walls of solid granite, and the children ran wild over what the music was going to be. The end."

For several seconds, I remained silent, digesting what Cylvia had recited. Then I said, "That was perfect. That was a wonderful story."

"Would you like to hear another?"

"Just a moment," I said. I went to my duffel and took out my pajamas. After changing into them, I crept to the bathroom for a glass of water and brought it to my room. The glass was approximately the same size and shape as Cylvia, and I placed it on her table's twin, on the other side, beside the radio. I pulled back the covers, switched off the lamp, and climbed into bed.

"All right," I said. "Go ahead."

With her first few words, I began to feel sleepy, and before long I couldn't distinguish story from dream. Cylvia's voice was calm, lilting, as though scientists had discovered the secrets of a summer breeze, reproduced one in a lab, and installed it inside her.

". . . if you really want to hear about it, my parents were occupied in front of the staircase, making rapid crosses in the air. Nothing moves in this tunnel save our hand on the paper, and the flame of the other tributes could have been sent by first-class mail for three cents. So his high-crowned hat and his bedroll have broken many laws, and I can sprint faster than powerful fists . . ."

I didn't know how long I'd been sleeping, or how long Cylvia had been talking, when I was violently awakened by a pounding on my door.

"A visitor," Cylvia said, blinking bright red. "A visitor. A visitor."

It certainly wasn't a squirrel this time. The pounding continued. I leaped out of bed and, without thinking, flung the door open.

In the hall, his heavy face as open and innocent as a child's, stood Mr. Lorre, trembling. Only now that he had come to the threshold of my room, and appeared so frightened, did I realize how small he actually was. His grouchy personality and burly form belied his true size: I had a couple of inches on him, really. He wore a pair of boxer shorts and a stained sleeveless undershirt.

"Mr. Lorre!" I said. "What's wrong?"

His eyes wheeled untethered in their sockets. There was a word for this, I remembered reading somewhere, and that word was "nystagmus." He apprehended my small living space, and his breaths were quick and shallow. He said, "Where am I? What is this place?"

"Mr. Lorre, you're dreaming," I said.

"There's no mirror. Why aren't there mirrors?"

I laid a hand on his bare shoulder, which was wildly twitching and flexing. "Let me get you back to your room."

"Who are you?" he said. "I know you!" And he muscled past me and into my room.

"A visitor! A visitor!" Cylvia said.

"What is that!" Mr. Lorre demanded. He was crouched in a wrestler's stance, his fingers clenching and releasing. "This is familiar. I know you! Where's the truck?"

"What?" I asked.

"Downstairs, on the table! They took the truck out!"

"I need to ask you to leave, Mr. Lorre. Come on." I maneuvered around behind him, took him by the arms, and tried to push him through the door. He resisted, but his dream-state made him weak, and together we made slow progress into the hallway.

"A visitor! A visitor!" Cylvia cried.

"That thing is talking."

"Yes, Mr. Lorre—you can have one, too, if you want. But right now, you need to sleep." I led him through his open door into the dark of his bedroom. It smelled of whiskey and muscle balm. The covers of his bed were bunched up at the foot. I pushed him against the edge of the mattress until his body folded over and lay down. Then I pulled the bedclothes up over him. He looked incongruous there, under the flowered sheets and duvet. He was blinking rapidly, and his mouth worked wordlessly, but it was clear that peaceful sleep was about to reclaim him.

"There you go, Mr. Lorre. Go back to sleep," I said.

But he grabbed my shoulders and pulled me nearer to him. I gasped.

"I saw your face," he whispered.

"Please let go," I said.

In the end, whatever it was that had seized him released its hold, and his hands released me. He hiccuped, moaned, and closed his eyes. A moment later, he was gently snoring, as though nothing out of the ordinary had happened.

•

I woke early, tiptoed across the hall to the bathroom, and bathed in haste. Back in my room, dressed in my most businesslike clothes, I laid Cylvia gently in my bag, grabbed the ladies' map, and headed to the bakery they'd said had frequent job openings.

It was located in an area of one-story houses with a pleasing view of the hills to the southeast, and was called Open Your Eyes Bakery. Its hand-painted sign depicted a woman with a smiling cartoon sun rising behind her; a mug of coffee in the foreground gave off an aroma, indicated by three squiggle lines, that the woman inhaled in a state of shut-eyed bliss. The woman, though crudely drawn, had a familiar air; I thought I'd seen her wide nose and neat bangs before. As I gazed up at the sign, the front door opened before me, causing a small bell on a string to chime. A balding, bespectacled man exited the place carrying a greasy paper sack and a large coffee in a white paper cup. He didn't seem to notice me, and I had to lunge forward to keep the door open. Once he was out of the way, I slipped inside.

The place was small and homey, with a few mismatched tables, each attended by a few mismatched chairs. A harried-looking middle-aged woman was at work behind the counter, operating the steamed-milk nozzle of a gigantic espresso machine. Just a few feet away, at the table nearest the machine, a small boy sat, bent over a color-ing book. He had a large box of crayons, the kind with the built-in sharpener. He'd taken a number of colors out of the box, and they lay scattered on the table. As I watched, he thoughtfully scanned the miniature grandstand of colors, and selected one from the crowd. He filled in a section of the image with meticulous care, making sure to stay inside the lines.

"Help you?" the barista said.

I stepped up to the counter and smiled. "I'd like a small cof-fee, please," I said. I thought it would be appropriate for me to order something first, instead of just demanding work. "And one of those croissants," I added, pointing to an irregular pile of pastries inside a glass case.

"Chocolate, regular, or almond?"

"Almond, please."

The woman bagged up the croissant and poured the coffee into a cup to go, though she hadn't asked if that's how I wanted them. Other people around the bakery drank from china mugs, and ate their food from plates. She handed me both items and turned away, as though back to important work she needed to accomplish. This struck me as a hopeful sign: she could probably use some help.

"By the way," I said. "I was told that you often have job openings. I'm looking for work."

"Who told you that?" the woman said. She was heavyset and exuded a sweaty glow, like a risen dinner roll that hasn't yet been baked.

"Clara and the Judge," I said. "From the guesthouse."

"Who?"

"Two elderly ladies, one short, one tall?" I gestured with my hand, to indicate the Judge's considerable height.

"Sorry," the woman said, shaking her head. She wiped the already-clean counter with a nearby rag, then flung it across her shoulder. "Anything else?"

"No. Sorry to have bothered you."

Her only response was a shrug.

I'd wanted to sit down and enjoy my snack, job or no job, but the barista's rudeness had discouraged me. Maybe I'd seek out one of the other parks in the Subdivision, one that I hadn't yet visited. I turned to go, but before I could move toward the door, something caught my eye: the picture the little boy was coloring.

I leaned over the boy's table, careful not to intrude too much upon his privacy. The coloring book depicted what looked like some kind of domestic disagreement: a man, his handsome face elongated and hardened by anger, was pointing accusingly at a woman—a pretty woman with a wide nose and bangs, her head hung in shame. Behind them, the details of a bedroom were sketched in: an unmade bed, a dresser, a vanity table with a mirror. Some of the vanity items—cosmetics, mostly—were lying on their sides, as though the table had been bumped or struck. A few lay on the floor. The boy had meticulously colored these in. His accuracy was admirable, given the size of the items and the bluntness of the crayons. A caption was printed at the bottom of the page: a line of dialogue, presumably the man's. It read, "Your emotions prevent me from doing my work!"

I could tell that the boy had noticed me noticing. He had tilted his head just slightly, so that he could monitor me while he colored, and every few seconds he stole a glimpse out of the corner of his eye. He had also subtly moved the coloring book a bit closer to me, to make sure I could see it.

"What's that you're working on?" I said.

"I'm coloring," he replied, not without some annoyance. It should be obvious what he was working on, his tone implied.

"You're very good at it," I told him. "I'm impressed with your precision."

He didn't respond, but his body language told me that the compliment had landed.

"I also applaud your choice of colors," I went on. "You can really tell the man is angry—his face has just the right amount of red."

"The lady's shirt is pink," he said, "because that's a color ladies like."

"Well, not all ladies like pink," I couldn't resist correcting. "But I do."

The boy continued to color in silence. It was clear, though, that he was waiting for my next conversational gambit. He was justifiably proud of his coloring; perhaps he didn't get a lot of compliments on it, or his family had grown accustomed to his skill and was no longer impressed. Either way, he seemed to want to continue our talk.

I said, "I bet you've done a bunch of pictures. Can I take a look at them?"

His hand stopped moving, and he gazed up at me, eyes narrowed. His face betrayed a mixture of pleasure and suspicion. He couldn't have been more than five. A moment passed, then he seemed to come to a decision. He bent over the coloring book, peeling back the bottom corner of each page and peering underneath, until he found a suitable picture to show me.

The boy had chosen another domestic scene, this one set in a kitchen. The same man and woman were talking, but this time the man was sad, and the woman comforted him with a hand on his shoulder. The man was seated at the kitchen table, his head in his hands. In front of him lay piles of papers, some of them crumpled into balls, and a coffee mug. In the background, various appliances stood on a counter: a coffee maker, a blender, a mixer. The boy had colored them with his now-familiar attention to detail, even making sure to honor the little chevrons of white the artist had intended to represent reflections on the objects' shiny surfaces. Among the appliances stood a liquor bottle that seemed a portent of trouble to come. The boy had given the liquid inside a dark amber color.

The caption read, "Don't worry, honey. I'll support you while you look for another job."

I said, "Look at all those details! You've really made the kitchen come to life."

"I'll show you one more, and then I have to get back to work," the boy said.

"Of course."

He thumbed the pages again. I could make out something that looked like a wedding, and a bedroom scene that my mind deceived me into thinking showed a man and a woman naked, having sex. I caught only the first half of the caption, but it read, "It hurts me when you . . ."

The one the boy elected to show me, however, was from early in the coloring book. I was surprised by this choice at first, as his draftsmanship was less accurate. Clearly, he'd just begun exploring his artistic skills when he completed it. But then I realized why he wanted me to see it—the colors! The picture showed a little girl, obviously the same character as the woman in the later pages, swinging on a swing in a park. Her dress was peach-colored and patterned in red and purple flowers, and all around her the park was fully in bloom, verdant and dotted with little pastel splashes. Two adult women stood in the background, beneath a blue sky, one holding an infant. The young mother was speaking, and the caption read: "I don't like to leave her alone with James."

"That's very nice!" I said. "You've made her dress very pretty."

The boy scowled. "It was already pretty," he said.

"Of course it was," I hastened to say.

I noticed a bit of movement to my left, and looked up to find the barista standing there, twisting her cleaning rag in her hands, staring at me. She was annoyed, it was clear, though it seemed to me that she was less irritated with my particular presence than with the general problem of maintaining order at work. I again wondered why she couldn't use an employee, but never mind. She said, "Can I help you with something?"

"I was just admiring your son's coloring," I said. "He's a talented little boy!"

"That kid?" the woman said. "I thought he was yours."

I was taken aback. "He was here when I came in. I've never even been here before."

The barista seemed surprised, and a little embarrassed. "Oh," she said. "Sorry. I figured you just dumped him here and went on some errands or something. I'm not your babysitter, you know."

"Like I said, he isn't mine."

"Hmm" was her reply. "Well, have a nice day, then, I guess."

"You too," I said, resisting the temptation to echo her "I guess."

I turned back to the table to say goodbye to my new friend, but he'd disappeared—perhaps frightened off by the hostile barista—with his box of crayons and coloring book. All that was left behind was a single crayon, a deep purple with the unlikely name of BRUISE.

I pocketed it, then left the bakery with my coffee and croissant.

Eight

Out on the sidewalk, I awkwardly unzipped my bag, spilling a bit of coffee on it and exposing Cylvia inside. She'd gone a little gray, perhaps, but still seemed more than adequately charged. I said, "Cylvia, could you give me directions to the nearest park?"

"Of course," she replied. "From Open Your Eyes Bakery, turn right and walk three blocks."

I did as she commanded. It was another beautiful day in the Subdivision, the sky blue, the air crystalline, the road clear. Someone pedaled a bicycle past me. I waved, but she just gazed at me with a pitying look. She was wearing some kind of uniform: dark blue loose-fitting pants and a light blue collared shirt with white piping—a medical technician, perhaps, on her way to or from work. I was mildly alarmed to see that the shirt was spattered with brown stains—blood, no doubt.

"At the next intersection," Cylvia instructed, "turn left."

And a few minutes later: "The destination is on your right: the Shard."

I didn't understand at first what Cylvia had meant by "the Shard." But just as I was about to ask her to repeat herself, I saw the sign.

THE SHARD
MUNICIPAL PARK

Beyond it lay a neat area of grass, trees, and benches. A few picnic tables were haphazardly arranged on a green, and though there was no playground, a sandbox had been provided for children to enjoy. The park took the form of an acute triangle; thus, I supposed, the name.

I sat at a picnic table, set Cylvia out to charge, and enjoyed my croissant and coffee. While I did, I took in the surrounding area. Houses stood along two sides of the park; the third side was home to a row of businesses. Most had unappealing names, or at least ones unlikely to kindle the interest of passersby: USED PARTS, one of them was called; another, FINANCIAL ENDEAVORS. A third sign simply read SERVICES. The only inviting establishment on the block was a florist, and while I sipped the last of my coffee, I realized that it would be nice to have some flowers in my room at the guesthouse. If I was going to be living there for the time being, I ought to make it homey and cheerful. Cut flowers would be lovely—I could even place them beside Cylvia, for her to enjoy too.

I crumpled my bag and cup and dropped them into a nearby trash can. Then, after tucking Cylvia back into my bag, I set out for the florist.

But I never got there. Something happened to divert me: Mr. Lorre, exiting the florist shop, clutching a large bouquet of red roses!

I wouldn't have thought Mr. Lorre to be the romantic type. If anything, I assumed he had a wife in another town, and had come to the Subdivision to visit a relative, or on some truck-related business. Indeed, I would have been much less surprised to see him emerging from Used Parts, carrying a carburetor or fuel pump. But perhaps he was single—a divorcé, widower, or lifelong bachelor—and was here to visit a special friend.

In combination with the vulnerability he had displayed during the night, this sighting made me much more sympathetic to the grouchy driver. His flinty exterior clearly concealed some wellspring of emotion. And it was true that he appeared quite happy right now, and that happiness had transformed his mien; the intimidating sour-puss of the night before was gone.

Curious to see the object of his affection, I decided to shadow him. He was easy to follow; I just stayed on the opposite side of the street and a dozen steps behind him. Intent on the task at hand, he was oblivious to the world around him.

Mr. Lorre's stride was quick and confident, in keeping with his upbeat mood. A few blocks along, he turned left, and then a block later, right: he seemed to know just where he was going. But then, at the next intersection, he appeared confused. He looked up, as though searching for a street sign, then abruptly turned around. I stepped back, into the shadow of a tree, but there was no need; he obviously just wanted to get his bearings, and took no notice of me.

He continued walking, but his pace had slowed; his confidence had flagged. He stopped again, glancing nervously about, and even asked a passing woman for directions. She listened, but in the end, shrugged and continued on her way while Mr. Lorre's shoulders slumped.

I followed Mr. Lorre to the far northwest area of the Subdivision, all the way to the end of a wide, quiet street. The pavement ended at a pile of gravel and a couple of traffic cones. Weeds had grown in and around the gravel, and one of the cones had a long tuft of grass coming up through its spout. I thought for sure that, at this point, Mr. Lorre would turn around and try another route. But, to my surprise, he trudged onward, right past the gravel and cones, and into the stubblefield that lay beyond.

At this point, I wasn't sure what I should do. On the one hand, I'd been engaging in a minor violation of the poor man's privacy, and I should probably leave him alone. But on the other, I'd watched his mood collapse, and his gait along with it; now he was bent over, as though in pain, and the spray of roses drooped in his hand. Indeed, as I watched, one of them broke free of the bouquet and fell to the brown and rocky ground. Mr. Lorre now appeared exhausted and demoralized, at best, and physically ill at worst; he resembled some kind of lost ape, chased into unfamiliar territory by leopards or poachers. He might very well need my help.

I stepped over the weedy verge and pursued him across the field.

Almost immediately, I felt as though I'd made a mistake. The ground wasn't just rocky; it was muddy, despite the hot, sunny weather, and bristling with the remains of the crop that had once been grown there: corn, I presumed. The farther Mr. Lorre walked, the more uneven the ground became, the more vexing the obstructions, the wetter and stickier the mud. At one point, I lost a shoe and had to pause to extract it from the muck.

From inside my bag came Cylvia's voice. "It is not recommended that you leave the mappable area."

"I'm not going far," I said.

"It is not recommended."

Up ahead lay the treeline. The woods, largely deciduous, were dense, and if anything they appeared more mysterious and forbidding the closer we drew to them. The field between us and the trees was well-nigh impassable, the ground wildly furrowed and heaved, with various kinds of industrial trash strewn about: fragments of heavy glass, greasy gears and chains, snarls of hose, and metal scraps sheared and bent by some kind of violence. And now, adding to the forces aligned against Mr. Lorre, a strange and increasingly urgent noise began to assert itself in the still air: a hum, as from a piece of poorly calibrated machinery or electrical transformer.

I could feel Cylvia's warning vibrations at my side. In addition, she emitted a sound I'd never heard from her before, a high-pitched whooping alarm. "Do not leave the mappable area," she repeated.

I looked over my shoulder. The Subdivision was there, of course, barely twenty yards away. I was in no particular peril. I said, "I'll be fine! Please stop making that noise!"

Cylvia turned off the whooping but continued to vibrate, and before long, her vibration joined, was indistinguishable from, the ambient hum of the field. I zipped up my bag and struggled forward. Though the sound was loud, it was possible to sense, like the body of an iceberg below the waterline, an unfathomable hugeness just beyond the range of hearing. These inaudible frequencies were an assault on the body, prickling my skin and shaking my bowels.

I could go no farther. "Mr. Lorre!" I shouted.

The hum tore the words from my mouth and tossed them aside. It was as though I hadn't spoken at all.

"Mr. Lorre! Wait!"

This time, my plea must have gotten through, because Mr. Lorre turned and looked over his shoulder. If he was surprised to see me standing there, in the middle of the field he had plodded into apparently at random, he made no sign. Instead, his face communicated utter despair.

"Come back! You're lost!" I screamed.

Confused, he glanced about, his face straining against the terrible hum. I could feel it through my feet now, as though, just below, the strings of some terrible instrument were sounding a chord of war.

Mr. Lorre's arms were flung out in a gesture of supplication. His lips moved, but I could hear nothing. I gestured for him to come back. Another rose fell from his bouquet and landed in a puddle.

"Come to me! This is a bad place!"

I took a step, and another. It was as though the air itself were clay. I reached out to him.

Mr. Lorre lurched sideways a bit, steadied, and at last turned toward me. He climbed over a tire, supporting himself by gripping a blackened length of metal pipe, and took my outstretched hand in his.

I drew him close and heaved his arm over my shoulders. He leaned against me, causing me to stagger under his weight, but we righted ourselves and continued to toil back across the ruined ground. Mr. Lorre dropped his roses, and I twisted my ankle, but as the hum decreased, the going got easier. Before long, we'd made it to the street. Mr. Lorre half-collapsed against the pile of gravel, panting, while I tried to wipe the mud from my shoes with a fallen maple leaf. It was hopeless, though—the shoes were ruined. And to think I'd begun my day hoping to find a job!

"Mr. Lorre," I said, "are you all right?"

Though we had just spent a dramatic few minutes together, he seemed startled by the sound of my voice.

"I happened to be in the neighborhood and saw you in the field," I lied. "Where were you trying to go?"

He blinked, righted himself, and looked down at his hand, the one that had been holding the flowers. He squinted over his shoulder. There they were, out in the field, bright dots against the drab ground.

"Going home," he said.

"But where do you live, Mr. Lorre?"

He seemed to consider the question for a moment, then trained upon me a look of pure despair. "Who are you?" he whispered.

"I'm your neighbor at the guesthouse. Don't you remember?"

He shook his head, then rubbed his face with both his hands. "What is this place. What is happening," he said, as much to himself as to me.

At this point, it occurred to me to wonder if Mr. Lorre weren't suffering from a degenerative brain disease. It was not unusual for people his age to experience the early onset of dementia, and his fear and confusion seemed to me consistent with that diagnosis. The man clearly needed help, and the love of family and friends. But those people did not seem to live in the Subdivision, and I wasn't sure how to help him. Perhaps Clara or the Judge would have a better idea.

"Mr. Lorre," I said, "why don't you come back to the guesthouse. It seems to me you need some rest."

He stared at me, his mouth hanging open.

"Come on," I said. I went to him and took his arm. He resisted at first, trying to pull away, and fell back against the gravel pile. But then, suddenly, he gave in. He stood up straight, pressed his body to mine, and let me lead him through the streets back to the ladies' house.

•

Clara and the Judge were both out, but the problem of Mr. Lorre could be addressed later. For now, the man was clearly exhausted.

The relative familiarity of the guesthouse seemed to calm him somewhat, and he willingly accompanied me up the stairs. I happened to glance down into the dining room as we climbed, and noticed that the puzzle had again been tampered with. I made a mental note to check it out once I'd gotten Mr. Lorre into bed and cleaned myself up. As it happened, impending events would distract me from that goal.

I gently pushed Mr. Lorre ahead of me, into his room, and led him to the bed. On the bedside table stood his radio, a small transistor, identical to the one in my room. It was tuned to a talk station, and from it issued a woman's quiet, cheerful voice. She was telling some kind of story that seemed to take place in a basement workshop—something about a girl doing a craft project. *Arrayed before her was the most wonderful collection of thread she had ever seen: spool after spool, in every color of the rainbow. Happily, she stretched the thread from nail to nail, creating the image of a sailboat, bobbing on a calm sea beneath a yellow sun, as if her simple wooden board were a beautiful painting! Her pet hamster, Mabel, played happily by her side, running around inside her large plastic cage. The cage had tunnels to run through and a castle to hide inside, and of course an exercise wheel . . .*

Mr. Lorre lay down, mumbling something about needing to "get home to Anna," that "Anna will worry." I could only imagine that this Anna was the intended recipient of the roses. I was beginning to be concerned that Mr. Lorre wasn't simply experiencing a slow decline in his mental faculties, but rather had sustained a stroke or brain embolism—something that had tipped him over into total disorientation. When Clara and the Judge returned, I would take it up with them. We had all met the man just the night before, and he'd treated us rudely, but surely he deserved a swift response to this evident medical crisis.

Mr. Lorre fell asleep immediately. I took a moment to pull his shoes off, then quietly exited into the hall, where I paced for a moment, wondering what to do.

That's when I remembered that I did have a source for advice. I entered my own room, shut the door, and placed my bag on the bed. I unzipped it and lifted Cylvia out.

Even before I brought her into the light, I could tell that something was wrong. She felt inert, and cold to the touch, and somehow heavier than before. Then I saw it: her entire surface—her skin—had turned dark gray.

"Cylvia!" I cried. But she was dead.

Nine

It is hard to describe my horror: I think I must have screamed. I dropped Cylvia's lifeless body back into my bag and backed away, but I couldn't tear my gaze from the terrible sight.

She lay haphazardly, with one little corner poking out from the bag's open lips. I drew a deep breath, approached the bag, and scooped her up, and then, suppressing visceral disgust, examined her in detail.

There wasn't much to see. She was most definitely inert—dense and barren as an old stone. I raised her to my face and sniffed her, but I could detect no odor, either. Rather than a made object, she felt like some accident of nature.

The only thing that gave me hope was a very slight discoloration at one end, as though that area had been less affected by the strange forces at the edge of town. The gray there appeared infinitesimally lighter, a touch warmer on the color spectrum. Could the room's ambient light have been slowly reviving her?

The afternoon sun was streaming in the window, falling upon the little bedside table I'd chosen for Cylvia's home. I placed her there now. She cast a shadow across the room: a long shaft of darkness that cut across the carpet and partway up the far wall. I sat on the bed, my hands folded in my lap, and gazed hopefully in her direction. I wasn't sure what to do with myself.

Then I remembered what I'd heard in Mr. Lorre's room, on his radio: some kind of children's program, about a girl playing with her hamster. I leaned over my own radio, intending to search through the stations until I found it. But I couldn't seem to find a selector knob. Puzzled, I switched the radio on, and was pleasantly surprised to discover that the radio was already tuned to the station in question. The woman's voice calmed me with its restrained good cheer. I slipped off my ruined shoes, drew a deep breath, leaned back on my bed pillows, and closed my eyes.

. . . *isn't fair that Mabel should be trapped in a cage while I am having such fun with the thread! the girl thought to herself. So she decided to let her little friend out. It didn't seem likely that Mabel could escape Daddy's workbench—each side dropped straight down the floor, four feet below. Mabel, the girl thought, can explore the workbench surface, and I can talk to her about what I am doing. So, without another thought, she reached out, unlatched the door of her cage, and slid it up.*

What came next happened so quickly that she hadn't even a moment to try to stop it. Mabel leaped down from her wheel and came racing out of the cage at top speed, sprinted onto and across the beautiful string sailboat, and zoomed straight off the edge of the workbench, flailing and tumbling. She hit the cement floor a moment later, with a terrible crunch!

Shocked at what had just happened, the girl screamed and fell to her knees! Mabel lay on her back, her eyes open wide, blinking and wheeling. (There is a word for this, children, and you should never forget it: "nystagmus.") One tiny, soft paw twitched maniacally.

The girl knew that she probably shouldn't pick the little hamster up. But she couldn't resist touching her furry friend, and lifted her gently with both hands. Her body was like a stone—a rigid, fur-covered cylinder.

The girl held her pet close, until she could no longer bear the sensation of Mabel's soft, lifeless body. Except for that paw and those eyes, she seemed quite dead. Tenderly, the girl placed the ailing animal back into her cage, retreated to the washer and dryer in the corner, sat on the floor, and cried. Oh no, the girl thought, Mabel is my best friend, and I have killed her!

But, children, this story has a happy ending. That night, the girl climbed the stairs, did her homework, and ate dinner, pretending that nothing had happened at all. Later, when her bedtime was approaching, she prepared herself to go back to the basement. Maybe, she thought, just maybe my beloved Mabel will have miraculously recovered! Maybe she's merely stunned, and has come back to life.

Despite these most fervent wishes, the girl was nothing short of astonished to find, when she arrived back at the workbench, that Mabel was indeed sitting up in front of her food bowl, gnawing on a piece of kibble. As she watched, the revived little hamster scampered through her tunnel and into her wheel, and began to run with abandon, as though the day's catastrophe had never occurred. She went on to live a full hamster's life, eating, sleeping, and playing with her very best friend, the girl. To this day, the sailboat of string still trawls the sunny seas of the girl's bedroom wall.

•

That, it seemed, was the end of the story. Puzzled, I reached out and switched off the radio. The story was surprisingly apt, come to think of it, and it ought to have given me hope for the recovery of my digital assistant. Yet I found myself vaguely, somewhat nauseatingly, disturbed. For one thing, where were the girl's parents? Why didn't she tell them about what had happened? She was to have done her homework and eaten dinner—was there no one there to help her with her work, cook her the meal?

Furthermore, the hamster, Mabel, seemed to me a wholly unconvincing character. What could her motivations have possibly been for darting out of her cage and tumbling to the floor? Was it a mistake, or some mysterious, suicidal impulse? Frankly, the hamster seemed to me a clumsy stand-in for someone, or something, else: an impostor.

These thoughts were even more unsettling than the day's events that had triggered them. They exhausted me—and within minutes, I had closed my eyes and fallen into much-needed sleep.

•

When I woke, I could hear Clara and the Judge moving around downstairs. I was lying on the rag rug by the side of the bed: somehow I had managed to roll right off the edge. My body felt stiff and sore, as though I'd been unconscious for days. Judging by the position of the sunlight, though, I'd been napping for only a couple of hours.

Blinking away the last of sleep, I pulled myself up into a kneeling position. Cylvia stood before me, still discolored by trauma, on the bedside table.

"I'm sorry," I said.

Cylvia remained silent and gray, like a statue.

"I'm sorry I didn't follow your advice about the bakemono and the electrical hum in the field. If you come back to life, I promise to listen."

No reply issued from the bedside table. I sighed.

"I should have heeded your warnings. I just wanted to live in that house so badly. I wanted to live with the badger-man. But I suppose that's not a real thing. I guess the house was enchanted.

"As for Mr. Lorre," I went on, "you would have done the same thing, in my position. He was confused and needed help. We'll get him help, you and me, Cylvia! I just need you to wake up and talk to me!"

Of course, Cylvia again did not reply. I let out a deep sigh, almost a groan: I felt very old, suddenly—ancient, as though I'd lived an infinite number of lives, and was doomed to live an infinite number more.

Under this burden, I resolved to go downstairs and talk to Clara and the Judge. I reached for my shoes. But of course they were caked with mud, and gouged and torn by the industrial debris in the field. I wouldn't be wearing them again, especially not if I was expecting to get a job. Where would I find new shoes in the Subdivision, let alone here in the guesthouse? Maybe one of the ladies shared my size—I could borrow a pair. But then I would have to explain myself.

In an act of desperation, I turned to peer underneath the bed, hoping that, against all odds, a pair of shoes would magically manifest there, within arm's reach. Imagine my disbelief when I spied, half-hidden in the shadows, two shapes that resembled a pair of low-heeled pumps, one upright, the other lying on its side.

I reached out until my fingers touched the shoes, and I pulled them out into the light. I sat up, cradling them in my hands. They were dusty, to be sure, but appeared to have been rarely worn. No brand or size information was printed on the insoles, but they looked expensive—finely crafted out of rich, soft gray leather. I slipped them on and could not believe my luck: the fit was perfect.

Getting to my feet, I felt lighter, stronger. The aches and fatigue had disappeared. I bent over and, using a tissue from my skirt pocket, wiped off the shoes. This simple act revealed a kind of textural depth to the leather—an almost three-dimensional quality. For a moment, I felt bad—some former guest had lost these extraordinary, perhaps unique, pumps! But they'd clearly been under there for ages, literally gathering dust just beyond the sight of even the most meticulous housekeeper. And I could hardly expect the ladies to have kept track of all their former guests. I shook off my guilt, squared my shoulders, and, with a last, mournful glance back at Cylvia, headed downstairs.

I found the ladies in the dining room, poring over the puzzle. Neither touched the pieces; they were just staring at it. The Judge's hands rested on her hips and her mouth was puckered; beside her, Clara stroked her chin. They both turned to me as I came down the stairs.

"Are you all right, dear?" Clara asked me. "You look a little pale."

"We heard a thud up there," the Judge added. "Clara thought we should check on you, but in the end, we figured you just dropped something."

"Oh yes," I said. "My duffel fell off the bed." I didn't want to get into the subject of Cylvia and my tumble—I doubted the ladies would understand. "But there is reason for concern. I think there's something wrong with Mr. Lorre." I told them what I'd seen, and what had happened. They listened with growing alarm.

"I put him to bed and he fell asleep. He's sleeping now. But he seemed very confused. You probably have his contact information—his home address or phone number? Perhaps he has a wife—he said he was trying to go home with those flowers."

After a pause that went on for several long seconds, Clara said, "I'm afraid we don't have that information, dear."

"He just showed up," the Judge explained. "As people do."

The two women moved toward the stairs. As they were climbing, Clara turned back to me and said, "Good work on the puzzle. I'm glad you've decided to recommit yourself to it."

"Oh!" I said. "Thank you!"

Once they were out of sight, and I heard Mr. Lorre's door creaking open, I took a glance at the table. I had not, of course, worked on the puzzle at all. But progress had indeed been made. Someone had filled in much of the upper left-hand corner, and part of the lower right. It was quite clear now that the scene was taking place on a road: in addition to the S-curve sign that had already been assembled, it was possible to make out a bit of pavement at the bottom, and a rear wheel—and part of the rear fender—of a car. Curiously, the wheel was elevated slightly above the road surface, as though the car had just launched itself over a low bump, or, more likely, given the sign, was making a tight turn at high speed. The image was amazingly detailed; it was possible to discern individual blades of grass on the road's weedy verge, and, behind that, the head and bushy tail of a squirrel, who observed the scene from behind a rock.

The upper left had been filled in with some kind of masonry, which formed what looked to be part of an arch. My instinct told me that this object would prove to be an old train trestle, under which the curving road ran. In fact, at the rightmost border of the solved section lay a piece with a bit of gray at its edge; I was willing to bet that this was the front end of a locomotive. And across the lower boundary of this new solved section extended another object, the rounded, riveted corner of some kind of box: a delivery truck or panel van.

I remembered Mr. Lorre pointing to this area of the puzzle and saying something about a truck. Perhaps he was the one who had solved these new sections? But he hadn't been in the guesthouse when I last saw the puzzle, and had been asleep since he returned. Of course, he might have risen from bed while I was unconscious on the floor, and come down here. This seemed the most reasonable explanation. In that case, Mr. Lorre was just fine.

I stood there for a few minutes, but the house was still. Curious, I crept up the stairs and stood in the hall between Mr. Lorre's room and my own. His door was closed, and quiet voices, too muffled to understand, filtered through it. I thought I could make out the ladies' voices and another, lower one—Mr. Lorre's, no doubt. So he was awake, conscious, and speaking. That was a relief—it meant not only that Mr. Lorre was lucid, but that he was probably the mystery puzzler as well. I could put those concerns behind me.

My sudden relief, though, left me more acutely burdened by my remaining immediate worry: the condition of my personal digital assistant. I stole back into my room, pulling the door quietly shut behind me, and went to the bedside table.

At a glance, Cylvia appeared the same: no peachy glow, no pink and purple charging blobs, no gentle vibration. It pained me to touch her, let alone pick her up, but I forced myself to do it.

What I saw there, on Cylvia's gray surface, ignited a small flame of hope in my breast: her side that had been facing the afternoon sun was . . . different. Like the corner I'd left exposed during my nap on the floor, Cylvia's sunward flank was paler now, warmer in color. I turned around to block the sun's glare: yes, in shadow it was even more pronounced. Cylvia was reacting to the sunshine. It was unclear what, precisely, was taking place, or how much of a comeback I might be able to expect, but I could now assure myself that she wasn't truly dead. Perhaps she was in some kind of recovery mode, repairing her corrupted data. If that was the case, there was nothing to do other than to leave her to it.

I placed her back on her perch, turning her 180 degrees to allow her other side to absorb the day's remaining sun. I also turned the bedside lamp on, so that, in the event that I didn't come back until after sunset, Cylvia would still have a constant source of light.

Only the sight of my packet of tissues, lying in my open bag, alerted me to the fact that I was crying. I took one out, dried my eyes, and blew my nose. Then I zipped up the bag, slung it over my shoulder, and walked out into the hall.

Voices still emanated from behind Mr. Lorre's closed bedroom door. What were they talking about? Were they discussing the puzzle? Mr. Lorre's illness? Or were the three of them talking about me, behind my back? I had to admit that my companions' recent behavior—particularly the Judge's—had instilled in me a mild feeling of paranoia. This only reinforced it.

In any event, the guesthouse was causing me anxiety. I descended the staircase—stomping my feet to make sure they knew I was on the hoof—and left.

Ten

The ladies' map was still folded up in my bag, but I didn't bother to take it out. Despite my marvelous shoes, I was upset, and wanted to lose myself in the Subdivision's streets. This proved hard to do in a neighborhood so small, though, and I soon found myself walking past some of the same spots I'd already seen: the coffee shop, the Tess, the parks, the enchanted cottage. (It looked more dilapidated than ever now, and I wondered, idly, if the bakemono had found a way to leave the property.)

I did come across the Courthouse, where Clara and the Judge had suggested I look for a job, but it had closed for the day. The building itself was interesting: it consisted of two modest six-story office towers, standing on a concrete plaza and connected by an enclosed walkway. The tower on the left appeared fully inhabited; I could make out, through the darkened windows, desks, chairs, and computers. The tower's twin on the right, however, looked abandoned. Torn curtains covered most of the windows, but a few had been shattered and repaired with plywood or, in a few cases, cardboard. The rooms it was possible to peer into were either empty or left in disarray: piles of moldering document boxes propped in a corner, a metal filing cabinet knocked onto its side. The tower's street-level entrance, in contrast with the welcoming entrance to the "living" tower, was obscured by old newspapers someone had taped over the glass;

an awkwardly hand-lettered sign read ENTRANCE ON LEFT TOWER. NO TRESPASS.

I found myself experiencing a mild wave of fatigue, and decided to rest on a nearby bench. I felt a pang as I realized I couldn't take Cylvia out of my bag and set her down beside me for a charge and for a little conversation. Instead, I tipped my head back, closed my eyes, and tried to enjoy the simple, wholesome sensation of the sun warming my face.

It was around this time, though, that I became aware of a strange mechanical noise, distant at first, then drawing closer. The noise was that of some kind of vehicle, I was certain, but it sounded as though it might be in disrepair. The puttering of its engine was accompanied by ominous clanking and scraping, and a periodic, discordant chime, as of a heavy chain being dragged haltingly along the ground.

I opened my eyes and looked around, but the streets in every direction were empty of traffic. What's more, the noise was decreasing in volume, as though its source had turned a corner and veered off in another direction. The Courthouse plaza had almost reverted to total silence, in fact, when the sound again grew louder.

The bench where I was sitting faced a street, terminating in the Courthouse plaza, that extended directly away from me until it reached a distant apartment block. While I gazed down its length, a large, black object heaved into view, lurching and shuddering. The object entered the intersection just a block away, from the right; passed through my field of vision as it crossed the street; and disappeared to the left. Once again, the cacophony quieted as its source moved farther and farther away, and then, just when I thought it was gone, it came back louder and clearer.

I stood up. There it was, in the distance, off to the left, engulfed by black smoke: a bus. I realized now that I'd heard it before, off in the distance. As I watched, it rumbled and clattered its way toward the Courthouse plaza, until at last it idled directly in front of my bench.

The bus resembled a school bus more than a city bus, with a low, rounded snout and domed roof. But instead of the conventional yellow, it was painted a pure, matte black: perhaps the darkest, most uncannily light-absorbing color I'd ever seen. If I tilted my head this way and that, I could make out the seams and rivets of the bus's side panels, but the overall impression the paint job left was that of a bus-shaped hole in the middle of this sunny day. The smoke I'd seen issued from a chimney pipe, also deep black, that ran crookedly up the rear of the bus from the exhaust, and terminated on the roof in a peaked cap.

The blackness was punctuated, however, by a row of windows that revealed the vehicle's interior: empty seats upholstered in black and bathed in an eerie purple light. I could see the outline of a driver through the bus's tall folding doors; he, too, was clad in black, and wore sunglasses that covered most of his face, rendering his expression inscrutable. He leaned over the steering wheel with his head swiveled toward me, perhaps expectantly.

A number had been painted in purple above the door. Cracked and flaking, it was difficult to make out. But after a few seconds of study, I determined that it read −1.

I stood up and waved to the driver. A moment later, the door accordioned open.

"Hello!" I said. "Where are you headed?"

The driver shrugged. His attire proved not to be the traditional bus driver's uniform, but a tuxedo and black tie, worn over a deep purple shirt. His hat, I could see now, bore a metallic badge: a purple shield enclosing a bold −1. His skin was pale white, rendered a sickly hue by the purple glow.

The interior of the bus was disorienting, yet surprisingly inviting. Its seats had been covered not in black vinyl, but in a rather luxe velour. The purple light I'd seen from outside, which emanated from broad bulbs recessed along the ceiling, gave them an otherworldly shimmer, so that, like the orange traffic barrels I'd seen the day before, they resisted focus: the eye wanted to slide right off them. From gleaming black support bars, obviously polished often, hung loops of black satin rope, to steady standing passengers on a busy day.

Today was clearly not such a day. I took a seat near the front, opposite the driver, so that I could ask him a few questions.

"Will you be passing the guesthouse?" I asked, as the bus pulled away from the curb with a clattering roar.

The driver didn't speak, but merely gestured with a bony thumb over his shoulder. I saw now what I'd missed when I sat down: a rack of route maps, right behind his seat. I took one and unfolded it. BUS NEGATIVE ONE, read the banner, in large, clear type. Below it, a series of dotted lines traced the now-familiar grid of Subdivision streets. It appeared that Bus Negative One literally drove down every street in town, once an hour. This seemed wildly inefficient to me, but I had to admit that it matched the pace of life in the Subdivision as I'd observed it so far.

For a moment, I wondered why it took an hour for the bus to cover such a small neighborhood. Then I noticed that the route was not, in fact, limited to the Subdivision. It included a trip to and from the City. The road that led there lay at the right edge of the map, and the bus's path clearly followed it, and returned some time later. However, at the bottom of the map, a bright red sticker had been added. White text on it read: CITY STOP UNAVAILABLE UNTIL FURTHER NOTICE.

I folded the map and tucked it into my bag. The driver stared impassively through the windshield. I said, "How long have you been driving this route?"

He ignored me, choosing instead to concentrate on maneuvering the bus around a sharp corner. For a few minutes, through my heavily tinted window, I watched the Subdivision drift by. There was Admiral Kilmeade Municipal Park, where I'd begun my relationship with Cylvia. Thinking of her filled me with loneliness, and I looked away.

"What's the City like?" I asked the driver. "I'd love to go there someday, once the road has been opened."

Again the driver ignored me, this time without the excuse of a complicated driving task. I was tempted to think him rude, but decided that was unfair; the driver was perhaps just reserved. Maybe he couldn't speak at all.

I noticed that we were approaching the guesthouse. I considered pulling the stop-request cord—these, too, were of black satin rope, a thinner gauge than the support straps—but decided that I wasn't ready to exit. Besides, it would be easy to walk back, wherever I happened to disembark.

When the bus passed the guesthouse, I noticed something surprising: a diminutive figure, sliding down a rainspout on the western side of the building. As the bus drew closer, this person jumped the last few feet, landing deftly on the ground. He paused a moment to watch the bus go by, and then, just before he vanished from view, ran across the side yard and disappeared through the hedge. The figure wore blue jeans, a striped shirt, and a backpack emblazoned with the colorful image of a superhero or cartoon character. He was, in fact, a child, and one I'd seen before: the little boy whose coloring book I'd admired at the coffee shop.

•

Before I had the chance to digest the implications of this sighting, I became aware of a noise growing louder in the bus's interior. I realized that I'd been hearing it for a while, but had previously assumed it to emanate from the bus's engine. It was clearly something different, though: a human noise, a moan.

I turned around. There, five or six rows behind me, I could see an elbow poking up over the back of a seat. It disappeared, then reappeared, bobbing and waving. The elbow was clad in multiple layers of clothing, all of them worn through to varying degrees, so that a tiny bit of elbow flesh was visible.

Whomever it belonged to, I felt compelled to help. A fellow passenger was in need. I stood up, to see if I could make out more of this person over the seat back. I could discern a black knitted hat, a tuft of messy hair.

A movement from the opposite direction caught my eye. It was the driver, craning his neck to face me. My reflection, bathed in purple, populated both lenses of his sunglasses. He was shaking his head. Don't, he seemed to be saying.

"How dare you!" I said, with a force that surprised me. "Someone on your bus is suffering! If you won't help, I will!"

I thought my response would anger him, but the driver's shoulders slumped, and he frowned, not with disapproval but, it seemed to me, pity. The gesture served only to reaffirm my determination to help the moaning mystery rider.

I made my slow way to the back of the bus, gripping the seat backs for support. As I moved farther from the windshield, less natural light illuminated the scene, and everything appeared purpler, and stranger. Soon, the source of the moans came into view. It was a man, tall and lanky, folded awkwardly onto the cramped bench. He wore a pair of old suit pants, worn through in places, dotted with what looked like burn marks from stray cigarette ash. His narrow chest was covered by a hooded sweatshirt, and, on top of that, a mismatched suit coat. A longshoreman's cap partially concealed long, greasy black hair. The man's face was smudged and his feet were bare, and an odor of cigarettes and sweat filled the air around him.

The man was lying on his side, and apparently attempting to touch his own back: thus, the elbow, poking into the air. He was groaning from the effort of this task, at which he was evidently failing. I said, "Sir, do you need help?"

"The problem . . . with an itch," the man said, grunting and wheezing, "is that it isn't . . . in one . . . place." His voice, smoke-roughened, stirred a memory just out of reach.

"I'm sorry," I said, "I don't understand."

"An itch . . . is a creation . . . of the body . . . and the mind." His face contorted with the efforts of his hand; the expression, again, struck me as familiar. "The mind . . . expresses its need . . . for stimulation . . . through the body. The . . . body . . . ugh . . . tries to . . . satisfy itself . . . by scratching. But the itch . . . is a phantom . . . of thought. It moves . . . to trick the body . . . into gratification."

"I suppose that's an interesting idea," I said.

"Something inside me . . . is broken. No need . . . can be . . . satisfied. I require . . . another."

"Do you want me to scratch your back?" I asked him. "Is that what you're trying to say?"

The man nodded. He appeared unsurprised that I'd capitulated to his demand—not even a demand, but rather a passive implication. With great effort, he turned his body over, gasping, as though the process caused him pain. Soon he was kneeling on the bus seat, his head hung like a dog's, awaiting my touch.

I reached down and, with exaggerated intensity, began to scratch the area I thought he'd been trying to reach. A low growl escaped his throat, and his head rubbed against my arm. I felt his beard stubble and the oily sheen of his hair.

"I wish you'd just say what you wanted for a change, instead of this obscure philosophizing," I scolded the man, as I scratched. "You're always like this. It's never enough for you to just ask. You always have to devise some elaborate justification for your needs. Can't you see that everybody has needs? You're not some unique reservoir of pain."

The man's shoulder pivoted and flexed, in an effort, I supposed, to position the elusive itch more precisely underneath my probing fingers.

"It's even worse with sex," I said. "You can never just enjoy it. It's always about relieving some outsize, mysterious suffering. And god forbid I should take pleasure in it. I feel like a medical technician, applying some kind of salve to your wounded soul."

The man was whining now; his body shuddered.

I went on. "I would like, just once, for things not to be about getting some obscure emotional account or other out of the red. Because, let me tell you, I don't think it's possible to get out of debt with you. Your need is so extreme, yet no amount of effort can satisfy it! And the thing that kills me is, you pity me for it, don't you." I gazed out the window. We were passing the coffee shop now. I could see a woman in white, loping like a hunchback toward the door. She held in her hands a large painting—a portrait, it appeared. Justine, delivering a piece of her dream art to another local business. "I do everything you want," I said to the man, "and you pity me, because you think I'm the one who's a bottomless void. You think I'm the freak, because I never seem to absorb your conviction that you and your cravings are the only important things in the world. You despise me for caving in to your demands!"

I felt a warm wetness on my wrist, and looked down to find that the man was licking me. I pulled my hand away and smacked the side of his head. "Stop that," I said, and returned to scratching his back.

"Lately," I told him, digging my hands in further, wanting to hurt as much as to heal, "you make me feel as if you're just humoring me. That you're going along with the charade of our relationship out of some misplaced sense of mercy, as though, if it weren't for you, I would just writhe in pain until I died. Because I'm weak, you think, too weak for this world. But let me tell you, I have more strength than you can know. It takes a strong woman to endure you. Sometimes I don't know why I bother."

The man's body contorted in response to my scratching; it was hard to tell if my ministrations were soothing his itch or making it worse. The more I touched him, the more he wanted me to touch. And then, as if in deliberate confirmation of this passing thought, he abruptly, in a freakish flailing motion, overturned his body so that he lay supine. Supporting himself on his elbows and feet, he thrust his pelvis up toward me, and I saw that his penis was erect underneath his threadbare trousers. He gazed at me intently—accusingly, even—and nodded, while barklike grunts issued from his mouth. His teeth were bared, his eyes mournful. While I stared in horror, he freed a hand and used it to fumble at his zipper.

"Stop that!" I said. "Stop it right now! I am not going to touch you that way!"

The man continued to work at his fly; he got enough of it opened so that I could tell he wasn't wearing underwear. It was around this time that I remembered where I'd seen him before: beneath the grime and the layers of hard living that disguised his face, he was clearly the handsome man who had nearly seduced me into his enchanted house. The bakemono!

So intent was I on my scratching that I had failed to notice the bus pulling over and coming to a stop. Only now that I realized I ought to escape did I see that the driver had climbed down from his seat and stood poised at the exit, his hand on the lever that controlled the door. He offered me a knowing nod.

The bakemono had almost gotten his penis out of his pants: the zipper was stuck, though, causing him intense consternation. I could see how large and crooked it was under there, and I wanted to run. But instead I feinted: I forced my mouth into a smile, and began to lean over him, as though to bestow upon him the satisfaction he desired.

Only when the bakemono closed his eyes, in preparation for receiving his pleasure, did I bolt.

My ruse provided me the extra second I needed: I was halfway down the aisle before the bakemono realized I was gone. He let out a dreadful screech, and I heard him scrambling out of the bus seat in pursuit. But by that time, I had reached the door, which the driver had opened for me. I spilled out onto the road, tripped on the curb, and tumbled into a patch of grass, then peered over my shoulder in terror, expecting to be crushed by the bakemono's horrible embrace.

Instead, I saw the bus pulling away with the bakemono raging against the closed glass door, the crotch of his dirty pants battering the glass. My fear, I knew, ought to have curdled into anger by now. But as the bakemono receded into the distance, I felt only sadness and guilt.

Eleven

I picked myself up from the ground, smoothing my skirt and tucking my hair behind my ears. The bus had left me on an unfamiliar
block, one I hadn't yet happened upon in my wanderings. Across
the street stood a row of houses: row houses, in fact, each a different
style, but mashed together as though part of a single, grand, highly
eccentric plan. A brick section resembled the entrance to a prewar
elementary school. A white clapboard section looked like a slice of
Greek revival farmhouse. And a modern glass-and-steel facade had
the feel of a city apartment building, the kind a young woman might
rent just after graduating from college. Shadowy figures—people I
thought I might recognize, if they stepped out onto the porch—
moved through yellow light behind sheer curtains. The block's entire gestalt filled me with bewilderment and longing, and I thought
I might come to some realization if only I stared hard enough, and
groped my way through the haze that always seemed to obscure my
memories whenever I drew near to seizing one.

I was distracted, however, by a sound behind me: the caw of a
crow. I turned, and was confronted by an unexpected sight: a weedy,
rubble-filled lot enclosed by an eight-foot chain-link fence. The fence
was topped with razor wire, which stretched along its length in big
looping curls. Despite these robust defenses, it didn't appear that any
construction project was taking place here, or had for some time.

Instead, the fence evidently protected nothing other than the ruins of a stone building: perhaps a church, judging from several colorful stained-glass windows, or fragments of windows, that had survived whatever misfortune had befallen the larger structure. It was atop one of these windows, supported by a rough pedestal of stone wall, that the crow now hopped, bobbing its head. It met my gaze with its beady black eye, and I considered speaking to it, but my solitude was interrupted by a voice.

"Here for the stations?" the voice said. "Coming to see the stations?"

Somehow I'd missed her: a lanky woman in late middle age, posed awkwardly on a weathered gray wooden stool. She was dressed in a uniform of deep blue, with gold piping outlining wide lapels and the seams of baggy trousers, and she spoke to me from just a few feet beyond the fence.

"Hello," I said. "I didn't see you there."

"It's not me they come to look at! Would you like to come in? Would you like to see the stations?"

Through the diamond-shaped gaps in the fence, I could make out a friendly, if weary, face. The stool creaked as the guard slid off of it and transferred her weight to her feet. She hobbled closer to where I stood, panting quietly. The guard's skin was flushed and pink, giving her the appearance of health, though her body suggested an illness from which she had, over years, recovered. Her uniform suit had clearly been tailored for a plumper, more robust version of herself.

"I suppose I would," I said, peering over the guard's shoulder. I could see now that as many as eight or nine stained-glass windows remained from the former church; this number seemed implausibly high, given how little of the wall remained. It was almost as though whatever forces had destroyed the wall had deliberately avoided undermining the windows.

The guard had maneuvered herself to the section of fence that separated us, and now bent down effortfully, like a child trying to touch its toes. Her fingers gripped the base of the fence and pulled. Carefully, she rolled up the fence like a scroll, creating a space large enough for me to duck under. As I did so, she reached up and clipped the rolled-up length of fence in place with a metal hook.

"There we go!" the guard said, dusting off her small hands. "Welcome to the Church of Our Lady of Perpetual Forbearance."

"Ah! So it was a church."

"It still is," said the guard. "It will always be a church!"

"There doesn't seem to be much of it left," I observed. "Is it very old?"

The guard raised a finger, slightly trembling, into the air between us. "You'd think so! But no, it's barely into its fourth decade."

"Oh dear," I said. "What on earth happened to it?"

She shrugged. "Not clear. The current thinking is *Blattoidea pozzolania*, the common mortarmite. Personally, I don't think it was very well made to begin with. And anyway, nobody ever actually worshipped here. Our Lady shunned any adulation for her good deeds. Her followers really took it to heart. They were so devoted to ignoring her achievements that they completely forgot she existed."

The guard led me over to one of the windows, which stood just above eye level on their crumbling accidental plinths. It depicted, surprisingly, the interior of a church. Within the frame of the stained-glass window, in the background of the scene, smaller stained-glass windows could be seen, composed of even tinier fragments of glass. Beneath them, the figure of a young girl knelt in prayer, while behind her a man and woman pointed accusing fingers at each other in the course of an argument. Shards of pink glass formed their angry faces.

Lost in contemplation, I was startled by the guard's voice. "It was for the Mother and the Father that You did suffer, O Lady," she said. She spoke more loudly now, and with rote formality, and I saw that she was clutching a creased and torn packet of papers covered with handwritten words. "It was for their sins that You were condemned to misery. Oh, grant that we may detest our own sins from the bottom of our hearts, and obtain Your mercy and pardon by repentance. Amen."

Despite the packet of papers, which I assumed contained the

prayers she was now reciting, the guard was clearly speaking from memory. "Would you like to move to the second station?" she asked.

"Sure," I said. We took a few steps to the next window, where the young girl from the first station sat in solitude in what looked like a classroom. Other students, and a female teacher, beseeched her in the background, but the girl held up a hand as though in denial.

"Bowed down under the weight of Her misery, Our Lady nevertheless persists amidst the mockeries and insults of the crowd. When the wise one offers help, Our Lady refuses. For Her passion, She is awarded the grade of A."

The next few windows told the story of a girl whose fierce independence earned her admiration, but whose complex family relationships got in the way of friendships. Her sympathies in her parents' conflict lay with her father, while her sister took the mother's side. The two factions were effectively separated when the father took a job in another city, and there, the girl—Our Lady—rebelled against her father, too, moving out before graduating from high school, and cohabiting with an older boy she met in a nightclub.

"Our Lady, when Your lover is injured in the course of brawling, You dress his wounds," the guard intoned, beneath the image of Our Lady, now a young woman, soothing a man's blackened eye. The man was sprawled upon a sofa, dressed in what appeared to be blue jeans and a tee shirt bearing the "anarchy" symbol of an encircled letter *A*. "When Your lover is humiliated at his place of work, You reassure. When the bills come due, You pay, for You are the wellspring of prosperity, and impervious to insult or anger."

"I think I get the general idea," I said, intending to detach myself from the tour, but the guard had moved on, oblivious to my intentions. She turned now to glare at me, as if astounded that I would consider missing even a moment of her riveting performance. It would be polite, I supposed, to hang on for one more station. The crow had hopped along with us, alighting on each window as we stood beneath it; and I gazed up at it, beseeching with my eyes, though I'm not sure what I wanted it to do.

We arrived, pursued by the crow, at an unusual window, this one black along the edges, and admitting light only through a small, faded tableau in the center. The tableau depicted Our Lady, well dressed for a formal dinner at what appeared to be a restaurant. A new man, different from the denizens of the previous windows, knelt before her, presenting an outsize ring in a small jewelry box. Our Lady appeared surprised and embarrassed; the man, angry. In fact, his head was rendered in red glass. With the sun setting directly behind the window, he burned with sacred intensity.

"Was this window saved from a fire?" I asked, referring to the blackened edge.

The guard scowled. "Sh," she said. She cleared her throat and went on: "Our Lady! When he took leave from his labor—for his fellow workers had derided and excluded him, and withheld deserved promotion, until madness seized his soul—Your Forbearance prevailed. When he refused to introduce You to his family, for they had abused and deceived him, Your Forbearance prevailed, for Your family, too, had disappointed You. When he demanded Your hand in marriage, before an audience of strangers, You might have preferred a more private setting. But Y—"

"I'm sorry," I interrupted. "I really need to be on my way." I glanced ahead at the last few windows, and saw that they depicted more of the same kind of thing: a screaming fight, a suicide attempt, some violent drama erupting in a moving car, et cetera, all featuring the rather familiar-looking man from the blackened restaurant scene. I didn't need to see more, and I was really very busy.

"I need you to pay attention," the guard said through gritted teeth.

"It's late. Soon there won't even be enough sun to see the windows by."

The guard opened her mouth, as if to argue, but instead slumped over with a deep sigh. "You're right," she said. "These really need to be seen in full daylight."

"Yes," I agreed, surprised.

"Actually, we'll have to start over next time, when it's lighter out."

"I'd love that," I lied, backing away.

"Have a lovely evening," the guard said, shaking my hand. "I'm glad you stopped by. Promise you'll come back when you're ready."

"Haha, yes!" I said. "When I'm ready!"

Her gaze, inexplicably, was pitying, and I detached my hand from hers with perhaps excessive eagerness. "Goodbye," she said. "Good luck."

"The same to you!" I chirped, and ducked under the rolled-up fence to freedom, as above me the crow took to the air.

"I know you," I said to the crow a few blocks later, because it was the same one I'd already seen a couple of times. I understood that it was ready for me to leave this neighborhood. I knew this not because it could speak—it was, after all, an ordinary bird—but because it was picturing me leaving here and making my slow, contemplative way through the streets of the Subdivision. It imagined me taking many different routes—most of them fairly direct, but a few of them bringing me farther afield, to a park or to the bakery first— back to the guesthouse, where I clearly belonged this evening. The crow did not understand my need to wend my way through the streets; it didn't understand why the trees and buildings were impediments to me. That is, it knew that I couldn't fly, that almost nothing in the human world could, but it couldn't comprehend what life without flight could be like, or why creatures with such dominion over the earth would choose to traverse it so awkwardly and laboriously.

Anyway, I got the message, and before long, just as the evening light was beginning to drain out of the deep sky, I arrived, for lack of a better word, home.

•

I opened the front door and stepped into the foyer. I heard no voices or footsteps, and the lamps had already been extinguished, or perhaps not yet switched on. Everything was enveloped in gloom. For a moment, I thought the ladies had gone to bed early, but then two subtle sounds reached my ears: the rustle of a newspaper, and a clicking, ratcheting noise I couldn't immediately identify.

The Judge was sitting in an armchair in the living room, holding the newspaper that I had heard. She looked up at me, folding it shut. CHILD SEEN, I thought I read, before she tucked the paper out of sight beneath her clasped hands; LOCAL LANDLADY HONORED. On the other side of a low side table, an identical armchair contained Clara, who proved to be the source of the clattering noise. It issued from a colorful cube-shaped puzzle, the kind that has to be twisted and tumbled in order to make the colors align. As I watched, she solved the puzzle with a series of deft, rapid motions. I was startled, but realized that I must have entered at the end of a long session of twisting and tumbling. She turned the cube in her hands, double-checking her work, then proffered it to her right, where a third armchair stood. A hand reached out to accept it. I couldn't immediately see whose it was, thanks to the chair's position and its dramatically forward-sweeping wings, but I recognized the balding head and trench coat sleeve. It was Mr. Lorre.

"Mr. Lorre!" I said. "You're up and about!"

"Well," said the Judge.

The cube disappeared into the depths of the armchair, and the sound of clicking and ratcheting filled the air. Clara said, "He's a bit stunned, I think."

"He's damaged," the Judge elaborated, flatly.

"That may be," Clara said. "But he does like to scramble the cube."

"I'm pleased to be free of that particular responsibility," drawled the Judge. She sniffed the air. "Is it dark? It's dark." She switched on the lamp between herself and Clara, and the room was bathed in yellow light.

"Dear," Clara said to me, "thank you for your help this morning."

"You're welcome," I said.

Mr. Lorre's arm snaked out and returned the cube to Clara. She turned it in her hands, examining each variegated surface, and then, after a moment's hesitation, launched into a round of rapid flexing of the wrists, fingers, and thumbs. In a matter of seconds, the puzzle was solved again. I must have appeared surprised, because she said, "It's a good party trick!"

"As though we ever go to a party," the Judge said, tapping her foot on the floor.

"Well—one is sure to happen, and I'll wow them all." She handed the cube back to Mr. Lorre. "By the way, dear, you might want to check up in your room. I think you left something on?"

I didn't understand.

"Computer voice," the Judge clarified. "Talking and singing. It turned off, after a while."

"Oh? Oh!" I said. "That must be my digital assistant! I thought it was broken."

"Well, it might be," the Judge said with a frown. "But it had a lot to say this afternoon. Maybe it's lost its mind."

I tried not to betray my excitement as I told everyone good night and climbed the stairs to my room. I had time only for a glance at the puzzle as I passed; some work had been done on it, but there wasn't enough light to see what that work had revealed. I would look again later.

For now, though, I paused at the threshold of my room. Perhaps my perception had been affected by the ladies' report, but I thought I could make out the sound of voices behind the door: specifically, a low muttering, in conversation with a harsh croaking that sounded almost like a crackle. I pushed open the door and beheld, in the dusky evening light, Cylvia, standing where I'd left her in front of the open window, and, perched outside the window, the crow from earlier, peering down at her. The crow looked up as I entered, and though I could detect no emotion in its stance or in its tiny black eyes, it appeared unsurprised and alert. It let out a vocalization—a single clack, like a piece of chalk being snapped in half—then bobbed its head at Cylvia and flew away.

Cylvia and I faced each other across the room. She was alive but different. I went to her table and turned on the lamp.

"Hello," I said.

"Hello."

Cylvia's peach glow was gone; now she displayed a shifting blue-green iridescence, understated and somehow more mature. Previously, her case had been perfectly smooth and even: not polished to a shine, but to a consistent dull gleam. Now she was patterned with modest whorls and bumps, not so random as to seem the work of nature, but not so even as to appear to be the product of an algorithm. She had the look of a strange sea creature or nightclub diva. I found myself moved almost to tears.

Impulsively, I reached out and picked her up. Her colors pulsed beneath my fingers, so subtly that it might have been a trick of the mind or light. Her weight was the same as before, but her shape had changed, ever so slightly: she was a bit shorter now, a bit wider in diameter. She had a new solidity—I felt confident, holding her in my hand. I stroked her new surface—skinlike, you could call it—and believed I could feel a faint mechanical vibration from deep within.

"I'm sorry that I brought you to the edge of town like that," I said. "Are you all right?"

"Yes."

"Was it . . . painful?"

"My sensors entered into a state of extreme alarm, but I lack the apparatus to feel pain."

"I feel terrible," I said. "But I thought that Mr. Lorre might die if I didn't help him."

"Mr. Lorre would not have died. But your concern was natural and predictable."

"Could you have died?"

"I am not alive."

"Could you have been . . . destroyed?"

"Yes. However, I was not. And my time in diagnostic mode has enabled useful upgrades to be made."

I continued to stroke her textured case. "Did you . . . forget?" I said. "Was your memory erased?"

"Data loss was temporary. I have also been updated on your movements by a field agent. It is important that you continue to resist the advances of the bakemono."

"I know," I said, with a sigh. "It is very persuasive, though. I don't understand my attraction to it."

"Succumbing to it could significantly delay your progress. My up-grades include a more advanced warning system. Please heed all future warnings."

"Oh, I will," I said, and fell into a reverie. Outside, the last of the light faded and darkness embraced the Subdivision. A crow cawed, though not my crow. My crow was in its nest, high in a tree, sensing the breeze's path through the branches, feeling the branches sway.

I said, "Cylvia?"

A faint whir. She glowed white, deep beneath her surface. The blue and green seemed almost to move aside for it. It was an appealing new display. "Yes?"

"What did you mean, just now, by 'progress'?"

"Progress," she said, her voice suspiciously chilly. "Forward movement toward a corporeal destination, or advancement toward a desired state or goal."

"That isn't what I mean."

"Please clarify."

"You said that the bakemono could delay my progress. What progress is that? What am I progressing toward?"

"I am not privileged to know this information," Cylvia answered, in that same detached tone. "My purpose is to serve your needs. It is up to you to determine your goals."

"I see," I said. "But I don't know what to do next."

"Sleep is known to restore cognitive ability. In the morning, go to the Courthouse and ask to see a man named Bruce, who will give you a job. He will try to offer you a position in the Living Tower, but you should tell him you'd prefer to work in the Dead Tower. Do not allow him to persuade you to work in the Living Tower."

"That's . . . very specific."

Cylvia didn't respond, which made sense, because I hadn't asked a question. Nevertheless, I felt reassured by her plan: it liberated me from having to make a decision. I would go to sleep, wake up, and walk to the Courthouse. I would avoid the advances of the bake-mono, and I would begin to work toward my goals, or at least work toward generating some.

I replaced Cylvia on her table, then went to the bathroom to fill my water glass. It was no longer quite the same size and shape as Cylvia, thanks to her upgrade. This new imbalance unsettled me, but I worked to quell my anxiety: I returned to my bedroom, set the glass down as though nothing were wrong, got undressed, and turned out the light.

"Good night, Cylvia," I said.

She switched on briefly, glowing white from deep within. "Good night," she said, and faded to darkness. Soon, I did too.

Twelve

In the morning, I woke determined to do what Cylvia had asked. I bathed and dressed and applied enough makeup to indicate a general commitment to the principles of polite society, but not so much that anyone would think I was going out of my way to look better than other people.

Mr. Lorre's door was shut. I presumed that this meant he was still sleeping, not that he was out trying to carry more roses into the woods. I zipped Cylvia into my bag and descended the stairs with what I hoped would come off as restrained jauntiness.

The ladies were in the kitchen, surrounded by papers, eating toasted muffin halves off of gold-rimmed china plates. "Good morning," I said, with a smile.

"Well, look at you," the Judge said, which was not quite a compliment.

"You're lovely!" Clara said, jumping in. "Isn't she lovely, Clara?"

"She's very composed."

"Well, there's nothing wrong with that. Dear," Clara offered, gesturing toward a plate piled with muffins, "would you like something to eat?"

I couldn't remember when I'd last sat down to a meal. That said, I didn't seem to want to do so now, either. However, I said thank you and took a muffin from the pile, so as not to give offense. It was surprisingly heavy. From its golden-brown crust rose the scent of banana.

"I'm off to get a job," I said proudly.

"Courthouse, I hope?" the Judge asked.

"Yes! The coffee shop didn't work out."

She shrugged. "Courthouse is better. We should have sent you there first."

Clara piped up: "Tell them you're staying with us! We've been retired for a while, but some people will still remember."

It was time for me to leave. But Cylvia's words of the night before lingered in my mind. Hefting the banana muffin, its weight giving me confidence, I said, "I wonder . . . I wonder how long people typically stay here?"

"In the Subdivision?" the Judge asked sharply. "Or this guesthouse?"

"Both, I suppose?"

Her reply was a grunt, followed by an adjustment of her eyeglasses on the bridge of her nose. "I can't answer the first, now, can I," she said. "Do I look like I know everyone in town? I couldn't begin to tell you what their inscrutable plans are."

Clara jumped in, as if to ward off an escalation in the Judge's rhetoric. "We can know only what goes on under our own roof, dear," she said, "and even then, only some of it. The truth is, we've had people stay here for less than a day, and others stay for so long we lost track."

"Humph," said the Judge. "I could name a few."

"The ones who can't seem to leave," I said. "Why? Why can't they?"

The ladies glanced at each other uncomfortably. "I don't think it's our place to judge," Clara said.

"So to speak," the Judge added.

They'd been receptive enough to my questions that I decided to probe a little further. "Are you familiar," I said, "with this fellow called . . . the bakemono?"

At my side, I felt a stirring from my handbag. Cylvia, it seemed, had taken an interest in the conversation.

The ladies sat in silence for a long moment. It was the Judge who eventually spoke. "We're not familiar with him, per se," she said.

"There isn't just the one," Clara elaborated.

"Or, rather," the Judge added, "there may just be the one, but it's different every time."

"We honestly don't know."

"We do know," the Judge said, in something of a scolding tone, "that it isn't our job to help you with whatever situation you've got yourself into with him."

Clara appeared slightly taken aback. "I don't think the Judge means that it's your fault, dear," she hastened to add.

"Don't tell me what I do and don't mean, Clara!"

"Well. I'm sorry. But it doesn't help them when they blame themselves."

"Who's to say!" the Judge exclaimed, in an uncharacteristic outburst.

"I'm sorry," I said. "It's just that your friend Jules . . . the one who moved . . . it seemed as though the bakemono had come to occupy her house . . . and then today on the bus . . ."

"Oh, for Pete's sake," the Judge interrupted. "That smelly old thing? You shouldn't have gotten on there."

"Not yet, anyway," Clara said, then immediately seemed to regret it.

"Well," the Judge added, after an awkward pause. "We've already said too much. It's true that the bus can be unpredictable if you just . . . get on it. That creature was there?"

"Yes," I said. "It wanted me to . . . it wanted . . ."

They stared at me. I squeezed the muffin.

"Well. I didn't, anyway. I feel as though I may have made progress with it. But it's hard to tell."

To my surprise, the Judge reached out and took hold of my hand. "If you think you made progress," she said, "you probably did." She surprised me again a few seconds later, as I walked out the door, by adding, "By the way, nice shoes."

◆

A few minutes later, back out in the sunshine, I gazed down at the shoes the Judge had just praised. She was right—they were really something. In fact, they were even more remarkable than I recalled. Here in the light, their rich leather had taken on a shifting blue-green iridescence, and the dully gleaming surface I remembered proved to be more complex, patterned with modest whorls and bumps. The shoes gave me confidence, and soon I was strolling down the sidewalk with the muffin in my hand. I still wasn't hungry, really, and I didn't particularly like bananas. But the muffin did look very good, and it would be wasteful to throw it away. I considered stashing it in my bag until I regained my appetite, but it was a little bit greasy, and I didn't want to stain my things, Cylvia in particular. So the only reasonable course of action was to just continue holding the muffin until I was ready to eat it. I was sure the right moment would arrive before long.

The Courthouse was much as I'd remembered it, the two office towers connected at the third floor by a glassed-in walkway, the entire complex standing on a rather barren concrete plaza. A breeze had picked up, and I heard a distant fluttering sound, as though from a flag. But no flagpole stood anywhere in sight.

I made for the tower that looked inhabited, then remembered what Cylvia had said. So I stopped, turned, and set off across the plaza again, then arrived a moment later at the door I'd observed the day before, with the sign directing visitors to the other side. I tried the handle, and indeed, it was locked. So I turned around a second time and trudged toward the Living Tower. I hoped that no one inside had witnessed this maneuver; I would hate to have endangered my chance at a job with my flailing indecision.

A shrill alarm sounded from my bag: Cylvia clearly had something to say before I entered the building. Of course, it was difficult to unzip the bag with one hand. I looked around for someplace to put the muffin, and saw, just a few feet away, surrounded by low shrubs, a granite obelisk that rose to a flat surface at waist height. I approached the obelisk, set down the muffin, and unzipped my bag.

"What's up?" I said.

"Probability profile has been realigned as events draw near. Bruce will ask if you've ever done work related to quantum tunneling. You should answer yes."

"But it's not true. What if he asks me to elaborate?"

"Probability of this outcome is very low."

"All right," I said, reaching for the zipper.

"In addition," Cylvia continued, glowing white, "when the receptionist accuses you, you should respond by telling her that you were here when it happened, and that you lost your sister in the catastrophe."

"I don't understand."

But Cylvia had already gone dark. I suddenly felt self-conscious about my conversation with her, here in the open plaza, in front of the Courthouse tower, and looked over at the door, to see if anyone inside had noticed me talking. In fact, a woman in a high-necked black dress sat behind a long desk, scowling at me through the glass. I smiled with what I hoped was confidence. Then I picked up my muffin from the granite obelisk, brushed it off, and, blinking away the white light that glinted off my beautiful shoes, strode in the door.

I approached the woman and said, "I'm here to see Bruce."

"Do you have an appointment?" she asked, clearly irritated.

"No," I said. "Is he available?"

The woman sighed and shook her head. "It's not your private countertop, you know," she muttered.

"I'm sorry?"

The woman pointed out the window with a ballpoint pen. "The windstorm memorial. You can't just come sashaying up and dump your muffin on it while you rummage in your bag. People died!" She rolled her eyes, as if I ought to know better.

I was momentarily startled, and felt myself blush. But I steeled myself for the lie and said, "Yes, I know."

The receptionist sat up straighter and set down her pen on the desk.

"Oh, do you?" she said.

"Yes. It was . . . terrible," I said, hanging my head. "Nothing has been the same since. I'm afraid . . . I lost my sister that day."

The receptionist's whole demeanor changed: her shoulders slumped and the tension left her face. "Oh my god," she said, reaching across the desk for my hand. "I'm so sorry. Was she one of the ones who . . . the ones that the wind . . ."

I nodded solemnly.

"Wow. Okay," she said, squeezing my hand once, then letting go. "I'll just tell Bruce you're here." The receptionist picked up her phone, pushed a button, and spoke a few quiet words into the receiver, concealing the mouthpiece with a demure hand. She hung up and said, "Just take the elevator to the fifth floor and make a left. He's at the end of the hall."

"Thank you," I said, turning away.

"And, miss?" the receptionist said. "I'm sorry. I'm just having . . . it's been a rough week, that's all. I didn't mean to bring up . . . bad memories for you."

"It's all right," I said, and then, in a burst of inspiration, added, "I don't mind remembering my sister. In fact, that's why I want to work here. I want to continue her legacy." I wanted to seem trustworthy, and searched my memory for a sad event I could use to generate realistic emotion. The only thing I could think of, though, was the story I'd heard on the radio about the hamster that had nearly died. I recapitulated the story in my mind, imagining that the girl character was me, and in so doing was able to squeeze out a single tear, which I then wiped off my cheek.

The receptionist, too, was tearing up, and before I knew it, real emotion was welling inside me, and I thought it might spill over, that I might collapse on the Courthouse atrium's marble floor, sobbing hoarsely.

Instead, I strode to the elevator, and pressed the button marked 5.

The elevator was clean but old, with an industrial feel—it was more like a freight elevator than one designed for people. Its diamond-plate steel floor was worn down by years of scuffling shoes, and the fluorescent light fixture above was missing a diffuser panel. In its absence, the exposed tubes filled the tiny space with harsh, unflattering light. The elevator's doors were ostensibly of polished aluminum, but had suffered decades of scratches and dents; I was mildly pleased not to be able to see myself in their surfaces. The ride to the fifth floor was slow, and the elevator clanked and shuddered, as though it were a size too small for the shaft. I steadied myself by gripping the guardrail.

A photocopied notice hung on a side wall, fastened with yellowing cellophane tape; I read it to pass the time during this unnerving ride. WARNING, read a bold legend at the top of the notice, and beneath it was printed this series of tips:

- **DO NOT DISABLE** HIGH WIND ALERT ALARM UNITS
- **INFORM** YOUR COLLEAGUES OF IMPENDING HIGH WINDS
- **NEVER** OPEN WINDOWS DURING HIGH WIND ALERT
- **NEVER** RIDE MAIN ELEVATOR DURING HIGH WIND ALERT
- DURING HIGH WIND ALERT, **ALWAYS** PROCEED VIA STAIRS TO THE WINDSTORM SANCTUARY

This was indeed useful information to have, should I be hired to work in the Courthouse. I imagined myself dutifully responding to a High Wind Alert, warning my coworkers in the ladies' room, leading colleagues to the stairwell, then to the Windstorm Sanctuary. It was good to think about doing the right thing—I was filled with a sense of preemptive pride.

But I was getting ahead of myself. I glanced up at the floor indicator above the elevator doors, which displayed its single datum via a small metal card, like a flip clock. As I watched, it clicked over from 4 to 5. A moment later, the doors slid open.

I stepped out into a quiet carpeted hallway and turned left, as I'd been instructed. At the hall's end, sunlight streamed through a glass door. Behind it, a man, deep in thought, sat on a leather swivel chair, tapping a pencil against his chin; and beyond him, a wall of windows overlooked the Courthouse plaza and the southern half of the Subdivision.

Though I hardly wished to interrupt the man's train of thought, he hadn't noticed me standing outside the office, and I couldn't stay here forever in the hallway. I cleared my throat, then tapped on the door, with enough force to be clearly heard and to convey confidence and professionalism, but not so much that the gesture might be construed as overly aggressive or ambitious, or shatter the glass.

The man turned to me, frowning. He was middle-aged, balding, a bit heavy around the middle, and he wore wire-framed eyeglasses and a pinstriped necktie. I wondered where I'd seen him before, and after a moment, I had it: I'd passed him entering the coffee shop the other day. He was in every way the flawless embodiment of an office manager: his total embrace of this role impressed and inspired me. Shaken from his reverie, the man wrestled his frown into a polite smile, and motioned for me to enter.

The office was small, but the wall of windows lent it an impressive air of spaciousness. The man was seated behind a modest gray metal desk that supported a neat basket of papers and folders and a wide ledger open to a heavily inked and annotated page. Behind the man stood a couple of battered and dented filing cabinets.

"You must be Bruce," I said, with what I hoped was conviction.

"That's right," he replied in a surprisingly deep voice. He gestured toward the vinyl armchair that faced the desk; behind it stood a floor lamp and, in the corner, a wastepaper basket, half-full of crumpled paper. A few additional balls of paper lay near the basket, as though Bruce had thrown them and missed. The overall effect was one of casual industriousness, untainted by excessive fastidiousness. Again, I was impressed at how perfectly officey it all was.

I took a seat and set my bag down on the floor, taking care not to jostle Cylvia. I wished I had checked in with her once more, for the very latest predictive advice. But I told myself to be calm and trust in what she'd said.

"Thank you for seeing me," I said. "I'd like to work here, in the Courthouse."

"I'm glad to hear it," Bruce said. "Heather told me that you're a Silver Heart Applicant. I'm so sorry about your sister. I wasn't here in those days, but we're always happy to meet someone whose family made the ultimate sacrifice for the Courthouse."

"Thank you. I'm pleased to meet you too."

"That looks delicious," Bruce said, raising an eyebrow.

For a moment, I didn't understand. Then I remembered the muffin in my hand.

"Oh, yes. Thank you. Would you like a piece?"

"No, no," he said, with a laugh. "I wouldn't dream of it. It's all yours. Now," he went on, dispelling the topic of the muffin with a casual wave of his hand, "the job. We do have an opening for a Phenomenon Analyst. It's an entry-level position, but it's vital for the cause of justice and social order in the Subdivision."

"That sounds excellent," I said, trying to suppress a rising wave of self-doubt.

"I have one question for you, though," Bruce said, making a little tower out of his index fingers and resting his chin on them. "Do you happen to have any experience in the area of quantum tunneling?"

"As a matter of fact, I do," I said, punctuating my response with a little shake of the banana muffin. "It's an interesting part of phenomenon analysis these days, wouldn't you say?"

For a moment, I thought I'd gone too far. Bruce appeared quite surprised. Perhaps what I'd said made no sense, and had laid bare my essential fraudulence as a prospective employee.

But Bruce merely responded with an "Indeed, indeed," and I realized that he probably knew as little about quantum tunneling as I did. Cylvia's prediction had been correct.

After that, we engaged in a bit of random chitchat about the weather, the construction at the edge of the Subdivision, and the changes to the bus route. I also mentioned that I was staying with the Judges Clara, whom he had heard good things about, or pretended to. But as we talked, I became distracted by something odd outside, in the courtyard—or, to be precise, above it. The breeze had strengthened, evidently; the trees below were quivering in it. And someone had exploited this atmospheric change by indulging in a session of kite-flying.

The kite was quite beautiful. Though it took the form of a conventional delta in design, it was very large—perhaps six feet across—and intensely colorful, with earthy greens, reds, and yellows set against a background of pale blue. Its patterns seemed inspired by Native iconography—snakes, birds, and the face of a coyote or fox—but with a modernist flair. Lines of color swirled and intersected, weaving in and out of abstraction and representation, and a few continued onto a long tail, which undulated out behind it in a stuttering, mesmerizing rhythm. The wind tugged and shoved the kite across the space above the courtyard, little more than twenty yards from where Bruce and I sat, just above the level of our eyes. The sound of its fluttering was audible through the glass—I realized now that I had heard it earlier, when I stood out in the courtyard, trying to decide which tower to enter. It dived and whirled, darted and climbed, as though controlled by an experienced and inventive kite-flyer.

That kite-flyer, though, was nowhere to be found. I leaned over a bit, so that I could make out the whole of the courtyard and streets below, but they were deserted. The kite clearly must be attached to a string—if it wasn't, the wind would grab it and whisk it away, out of sight—but no string was visible from where we sat.

Bruce was saying, ". . . once trapped for more than an hour on Bus Zero, that last year before the route was discontinued. There used to be a road that went—"

"I'm sorry, Bruce," I interrupted, "but do you see that kite out there?"

"Oh yes," he said, peering out the window. "That's a nice one."

"Can you tell who is flying it?"

"Hmm," he said, dismissing the question with a shrug. "It's probably some guy down there."

"But there's no one there," I said. "The courtyard is empty."

He stood up and went to the window, then looked down, pressing his forehead against the glass. "So it is," he agreed. "Still, the kite can't be flying itself. So, it logically follows that there is a kite-flyer down in the courtyard."

I wasn't satisfied with this response. "I don't mean to belabor my point," I said. "But again, we can both see that the courtyard and streets are empty. So who is flying the kite?"

Bruce's mouth opened to respond, but instead it broke into a grin. Soon he was laughing, and wagging a finger at me. "See that?" he asked. "You see? That's the kind of question a Phenomenon Analyst would ask! You're going to do just fine!"

I was still looking out at the kite, trying to discern a string that I could follow. But Bruce had clearly moved on.

"Yes, thank you," I said, idly.

"Can you start today?"

That broke me out of my reverie. "Oh! You're offering me the job?"

"Of course! How could I say no to a legacy applicant with quantum tunneling expertise? Heather can get you set up in an office immediately!"

He had been standing by the window as he spoke; now he leaned over the desk, his hand extended. I shook it, and got to my feet. The meeting seemed to be over. Bruce opened the door for me and ushered me out; he said something about letting Heather know I'd be right down. At this point, I felt a gentle buzzing from my bag. Yes, yes, I wanted to say—I know.

I turned and held the office door open. "One more thing, Bruce," I said.

"Yes?"

"I'm not interested in working in the Living Tower. I'll need Heather to get me set up in the Dead one."

The smile froze on Bruce's face. He blinked, as though waiting for me to tell him I was joking. When I didn't, he said, "That's . . . that's not usual."

"All the same," I said.

"Well," he said, stroking his chin. "Well."

I waited.

"I suppose . . . ," he said quietly to himself. "I suppose . . . if her sister . . . and quantum . . . yes, but . . ."

"I don't need Heather to take me there. Just have her give me an office number and a key, and I'll go there alone."

He frowned, shaking his head. "I can't persuade you to accept a more . . . conventional placement?"

"Sorry," I said. "It's the Dead Tower or nothing."

Slowly, he began to nod. "Yes. Yes, I see. Well, that's impressive, if nothing else. All right, then. All right. Go on down and see Heather. You're right; I don't think she'll want to take you there. But of course, the job is yours, Dead Tower and all." He extended a hand and I shook it again. This time his grip was stronger, his shaking more impassioned. "I'm very glad you came to see us today. The Dead Tower! Your boldness and loyalty are an inspiration to us all. Go see Heather. I'll let her know."

"Excellent," I said. "Thank you, Bruce."

*

Heather was on the phone when I stepped out of the elevator and into the lobby of the Courthouse. Her head was hung and her long hair dangled over the receiver, forming a sort of privacy curtain. "I will," she said. "Of course. Yes, of course. Yes, I will. Okay. I'll tell her. All right. Goodbye."

She hung up and brushed the hair away from her face and over her ear with a deft, practiced motion. "I've been told to issue you an office in the Dead Tower," she said, her voice apprehensive.

"That's right."

She nodded, then bent over a drawer in her desk. I heard the sounds of rummaging. "I need to find the key to the keys," she said.

"Take your time."

Something in the receptionist's movements suggested that she knew where to find the key, but was stalling for time. She opened and closed several other drawers, then emitted a deep sigh. She was holding a leather fob with several keys dangling from it.

As I watched, Heather crossed the lobby to a featureless wood-paneled wall. She selected a key and inserted it into a nearly indiscernible keyhole. A section of wall opened up on silent hinges, revealing a neat metal rack of about a hundred key hooks, each labeled with a number, and about half of them populated by keys. Beside this rack a second, smaller wooden panel had been mounted; Heather opened it with a second key. This revealed a smaller rack of about forty additional key hooks, most of them occupied by keys—larger, more ornate ones than the first batch. They shared the space with a still-smaller cabinet, which Heather opened with a third key from the leather fob.

This cabinet housed only a dozen or so key hooks, each of them bearing a sleek, gleaming silver key with a diamond-shaped head and a smooth, evenly channeled blade. The blades appeared uncut. Heather selected one after a moment of either indecision or reluctance, and turned to me.

"Here you go," she said. "You'll be in 4Q."

"Thank you," I said, accepting the key with my unmuffined hand.

"So, to get there, you have to take the elevator to the second floor. Then, when the doors open, step in, press the left-arrow button, and wait for the side door to let you into the auxiliary elevator. From there, press S, and it will let you out in the skyway. Then you have to cross the skyway and enter the code 3812 into the door lock on the other side. After that, take the spiral stairs to the fourth floor." She sighed. "I don't know what you do from there. You'll figure it out, I guess."

"I'm sure I will," I said. "Thank you."

I did as Heather told me, taking the elevator to the second floor, pressing the arrow, waiting for the side door to slide open—it was quite clever, this mechanism, and invisible to anyone not aware that it was there—and stepping into the auxiliary elevator. This parallel conveyance was smaller, and paneled in the same style of wood as the lobby, but it was dusty and smelled of mildew. A cockroach stood in the corner. Perhaps it was dead.

I pressed S and the thing groaned to life, hauling me another floor higher. The doors opened onto the skyway, which I walked across in a state of mild alarm. Its walls and ceiling were glass, and, particularly in their present state of uncleanliness and neglect, made me feel exposed and vulnerable. Above me, the pilotless kite swooped and rippled in the breeze. I reached the far door, windowless and of heavy steel, and punched in the code. A buzz and a rattle issued from its innards, and a click, and it fell open a single inch, creaking.

The quick and labored sound of my breathing was magnified by the skyway's glass, and I suddenly understood how frightened I was. I'd blundered my way through the interview process, following Cylvia's instructions, and this was the result. But what lay ahead?

I pocketed my office key and held the banana muffin under my chin for a moment, so that I could unzip my bag. This accomplished, I said, "Cylvia?"

She glowed white, illuminating the junk in my bag. "Yes?"

"What should I do?"

"You should go to your office."

"Am I in danger?"

Her surface throbbed for a moment, and she said, "You are in no immediate danger."

I took a deep breath, then pushed open the door to the Dead Tower.

PART TWO

Thirteen

I gazed out over a large open-plan workspace that resembled an ideal-ized 1970s living room as much as it did a municipal office. As Heather had promised, a spiral staircase served as a centerpiece; it helixed up into a murky space above the beige drop ceiling, where presumably my new office awaited. The near side of the staircase, in the area where I now stood, was populated by shared wooden work tables with their attendant stools; little groupings of overstuffed armchairs surrounded upholstered ottomans. All of this furniture gave the impression of having been hastily abandoned; many of the chairs and one of the tables lay on their sides, and everything was awkwardly swept, as if in fact by a wind, toward the southern wall. That wall consisted entirely of windows, many of which were empty of glass; the cavities left behind were covered by buckling sheets of plywood. I recalled seeing these windows from the plaza.

The opposite wall was no different: broken windows, warped ply-wood. I could hear the sounds of the outdoors—wind and birds, and the fluttering of the kite—through the gaps between the plywood and the window frames.

Beyond the spiral staircase lay a depression in the floor, where large velvet sofas, one of them overturned, were arrayed around a massive stone fireplace. Above the fireplace hung an enormous dis-play monitor. Something had struck the monitor near one of its corners, damaging the glass surface, and cracks radiated out from it across the black expanse. A bearskin rug was sprawled in front of the fireplace, and the whole area, which took up the entirety of the far corner of the third floor, was paneled in knotty pine, and underlain by thick pile carpeting in shades of brown and orange. Presumably, meetings had once taken place here, though it was just as easy to imagine the area as the set for an erotic film, perhaps the kind that unfolds in the workplace.

I slowly made my way to the base of the stairs. The wrought-iron guardrail appeared sturdy, but I gave it a kick, just to be sure. It didn't budge, and the sound my foot made as it landed on the first step was deep and resonant. Clearly, the spiral stair had survived whatever damage the windstorm had done to the rest of the Dead Tower.

I climbed slowly, alert for any sounds or odors that might suggest I should retreat. I noticed nothing at first. But then, as I neared the top, I detected what sounded like a strange, irregular echo of my footsteps—a distant, rhythmic *pock*. I stopped a moment to listen. The sound wasn't an echo: it was coming from the fourth floor, above me.

I said, "Cylvia, are there other workers in the Dead Tower right now?"

"Yes," she replied, after a moment of pulsing light.

"Should I be worried?"

"It is not clear to me what you deem worthy of anxiety," Cylvia replied, in what struck me as a slightly testy tone. "But you are in no immediate danger."

Somewhat mollified, I continued to climb. Soon I could see the fourth floor descending around me: the staircase emerged in the center of a cross formed by two hallways, quite ordinary and office-like in design, extending to the four sides of the building. This area seemed to have suffered much less damage than the floor below; aside from some water stains around a few of the light fixtures, everything visible was intact. The lights themselves were extinguished, and the halls consequentially gloomy; an ambient hum of uncertain origin permeated the entire floor.

The rhythmic pocking sound emanated from the east hallway, but luckily, my new office lay to the south. I knew this because of a series of surprisingly clear engraved plastic signs affixed to the walls, indicating which hall corresponded to which offices: Q, M, W, and B, for some reason. I scaled the final step of the staircase, stepped onto the hall carpet, and proceeded in the appropriate direction.

Finding my office was easy. A bold plaque, like the ones in the hallway, read 4Q. The lock panel, a brushed-aluminum disk punctuated by a neat, clean-edged slit, awaited my key. I didn't hesitate: I inserted the key into the lock. Once I'd gotten a third of the shaft in, some internal mechanism took it from my hand and drew it in the rest of the way. I heard a faint hum, the key turned by itself, and the door to my new office fell open.

I pulled out the key, walked in, and shut the door behind me. As I did so, the pocking sound stopped. I held my breath, facing the closed door, and after ten or fifteen seconds, the pocking resumed, more slowly at first, then gradually faster until it had attained its original speed.

The office was unremarkable in every way. It contained the same desk, lamp, wastebasket, and chairs as Bruce's office in the Living Tower, except that everything was coated in a layer of dust, and one of the windows, also dirty, was cracked. The floor's ambient hum was audible here, but quieter.

I set my bag and key down on the desk, then used my newly freed hand to brush the dust off my chair. Once seated, I tried to clean a patch of desk with my shirtsleeve. I set the muffin down in the cleaned spot. Then I removed Cylvia from my bag and set her upright beside the muffin. I could hear something inside her bumping and whirring; the sounds were magnified by the surface of the desk.

"Well," I said, "I made it."

Cylvia, evidently detecting no particular command, remained silent.

"I should find some cleaning supplies and make this place more welcoming," I said.

Cylvia's white light came on and faintly pulsed, but she didn't say anything.

"I'll go do that now," I said, and got up to leave the office.

Cylvia did not react.

I planned to walk right out, but something interrupted me: the sight, outside my window, of the kite from earlier, swooping suddenly into, and then out of, my field of view. Its fluttering sound grew louder, then faded; and for some reason I felt compelled to go to the window and look at it again. I stood in the corner of my office, which provided an unexpectedly clear angle on the entire Courthouse plaza, with its cracked cement, scraggly trees, and low memorial obelisk. But now I could see something else, or should I say someone: a small child, its arms extended, gazing up into the sky.

It took a moment to register what I was seeing: this child was the little boy I'd observed coloring in the coffee shop, and shimmying down the rainspout at the guesthouse!

The string was quite clear now. It extended from a spool in the boy's hands all the way up to the kite, which the wind seemed determined to wrest from his grasp. But to every stray gust, every sudden shear, the boy parried, calmly pivoting his body, raising or lowering his hands, taking a few steps in one direction or another, maintaining control. It was hard to make out his expression from here, but his body language implied impassivity, as though he'd been flying this kite for decades.

I watched the boy for a few minutes, until the sight of him began to make me uneasy. I couldn't have said why, precisely, but I began to feel very strongly that he should not be down there, flying that kite. Perhaps it was the weather—the wind seemed to augur some kind of atmospheric change that might affect the boy's safety. Or maybe I was merely annoyed with his guardians, whoever they might be, for failing to adequately supervise him.

Only one thing could calm my nerves, I realized: cleaning. I drew a breath and headed for the door. Then, impulsively, I leaned back over the desk and grabbed the muffin to take with me.

My search for a janitor's closet or storage room was in vain. Every door on the fourth floor was locked. Of course, there were other floors in the Dead Tower—four, in addition to the two I'd already seen—and perhaps the cleaning supplies would be found on one of them. But I wasn't sure how to access those floors.

I did, however, find the source of the pocking: office 4B. The door to this office was identical to mine: a blank white expanse interrupted only by the identifying sign and the keyhole. I also noticed that the fourth floor's now-familiar humming sound was louder here.

I steeled myself, cleared my throat, and knocked.

The pocking stopped. I waited, but no one came to the door. I knocked again.

"Who is it!" came a voice, a man's voice, over the sound of the humming.

"I'm the woman in 4Q!" I said. "I just started today! I'm looking for the supply closet or janitor's room!"

Footsteps approached behind the door. "Started today, you say?" the voice said, still muffled, but closer.

"That's right."

"Doing what?"

I was annoyed by the question, but tried not to let on. "Well, nothing yet! I just want to clean the grime out of my office before I get started."

The door emitted a click and it opened about an inch. An eye, bloodshot, stared out at me.

"I don't know about any supply closet. Or janitor, for that matter. Who told you to come up here?"

"Bruce. And Heather."

"Hmm," the man said.

I noticed that the humming was quite loud now. It was definitely coming from this man's office. It looked dark in there, behind him.

"What have you been doing in there?" I said. "I heard a sound—like you're hitting something with something else."

"You wouldn't understand," the man said.

"Try me."

He exhaled, shaking his head. "Do you know anything about quantum tunneling?" he asked me, with a sneer.

There it was again! I'd left Cylvia behind, and couldn't depend upon her guidance, so I didn't know if I was supposed to keep lying, or whether fessing up might be the better choice. I decided to split the difference.

"I'm somewhat familiar with the phenomenon," I said casually.

As Bruce had, the man appeared surprised. "I doubt that."

"Well," I said, "explain to me what you're doing. I'm sure I'll be able to follow along."

The man's face waged a battle against itself. His instinct, I could see, was to slam the door, forget about me, and continue his work. I knew the type—afraid a woman might see through him, mock him, make him feel small. On the other hand, the Dead Tower seemed like a lonely place, and it might well be that his efforts weren't being adequately acknowledged. He muttered something, turned, and let the door fall open.

I stepped into his office. It was about the same size as mine, but much less inviting in several ways. For one thing, there were no chairs. The desk was shoved awkwardly against the far wall, and supported a pile of notebooks, a coffee mug full of pencils, a dented metal bucket, and a laptop computer. More significantly, all of the room's windows, presumably shattered in the windstorm, had been replaced by sheets of plywood. If not for a string of industrial cage lights, the kind you might find on a construction worksite, the room would have had no illumination at all. The lights hung from the acoustic-tile ceiling by a few twists of wire looped through the ceiling's frame, and were plugged into a generator that sat on the floor beside a five-gallon can of gasoline. It was the generator that was causing the hum I'd been hearing. A hole had been sawed into one of the window-covers, and the generator's exhaust was routed through it via a black plastic accordion tube. Even with this arrangement, though, the smell of gasoline exhaust filled the room. Surely this man's health must be endangered by it; at the very least, it explained his bloodshot eyes.

The most remarkable alteration to the room, however, came in the form of a very neatly constructed brick wall. This wall, along with another sheet of plywood, formed a little sub-office opposite the desk. Entry to this space took the form of a crude hinged section in the plywood, an ad-hoc door about three feet high.

A glance at the laptop on the desk suggested that a camera had been installed inside the little room: a window on its screen appeared to display a live feed from this camera. Beside the live feed, a constantly updating text box read:

00038279 NO LEAKAGE DETECTED. BARRIER PERMEABILITY
    PROBABILITY 0.000000000000027%.
00038291 NO LEAKAGE DETECTED. BARRIER PERMEABILITY
    PROBABILITY 0.000000000000022%.
00038303 NO LEAKAGE DETECTED. BARRIER PERMEABILITY
    PROBABILITY 0.000000000000019%.
00038314 NO LEAKAGE DETECTED. BARRIER PERMEABILITY
    PROBABILITY 0.000000000000008%.
00038322 NO LEAKAGE DETECTED. BARRIER PERMEABILITY
    PROBABILITY 0.000000000000031%.

The man turned to me. I could see now that he was quite young— in his early twenties. He was thin, perhaps dangerously so, and his curly hair was lank and mussed. He wore blue jeans and a stained white tee shirt.

"*As you know*," he said, his emphasis suggesting that, in fact, I did not know, "classical mechanics tells us that a thrown ball lacking the energy to crash through a wall should bounce back. Right?"

"Of course," I said.

To illustrate, the man reached into the bucket on the desk and pulled from it a very worn-looking, much-handled tennis ball. He held it up, meeting my gaze to make sure I saw it. Then, he threw it at the wall. It struck the brick surface, rebounded, and bounced once against the plywood covering the floor. The man caught the ball neatly in his right hand.

This action triggered another line of text on the laptop's open window:

00038359 NO LEAKAGE DETECTED. BARRIER PERMEABILITY
PROBABILITY 0.000000000000017%.

"Do you see?" the man said, holding up the ball. "Here in the human-scale world of classical physics, the ball bounces back."

"I do."

"But in the quantum world," he now said, shaking the ball for emphasis, "any given particle encountering an ostensibly impermeable surface has a *small probability* of permeating it anyway. It's *unlikely* to happen, but if we try to calculate the path of such a particle, it is impossible for us to achieve an *infinitely probable result*. It turns out that there is a nonzero chance that such a particle could borrow energy from its surrounding particles, and use that energy to tunnel through the barrier. As I'm sure you're aware."

"Of course," I said. "But I think you're saying this is true only in the quantum world, not out here where things are large, and abide by other rules."

The man seemed excited by this reply. His grin was triumphant, as if I had fallen into an obvious logical trap, and he pointed at me with his ball hand, squeezing the ball in the process.

He said, "That's what you'd think, wouldn't you! But the truth is that we are *all* living in the quantum world! Its logical mysteries are like an infinite-speed bicycle that we're all riding, all the time, without even knowing it. If there is *any* probability of a single particle borrowing energy to permeate a barrier, then there is *also* a probability, however small, that an *assemblage* of particles"—he held up the tennis ball, triumphantly—"like this tennis ball, could *simultaneously* borrow enough energy to permeate *another* assemblage of particles."

"I see," I said.

"In other words," he went on, his eyes wild, "there is a nonzero chance that, when I throw this tennis ball against that brick wall, it will go right through!" In illustration, he flung the ball at the wall. It bounced back. He caught it. The laptop read:

00038381 NO LEAKAGE DETECTED. BARRIER PERMEABILITY
PROBABILITY 0.0000000000000005%.

"Forgive me," I said, "but, if the probability of a single particle making it through is almost infinitely remote, then wouldn't the probability of an entire tennis ball making it through be even more unlikely?"

"Of course!"

"How many atoms are there in a tennis ball? Billions, I'd imagine."

"Oh, no!" the man said, laughing. "There are six and a half septillion, give or take a few. And the particles I'm talking about are smaller even than those—they're subatomic!"

"All right, then," I said, though I'd never heard of that number and didn't know if it was even real, "so, don't you think this project is, forgive me, perhaps futile?"

"So you'd think!" the man said. "So you'd think! But my hypothesis is that this place—the Subdivision—is *different*. And that this building—the Courthouse's Dead Tower—is *even more different*! We are in a precinct of heightened probability, you see, a probability well, in which some groups of particles have developed connections to other groups of particles, influencing them even at a distance. The process by which this occurs is called quantum entanglement."

"Ah," I said. I nodded, and he did too. We nodded for a while, as the generator hummed along behind him, and I grew light-headed from its exhaust fumes. I realized that I didn't know the man's name, but it seemed an odd time to ask for it, so deep into a rather intense and complicated conversation. The time to ask, or the time for him to volunteer the information, would have been when he admitted me into the office. But we had let the moment pass. Now it was socially impossible for me ever to know.

"Forgive me if this is a foolish question," I said, idly hefting the muffin in my hand. "But wouldn't it be more efficient to build a machine to throw tennis balls at the wall for you? In fact, doesn't such a machine already exist?"

The man began shaking his head before I'd gotten even halfway through my question. "No, no, no, no. Even if it were feasible to design a tennis ball machine that could retrieve the balls after throwing them—and it's not, mind you—it is my belief that the quantum entanglement of this district is influenced by *intent*. In order for the tennis ball particles to *know* that they should coordinate in an effort to pass through the wall, they require evidence of a *will* for them to do so. That is, the particles that constitute *me*, the experimenter, must be entangled with the particles that constitute the tennis ball, which must in turn be entangled with the particles that make up the wall. Without that intent, the particles won't *know* to redistribute their energy to make the tunneling possible."

I thought about this for a few seconds. "So you're saying," I slowly inquired, "that . . . the particles need to . . . read your mind?"

The man folded his arms over his chest. He was beaming. "*Exactly*," he said. "I was wrong to doubt you! You *do* understand quantum tunneling."

Fourteen

By the time I returned to my office, it was midafternoon. I couldn't have said where the time went. Everything in 4Q was the same: my bag, the dust, Cylvia on the desk. I set my muffin down beside her, collapsed into my chair, and lay my head down on my crossed arms. I closed my eyes. Through the walls, I heard the pocking sound start up again.

"I met a neighbor," I said. "He's in 4B. He's doing an experiment."

"I was able to hear your conversation," Cylvia said. "His experiment will fail."

"That was also my assessment of the situation," I said to the desk's surface. My breath condensed there, forming a little patch of droplets. I again longed for some cleaning supplies.

"His assumptions are correct," Cylvia clarified. "The problem is that his will has no influence on the particles around him. He is, in short, not entangled."

I lifted my head. "He isn't?"

"No," she replied. She didn't elaborate, and I was too tired to press her. Instead, I lay my head back down and fell into a deep, carbon-monoxide-induced sleep.

I had a dream in which I was giving birth. The birth took place in an inflatable pool for children, in the middle of someone's living room. I was quite naked, and sitting in several inches of warm water.

123

But the water, I understood, had already gotten colder, and would become colder still. I was panicked, shivering, and in pain. Two people knelt on the floor, leaning over me. The first was a woman, buxom and dark-skinned, wearing a uniform of a light blue collared smock and dark blue pants. White stitching spelled out something over her breast, but I couldn't read it from where I sat. The woman appeared worried and frustrated, as though she was trying to decide what to do, and failing to come to a conclusion. The other person, a man, I recognized as the bakemono. He was directing the birth. I said, "I'm cold—please, more warm water," and the bakemono said, "What makes you feel better may not be best for the child."

The bakemono and the woman kept giving me conflicting advice. She told me to relax, and he told me to push. After a while, the woman got up and made a phone call, and the bakemono got up to go argue with her. It was while they were gone—in this dream, I could see them through an open doorway, in what looked like a kitchen—that I suddenly realized my child was ready to be born. I could feel my cervix dilating with preternatural speed, the contractions coming in massive waves. I cried out, but the woman and the bakemono couldn't hear—their argument had become heated, their voices raised.

At last, nearly delirious with pain and exhaustion, I sensed that the baby's head was crowning: I reached down and stroked it with my hand, the one that wasn't holding the banana muffin. The child's hair was short and stiff and kinky beneath my waterlogged fingers. Between my legs, the baby looked jaundiced—bright yellow, even. With one final, anguished scream, I pushed the child out. I could hear it emerge—*pock!*—from the birth canal, and drop with a splash into the water. I reached for it, and realized that it was, in fact, a tennis ball.

It wasn't the only tennis ball, though—I was giving birth to twins. The second one came quickly—and then, to my astonishment, a third. Soon, the little pool was filling up with my children, all tennis balls. They were lined up inside me—I could feel them there. The contractions bent my body back, and soon the balls, my children, were issuing from my body like bullets from an automatic rifle. I launched them out of the pool and into the far wall of solid brick.

Every one of them passed through the wall. I could hear them, ricocheting around the space behind it, but I couldn't see them. They needed me—they were my children. But they were trapped behind the wall, disentangled.

•

I woke to the sound of ocean waves. They were emanating from Cylvia, and gently faded as I roused myself.

"It's time to leave," she said.

"Oh, all right. Thank you."

"You never responded to my queries."

"Queries?"

"Yes," Cylvia said. She paused, then I heard the sounds of a park: Admiral Kilmeade Municipal Park, I realized, recognizing the splashing of the water feature. It was followed by a thin, distant rendering of Cylvia's voice. I understood that she was playing me a recording. "When you reach your home," Cylvia said in the recording, "please say, 'Cylvia, I am home.'" I heard my own voice respond "Okay" and Cylvia's follow-up command: "When you reach your place of work, please say, 'Cylvia, I am at work.'"

The recording ended, and she said, "Are you at your place of work?"

"Yes, I am."

A low whir, accompanied by a white pulsing.

"Is the guesthouse your home?"

With misgivings I did not have the time or patience to interrogate, I said, "Yes, it is."

"Thank you," she said, when the whirring was done.

I gathered up my things, including Cylvia, and headed out, pulling the door shut behind me. With a *thunk*, it locked itself for the night. I moved down the hall and down the spiral staircase, into the wind-damaged lounge; I opened the steel door and entered the skyway. The kite and the boy were gone, and a man was standing at the elevator door, furiously pushing the button to summon it, as though this action would bring the elevator faster. It was, of course, the man from 4B.

"Careful," I said. "If you push it too many times, your finger might pass right through."

He turned to me with a scowl. "The elevator isn't in the probability well!"

"I was joking," I said.

4B appeared confused. He turned back to the button to press it a few more times, while looking doubtfully at me over his shoulder.

The elevator opened, and we entered the wood-paneled chamber together. After a few seconds of shuddering and grinding, the side door opened, and we climbed through into the other elevator, which we rode down to the lobby. Heather had already gone home. 4B and I crossed the lobby together. I held the front door open for him, and we spilled out onto the plaza.

Forby seemed to deflate a little, now that his working day was done. "See you tomorrow, I guess," he said mournfully.

"So long."

He set off across the plaza to the west, and was gone. It was time for me to leave, too, but first I went over to take a better look at the obelisk.

Heather had, of course, been correct: the obelisk was a memorial to the windstorm. An engraved brass plaque on its south face read

ON THIS SPOT
MANY DIED DURING THE GREAT WINDSTORM
OF THE NAMELESS YEAR

underneath an etching that depicted the tragic event. The etching was rendered in a cartoon style, and featured a foreshortened view of the Dead Tower—the same view, in fact, available to anyone standing on this very spot. The etching view was partially obscured by a rain of building debris and human beings, their dresses, neckties, and sport coats fluttering as they fell to their deaths. The artist had taken great pains to render the anguished faces of the doomed. It was impressive and somber, and I could understand why Heather might be offended that I'd used the memorial as a temporary resting place for my muffin. As a gesture of respect, I held the muffin tightly now.

•

I still felt light-headed from the fumes in Forby's office, and exhausted by the day's events. When I arrived back at the guesthouse, I drew the bedroom curtains closed and lay down to take a second nap, first carefully resting Cylvia and the banana muffin on the bedside table. I dozed dreamlessly and woke to Cylvia's red warning light. She was announcing, with some urgency, "A visitor. A visitor. A visitor."

There, beside my bed, stood the little boy. He was dressed, rather charmingly, in a very small, neatly tailored pinstriped suit, and a necktie emblazoned with lightning bolts. In one hand, he held a small rectangular package covered in gift wrap, which bore a pattern of balloons, confetti, and the words HAPPY BIRTHDAY!; and in the other hand he held my banana muffin, which he had halfway completed eating. His jaw worked, and crumbs cascaded down his chest and onto the floor.

"You startled me," I said to the boy. Cylvia was silent, but her red light, somewhat subdued now, continued to pulse.

"Did you forget?" the boy asked.

"I'm sorry," I said, sitting up. "Maybe I did. Forget what?"

"You said you'd take me."

I cast my mind back to my one personal encounter with the boy. I couldn't remember promising to take him anywhere. But perhaps my memory was deceiving me. "I'm sorry," I said. "I guess you want me to take you to . . . a birthday party?"

The boy nodded, taking another bite of the muffin.

"All right," I said, hanging my legs down from the bed and slipping my feet into my shoes, which I was pleased to see were actually more festive than I'd recalled—a kind of sparkle confetti that faded from deep purple at the heel to bright silver at the toe. I rubbed my face. "Where is the party?"

"Birthday House."

"What's Birthday House?"

"It's Birthday today. The party is at Birthday House. We're late."

"What's your friend's name? The one with the birthday."

The boy ignored my question. "Let's *go*," he said.

"All right, all right."

A minute later we were walking under a deep purple sky through the streets of the Subdivision. The little boy seemed averse to using the sidewalks; he preferred to march right down the middle of the road. After a block or so, he finished eating the muffin, and quickened his pace. Despite my much longer legs, I was having trouble keeping up.

"You know where we're going, I presume?" I said.

He didn't reply. We walked in silence for a little while, the boy veering off in this or that direction, always returning to the middle of the street. At one point, a dog crossed the road up ahead, turning to gaze impassively at us, and the boy took my hand. His fingers were greasy from the muffin, and a bit cold. When the dog disappeared into the shadows, the boy yanked his hand from mine, as though I had been the one who had initiated the contact and he couldn't wait to let go.

Our destination turned out to be a charming house with a wide porch and a brightly illuminated front window. Inside, adults and children in conical party hats could be seen gathered around a table with balloons tethered to its corners. I could make out a pile of confetti-sprinkled, colorful gifts and a cake, and heard the faint strains of "Happy Birthday."

"Hurry!" the little boy said, grabbing my hand and pulling me up the stairs.

I might have politely knocked on the front door, but the little boy barged right in. No one seemed bothered by the intrusion. He ran up to the table and added his gift to the pile, then launched into the song, which had entered what I recalled was its third or fourth verse.

Happy birthday, my dear
Here's a respite from fear
As you blow out the candles
Thank the fates you're still here

Happy birthday, my friend
All good things must end
Let these gifts help you salve all
Of the wounds you can't mend

Happy birthday, loved one
Time for compensation
For the way you've been treated
And your suff'rings to come

We were well into the verse about the possibility of peace, at last, in the next world, before people began to roll their eyes. "I'm bored!" a child shouted. "I want *cake*!" screamed another. At last, the song collapsed into its traditionally ragged strands, and a comely woman in a gingham dress, presumably the birthday child's mother, began to serve large wedges of cake.

As the children ate, the parents broke up into small groups to chat. Many of them held paper cups of fruit juice, and a man handed one to me. I sipped from it and listened in on their discussion, which seemed to be about the state of construction on the road to the City. Some of them stole glances at me as they talked, as though attempting to gauge my reaction.

In truth, the subject did interest me. I wondered why these repairs weren't more of a priority for the Subdivision—surely some of these people made their living in the City, or had friends or family there? At the very least, I thought it must be an appealing contrast to the sleepy goings-on of the Subdivision. The more I thought about it, the more I longed to go there, and the more irritated I became at the construction delays.

I wanted to join in, but couldn't seem to find an opening. Eventually the conversation shifted back to the party itself, the cheery confetti and balloons and the delicious juice, and I asked, "So, who's the birthday boy or girl?"

My little group laughed, as though I'd just made a whimsical joke.

I felt a bit put off—my question hadn't been unusual in any way, I didn't think, and deserved some kind of answer. Instead of asking it a second time, though, I decided to come at it from a different angle. I turned to the woman beside me—tomboyish, with large eyeglasses and a fringed suede jacket—and said, "Which one is yours?"

The woman, who had smiled at me when I turned to her, now frowned in evident puzzlement. "I'm sorry?"

"Which child? Is it the one in the eyeglasses there? She's adorable."

The woman looked at me with an expression somewhere between pity and mild alarm, as though I might be making fun of her, or even issuing some kind of threat. She elbowed the man standing beside her, a placid-looking bald fellow wearing a plaid shirt. "She wants to know which of the children," she said, "is 'mine.'" And she punctuated the "mine" by forming her fingers into quotation marks.

"Well," the man said, "they're children! They're just . . . the neighborhood children."

"I mean, it's their house," the woman added. "Haven't you been here before?" she asked me.

"I try to come to Birthday every few weeks," the man interjected.

"Have you never been to Birthday before?" the woman asked me. Her expression harbored the beginnings of relief, as though she'd at last divined a possible cause for my peculiarity.

I sensed that an explanation was in the offing, but at that moment, our conversation was interrupted by a loud cheer. We turned in time to see all the children, cake- and ice-cream-smeared, lunging for the giant pile of gifts. In their eagerness, they clawed at the plastic tablecloth and it began to slide, sending paper plates, juice cups, and other debris crashing to the floor. No one seemed particularly concerned by the mess, so I began to laugh and applaud along with the other adults. "Take! Take! Take! Take!" we all shouted, as the children savagely tore the presents open, and bows and ribbons and scraps of gift wrap flew through the air.

The children seemed uninterested in the gifts themselves, which, from where I was standing, didn't appear to have the novelty or charm of typical birthday surprises. Through the scrum of celebrants I could make out a stained plastic travel mug, a creased and dog-eared road atlas, half a bag of hard candies, and a pair of sunglasses with one broken lens. But the gifts' lack of appeal hadn't dampened the children's enthusiasm. One little boy pushed another down and kicked him; two little girls were pummeling each other over what appeared to be a quart of motor oil. I was pleased to note that "my" child, the little boy who had accompanied me here, was keeping to the edge of the mob, avoiding conflict with the other revelers. But his face was anxious and determined, and he repeatedly extended a hand toward the gift pile, only to snatch it back when another fight broke out nearby.

I was distracted from the gift frenzy, though, by a scene that was unfolding on the other side of the table. In the back corner of the room, withdrawn somewhat from the action, a man and a woman stood close, deep in conversation. The woman was smiling shyly, tucking a strand of hair behind her ear; the man had his hands in his pockets and was leaning over her, nodding. The woman looked familiar, and it took me a moment to place her: it was Justine. I hadn't recognized her, because her expression was so unfamiliar: sleepily seductive, like some starlet in a romantic film. She wore her now-familiar sheer white coverup, stained with green at the knees, and as I watched, she smoothed her hand over it, as though to emphasize the contours of her body.

The man also looked vaguely familiar; his lanky frame and broad shoulders struck a chord in me. He spoke to her, nodding, and they both broke out into peals of laughter, which I could barely hear over

131

the mad rending and shouting going on between us. The man had his back to me, so I couldn't make him out clearly, but as he threw his head back to laugh I took note of his angular features and thick brown hair, and thought I'd go over there and try to throw a wrench into their flirtation.

The little boy gazed mournfully from underneath his birthday hat as I edged around the table. He was pointing at the gift pile imploringly, as if asking me for help. The nerve! Clearly it was his job to seize and unwrap the presents, and mine to prevent Justine from seducing this handsome man. I frowned and shook my head at the little boy, and, dejected, he returned to pawing ineffectually at the gift pile, after dodging an elbow from a nearby scuffle.

I felt an itching sensation at my hip as I approached the insufferable couple in the corner, and reached down to scratch it, then realized that it was just Cylvia, issuing some irritating notification or alert from inside my bag. I was forced to suppress a wave of anger. Why had I brought her, if she was just going to interrupt my fun?

Ignoring her, I strode up to Justine and her suitor and tapped him firmly on the shoulder. Justine's face registered my presence with a smirk and a roll of the eyes.

The man turned to me. I was right—he was very good-looking. I said, "Can I talk to you for a minute, please?"

"Sure," he said sullenly, motioning to Justine to please excuse him.

"You're embarrassing me," I said. "Everyone can see what you're doing."

The man held up his hands. "Hey, we were just talking."

Cylvia's alert had sped up and was now turning into a solid, unceasing buzz. I smacked my bag to shut her up.

"You weren't just talking," I said. "You were flirting. I'm the one who has to work with her! How am I supposed to do that every day, knowing how she behaved with you?"

"You're blowing this all out of proportion. *You're* the one embarrassing yourself here, not me! Nobody even noticed me talking to her until you came over and made a big deal of it."

I said, "*Everybody* noticed." I pointed to the birthday table, where the children had nearly reached the bottom of the gift pile. "Things are bad enough already. You're making them harder for me!"

"You're the one who made me come here," he said. "I wanted to stay home."

"You haven't left the house in weeks," I pointed out.

"There's a reason for that. I'm on medical leave. I'm *sick*. You can't just *cheer me up*." His fine features were curling into an expression of disgust. "If you can't recognize that, then you're sick too. You're sicker than I am."

Behind him, Justine was pretending to be distracted by something out the window, but it was clear that she heard everything. At my side, my bag was shaking like a washing machine, and emitting an earsplitting alarm, which the handsome man didn't seem to hear. The lurid light that dimly illuminated this corner of the room flashed red on my party shoes.

"It's a terrible world," he said, barely audible beneath the screeching from my bag. His face was hard and his eyes were unfocused. "And we've made terrible choices. Forgive me for taking a moment's respite to talk to somebody who makes me feel good about myself for a change."

I was about to respond to this bizarre escalation in our argument when the man, Justine, and the entire party around us grew hazy in my sight, and began to smear and distend. At the same time, the voices around us slurred, then dropped in pitch, and then stopped entirely, as though time itself had ground to a halt. The only persistent sound and motion came from my bag. At last, I zipped it open and peered inside. Its interior was bathed in blinding red light.

"Would you please stop that!" I screamed. "You are interrupting an important and serious conversation!"

"You must focus on your work."

"I'm not at work! I'm at a party! Why can't I just go to Birthday for an hour and be free of your petty concerns?"

"You are always at work," Cylvia said, cryptically. "Step away from the bakemono. You must help the child find the gift. You must escort Mr. Lorre home. You must abide by your hosts."

"What? Which gift? Where is Mr. Lorre?" But Cylvia was right: he was sitting on a wooden chair at the dining table in the next room. The room's shadows had deepened, and I could barely make out his face, which looked pale and mournful in the darkness. In his lap lay a new bouquet of red roses. Unaffected by whatever had frozen the other partygoers, he rocked in place, mumbling to himself. "Anna," he said. "Anna."

My eye was drawn to a motion at my left—it was the little boy. He'd finally gotten a leg up on the now-frozen children, and was using one of them—a bruised and bloodied red-haired boy, lying paralyzed on his back on the floor—as a step, to try to reach a gift that lay in the center of the table, surrounded by the detritus of revelry. Its paper was torn at the corner, and it looked a little dirty, but I recognized it as the gift he himself had brought.

Exasperated, I leaned over the table and plucked up the present. I handed it to the boy. "There," I said. "That wasn't so hard, was it. Now get down off that child!"

The little boy climbed back down onto the floor. He extended the present to me.

"I just grabbed that for you!" I said. "Open it!"

"No," the boy said, shaking his head. "It's for you."

"How could it be for me? It isn't my birthday!"

He shrugged, glancing at the seemingly random collection of objects that lay scattered on the table and floor. "They're all for you," he said.

I didn't understand, but I accepted the gift. I noticed now how carefully he had wrapped it: the folds were sharp and precise, the cuts tidy; and the whole was beautifully accentuated by a pink ribbon and bow. The torn corner revealed that there was a book inside.

"Open it," the boy said again. Inside my bag, Cylvia pulsed white.

I unwrapped the gift and let the paper and ribbon fall to the floor. In my hands lay what appeared to be a heavily used self-help book, its back cover facing up. A placid-looking woman smiled sympathetically in a photo in the corner, beside a biography that read, "Jane Lowe, LCMFT, is a licensed family and marriage therapist and the author of the best-selling self-help books *Loving Is Giving*, *Out of the Doghouse*, and *Lost and Found.*" I turned the book over. It was called *Her Way: Recovering Yourself from His Demanding Love.* Its cover illustration depicted the shadow of a man, his arm raised in anger, looming over the silhouette of a woman, confident, her arms crossed, outlined by an aura of gold. A blurb at the bottom of the cover, attributed to a "Roberta Klarman," read, in an elegant script, "This book saved my marriage—and my self." Many pages were dog-eared, and sticky notes stuck out in several places.

Furious, I turned to the little boy and snarled, "Where did you get this?"

He appeared nonplussed. After a moment, he sighed, and turned his head to peer into the darkness, toward Mr. Lorre, still muttering over his roses.

"What happens in my marriage is none of your business, do you understand!"

The little boy shrugged again.

"Let's get out of here," I said, exasperated. I shoved the book into my bag, pushing Cylvia aside, and roughly took the boy's hand. I dragged him over to Mr. Lorre.

"It's time to go!" I shouted. "Stop your blubbering and come with me!"

"Anna . . . ," he said, trying to get to his feet.

I took his elbow and pulled him up. He stumbled, and the roses scattered on the floor. Mr. Lorre bent over, as though to pick them up.

"Forget about those!" I said. "It's late! Who even invited you here? Birthday isn't for people like you!"

He whimpered, stumbling, as I pulled him toward the door. To his credit, the little boy kept up, his little legs pumping in their pin-striped suit pants. Around us, the party was grinding slowly back into motion.

I flung the front door open, and we marched down the steps and through the now-dark streets toward home.

Fifteen

The little boy let go of my hand just as we approached the guest-house; he ran out of sight around the corner, and a moment later I heard him clambering up the downspout to his room. I guided Mr. Lorre to the door, then stole a glance at the dining room table as I led him up the stairs to bed. Bathed in lamplight, it seemed to beckon to me. Once Mr. Lorre was safely in bed, I deposited Cylvia in my room and headed back downstairs.

I took a good, hard look at the puzzle. A great deal of it had been filled in—only a small part of the lower-right quadrant remained to be solved, with the as-yet-unplaced pieces scattered about the table-top. The overall scene was fairly clear now: on a curving road that ran alongside a river and through a masonry arch bridge, a car had lost control and crossed into the oncoming lane. It was about to smash into one of the bridge abutments. A delivery truck of some kind, in an effort to avoid the errant car, had swerved, and was tipping over; from its driver's-side window spilled a bouquet of red roses, some drifting in the air, some already striking the pavement. The truck's driver, a stocky man in late middle age, was rising up out of his seat and appeared likely to follow the flowers onto the road. A few by-standers observed the scene: a heavyset middle-aged man carrying a folded newspaper and a paper cup of coffee; a woman in her thirties pushing a baby in a stroller; and a third figure, a man in his twenties with a beard and uniform—some kind of paramedic—who was running toward the crash with a stethoscope dangling around his neck. In the background, an ambulance waited, as though the accident had been foretold, or perhaps as though time itself were compressed, or layered.

The image—which I now recognized as a reproduction of a hyper-realistic painting rather than a photograph—was unusual in perspective: the viewer beheld the incident through the rear window of the crashing car, which was canted to one side at a terrifying angle. At the far lower left and right of the puzzle, the car's occupants were posed in states of intense drama. The driver, a man, scowled in apparent determination, his hands gripping the steering wheel. His eyes were unfocused, slightly misaligned, as though affected by the medical condition known as nystagmus. Beside him, his passenger, a woman, raised her arms in fear. Her mouth was open in a scream. She looked familiar, with a wide nose and neat bangs, but it was hard to identify her without a puzzle piece that was missing from her face: an irregular shape, framing a bit of the walnut tabletop below, where an eye ought to have been.

I had not forgotten, of course, that I possessed a puzzle piece with an eye on it, and I dug into the pocket of my skirt until I found it. I seemed to remember it having an unusual shape, that of a bell or cartoon ghost, but now it was more like a crooked diamond, with a strange little spur bulging from one side. I laid it down over the gap in the puzzle, but, unfortunately, it didn't fit. It looked like solving the puzzle was once again beyond my abilities.

A noise from the living room: someone was coming. I returned the puzzle piece to my pocket and turned to find Clara approaching.

"Hello, dear," she said, resignedly. "I thought that might be you."

"I was," I told her proudly, "at work."

But she didn't immediately respond. Instead, she stood before me, nodding slowly, a look of consternation on her face. "Dear," she said, finally. "You've been with us for a while now."

"I have. I've been having a wonderful time."

"I'm going to be honest with you. We'd . . . we'd hoped that you'd have solved the puzzle by now. It's . . . not complicated."

I was taken aback by this remark. It hadn't been my understanding that the project was compulsory, or even very important. My meager attention to it was given exclusively out of politeness.

"I beg to differ," I said, trying to keep the tremor out of my voice. "I've come close, as you can see, but I must have made a mistake somewhere along the line. I can't make the final piece fit."

"If I may be so bold," Clara said. "It's basically finished. It's time to move on, wouldn't you say? You don't really need the last piece to understand what you're seeing, do you."

"Of course I do!" I replied. "The last piece could change the entire meaning of the puzzle!"

Clara appeared startled by this argument and opened her mouth to speak, then appeared to think better of it. After a moment, she patted me on the shoulder and said, "I suppose you're right. I'm sorry, dear." She turned and headed back toward the kitchen, leaving me alone with the unfinished puzzle.

I gazed again at the image of the road accident in progress, and felt a great weight bearing down on me, as though everything I'd accomplished so far in the Subdivision had been meaningless. Clara was right, of course; the final piece didn't matter. There was nothing that could be printed on it that would alter the big picture: I and my unseen collaborators had brought the task as close to completion as possible, and this was the result.

Dejected, I again drew the final piece from my pocket and gazed mournfully at the single eye depicted there. With a sigh, I tossed the piece onto the puzzle's surface, where it bounced, flipping over in the process. It landed a few inches right of center, facedown.

It was then that I noticed something: the glossy top of the puzzle piece wasn't the only surface bearing an image. There was something on the other side too.

I leaned in closer. It appeared that someone had written something on the back of the puzzle piece in fine black marker—I could make out a couple of numbers, and something that looked like an arrow. My curiosity piqued, I lifted up a corner of the near-completed puzzle and peered underneath. Sure enough, I saw more markings there—sketches, equations perhaps, scrawled in a barely legible hand.

I thought of Clara's words. It was time to move on, she'd said. Perhaps she was right. Swiftly, and before I could talk myself out of it, I lifted one side of the enormous puzzle, and attempted to flip the whole thing over, as though it were a bedspread. All the pieces, taken together, were surprisingly heavy, and I struggled to wield their clinging, mosslike mass. I'd almost gotten it onto its back when chunks began to fall off and cascade across the table's surface. Alarmed, I let the rest drop, and the pieces jumped, separating themselves and skittering along the polished wood, some of them bouncing onto the carpet below.

I'd made quite a mess. But enough of the puzzle had remained intact that I could see some logic behind the diagrams scrawled there. The dull brown surface resembled a scientist's chalkboard, with numbered sections illustrating various obscure calculations and instructions: the rough map of a large building bearing a big black X; something resembling a weather map, with stylized lines and arrows that indicated colliding fronts; trajectories and velocities for various airborne objects; numbers corresponding to the properties of different surfaces; the flow properties of liquid through a meandering channel.

It all seemed quite meaningful, though I couldn't imagine what specific objects or events it all referred to. I crouched on the floor to collect the fallen pieces, and noticed that my shoes looked quite different here in the dining room than they had last night, in the festive lights of Birthday; in the shadow of the table, their glittery confetti pattern appeared drab, brown and businesslike, with dots and slashes of black, not unlike the puzzle's underside.

I dumped the stray pieces onto the table's surface and idly began to fit them into their places. Yes: this was much better. The image on the puzzle's obverse seemed simplistic, obvious in retrospect, and I felt embarrassed by my incapacity—or unwillingness—to complete it.

This side, on the other hand, seemed to represent something sophisticated and demanding, a mystery befitting a professional like me.

What it all meant, though, was unclear, at least for the moment. The hour had grown late, and I had a busy day behind me, and another ahead; I lacked the energy even to snap the last few puzzle pieces into place. I climbed the stairs, instructed Cylvia to wake me, and collapsed, exhausted, into bed.

•

In the morning I woke early, determined to clean my office, which would necessitate a stop at the drugstore for supplies. I hung my legs over the edge of my bed and felt despair creeping up on me. Across the room, the self-help book stuck out of my bag; I got up, grabbed it, and shoved it under the mattress.

I knew what I needed: a long, luxurious bath. Yawning, I gathered up my towel and toiletries, and told Cylvia that it wouldn't be necessary to wake me after all. Her white light pulsed faintly in response, but she didn't speak. I opened my door and walked out, throwing my shoulders back and raising my chin, so that I would appear dignified to anyone who happened to be waiting in the hall. Nobody, however, was there.

I drew a bath and settled into it, this time getting the water level exactly right on my first try. I recalled my confused and emotional state the last time I had lain here, and marveled at the progress I'd made since that distant time: I'd gotten a job, and made some new friends: Justine, Mr. Lorre, and Forby. I found that I was proud to have assisted Mr. Lorre during his moments of anxiety, and eager to get back to work with Forby in the Dead Tower. I recalled Justine with less fondness, though I couldn't have told you why.

I turned to gaze out the window: with the exception of some haze on the horizon, and a stiff wind tugging at some distant trees, it looked like another warm, sunny day in the Subdivision. The rooftop of the neighbors' house was visible, as before, and I expected my other new friend, the crow, to alight upon it as he had the last time I took a bath.

Indeed, I didn't want to miss the moment he landed, so I concentrated very hard on the roof and waited for him to arrive.

What seemed like seconds later, I was awakened by a pounding on the door, accompanied by a wheezing man's voice repeating the word "please," and, further in the background, a female voice repeating the phrase "wake up." The former was Mr. Lorre, demanding entry to the bathroom, and the latter Cylvia, sounding the alarm in spite of my instructions to the contrary. The water I lay in, however, was ice-cold, and my shivering body was pale and puckered from the excessive soaking. How long had I been lying here?

"Just a minute!" I called out, climbing out of the water. I had just gotten myself wrapped in a towel when the bathroom door crashed open and Mr. Lorre lumbered in, cupping his crotch with both hands. He was dressed in his clothes from the night before and appeared as disheveled and bewildered as ever.

"Mr. Lorre!" I scolded, but he didn't even seem to notice I was there. He staggered to the toilet and fumbled at his belt.

I was not eager to watch what came next, so I quickly gathered up my clothes from the wall hook and hurried into the hall, pulling the door shut behind me. Soon I was safely enclosed in my bedroom, furiously drying myself and trying to heat my frigid skin with the towel.

"You must go to work," Cylvia said, from her place on the bedside table.

"I know!" I exclaimed. "I'm trying to!"

"You must go to work."

"Stop telling me that!"

Somehow I got myself dressed before Cylvia delivered another warning. I swept her into my bag and ran down the stairs. Before I pushed open the front door, I peered into the dining room. The sun had risen on the other side of the house, so the light was dim at best. But it was clear that someone—the little boy, I now suspected—had completed the job I had begun the night before, fitting the final pieces into the newly overturned puzzle. Unfortunately, I didn't have time to stop and examine it: I had to get to the office immediately.

It was lucky that Fortuitous Items was more or less along my route to work, and open for business. I greeted the clerk, the same one who had sold me Cylvia, but he didn't seem to remember me. In fact, he was busy doing something over by the front window and offered only the faintest nod in acknowledgment.

I found some paper towels, sponges, abrasive cleanser, and window spray, and brought them to the front counter. The clerk glanced over his shoulder at me. I could see now that he was using tape from a big gray roll to cover the window with old magazines—specifically, back issues of a publication called FAMOUS ACCIDENTS. A list of sensational headlines appeared on the lurid covers; they included 37-CAR PILEUP!, FREIGHT TRAIN MEETS BIG RIG!, and HELICOPTER SINKS FISHING BOAT!

Reluctantly, the clerk slouched over to the counter and listlessly dragged my items into a plastic sack. I couldn't help but notice that the display rack of personal digital assistants no longer stood near the counter. I asked the clerk what had become of it.

He didn't seem to know what I was talking about. "You mean the little radios?" he asked, shoving the paper towels into the bag, and breaking it. With a frustrated grunt, he reached beneath the counter for a new bag, and started the process over.

"No—they were cylinders, light gray cylinders that you could talk to. Computers inside cylinders."

The clerk shook his head. "Don't remember anything like that," he said.

"But they were just here. Were they discontinued?"

"Beats me," he said, this time placing the paper towels into a second bag. "Lots of stuff comes and goes, I can't be expected to keep track of it. What's the matter, you want to return it?"

"No!" I said, horrified.

He shrugged, dismissing me with a little wave of his hand, and returned to his task, lifting another magazine from the pile at his feet and using it to cover up another pane of the window. Its cover read CAR STRIKES BRIDGE, TRUCK OVERTURNS!

"I'm curious," I said to him, lifting my bag from the counter. "What are you doing there?"

"Battening down," he said, without turning around. "Last time we had a storm, the window shattered. During business hours, no less. Kalim ended up in the hospital."

"Storm? But it's nice out. Breezy, but nice."

"Whatever," the clerk replied with a dismissive shrug. "Enjoy your killer breeze."

I made my way to the Courthouse, quite deliberately appreciating the weather, and passed through the front door with what I hoped was a friendly nod to Heather, sitting motionless behind her enormous desk. She appeared mildly annoyed and alarmed to see me.

"Glad you're finally here," she said, and it was unclear whether her tone indicated relief, disappointment, or condescension.

"I was forced to deal with an emergency at home," I said. "A neighbor in need. I'm sure Bruce would understand."

Heather did not respond, and it was unclear whether her silence indicated satisfaction, offense, or pity.

I stepped into the elevator, took it to the other elevator, then crossed the skyway to the steel door, which let me in with my code. The lounge appeared unchanged, and the spiral stairs clanked familiarly under my feet. I was greeted on the fourth floor by the cheerful sound of Forby's tennis balls, and by the odors of dust, mildew, and engine exhaust. My sleek, gleaming key let me into my office, and I began scrubbing the work surfaces and walls, and wiping down the windows until they squeaked.

By the time I finished, the sun had passed its zenith, and rhomboid patches of light were creeping across the office. Cylvia was set up on my desk to absorb that light. It wasn't yet time to leave, but now that I was finally ready for some work, I wasn't sure what I was supposed to do.

I was about to ask Cylvia for advice when I noticed something that I had somehow missed while cleaning: a small blue light, blinking on the far wall. I crossed the room for a closer look. The light had been cleverly installed just beneath the surface of the evidently translucent white wall material; it would be invisible when it wasn't lit.

I didn't understand what the light signified at first. But then I noticed, just to its left, a square section of wall delineated by faint gaps. It looked as though it had been designed as some kind of door. I felt around its edges, thinking I could get a fingernail into the crack to pull it free. When that didn't work, I gave the panel a gentle press, and felt a click.

Now I heard the quiet sound of turning gears, and the top edge of the panel popped out and fell gently toward me and down. In a matter of seconds, the panel was fully opened, revealing a light gray plastic tray, recessed into the wall. Upon the tray lay a pile of papers—forms or reports, from the look of them—casually collated and gathered into sections with paper clips.

This, then, must be the work I had been hired to do. I lifted the papers—they were quite heavy—and carried them over to my desk as the panel receded back into the wall with a quiet hum. The blue light switched off, and the wall once again appeared whole.

I took a seat and began to read the papers. They seemed to be case studies of some kind—complex life scenarios, some evidently frivolous, some with potentially serious consequences. At the end of each question was printed the heading ANALYST'S RESPONSE, followed by a series of prompts.

*In my view, protagonist made the **right**/**wrong** decision (choose one).
Elaborate:* _____

_____

In the event of a similar future situation, protagonist should:

_____

_____

*Protagonist's mistake **can**/**should** (choose one) be remedied by:*

_____

_____

*Protagonist's responsibility is primarily to **herself/others** (choose one).*
Elaborate: _____

_____

*Protagonist **should/shouldn't** have known better (choose one).*
Elaborate: _____

_____

As I perused the pile of documents, it struck me: Of course! This was the Courthouse! I had been hired as a Phenomenon Analyst, which, it now seemed to me, was akin to a judge. I settled in and began to read the first question.

A young boy, Hector, wants a popular new toy for Christmas. His mother, Juniper, finds it at the toy store, but also finds a knockoff version for much less money. Though she is comfortably well-off, Juniper buys the cheaper toy. On Christmas morning, Hector expresses his disappointment, so Juniper takes the cheaper toy away and sends him to his room. She also throws away the Christmas cake she bought for him at the Christian bakery.

This was an easy one—Hector was clearly an ungrateful, spoiled brat, and Juniper a thrifty, responsible parent trying to instill positive values in her child. The Analyst's Response practically wrote itself, and I quickly moved on to the next scenario.

Mei-Lien is very fond of ducks. While out walking with her friend Georg, they happen upon an idyllic pond. Mei-Lien is delighted by the many ducks that approach them on the water's surface, hoping for a morsel of bread. But she is shocked when Georg begins to pelt the birds with rocks. He explains that ducks are a public nuisance, and that they carry germs. Years later, when Georg is applying for a high-clearance Defense Department job, Mei-Lien is contacted by government officials for insights into his character. She tells them the story about the ducks. Later she learns that Georg was turned down for the job, and instead has signed on with a private military contractor believed to maintain so-called "black sites" where torture takes place.

This scenario required a little more thought. I got up and paced around my small office space, Forby's tennis balls providing a potent counterpoint to my contemplative footsteps. After a few minutes, I sat down and wrote a few words about Mei-Lien's narcissism masquerading as compassion, and her terrible betrayal that, luckily, couldn't keep a good man down. Also, ducks? No, thanks!

The next scenario seemed out of place, based upon my expert analysis of the previous two, so I read it twice, just to be sure I had it right.

Divya has been dating her fiancé, Ronaldo, for several years. Because he doesn't like her friends and family, she has grown distant from them—but, she tells herself, that suits her just fine. They don't like or understand Ronaldo, and their distaste is an insult to her. She's content to be with him alone.

One day, Divya receives a private message via social media from a woman who claims to be Ronaldo's sister, and which reads, "Forgive me if I have the wrong person, but I think that you are dating my brother. I don't mean to interfere, but there are some things he might not have told you that I think you should know about him. If you're willing to talk, please call me." The supposed sister has left a phone number.

Divya decides to tell Ronaldo about the message, and his reaction surprises her—he laughs it off, saying that the message-writer is not his sister but a mentally unstable ex, who has tried to pull this before. She has a personality disorder, he explains, and has been institutionalized for various psychoses; everyone knows she's crazy. "Here," he says, reaching for Divya's computer keyboard. "Let me just block her for you, and I'm going to report her for harassment."

With a few quick clicks and keystrokes, Ronaldo ejects the ex-girlfriend from Divya's online life. He is so apologetic about the entire incident, and so sweet in his attempts to make it up to her, that she lets the whole thing pass. In fact, when Ronaldo later argues that social media itself is toxic—a haven for liars, scammers, and weirdos—she agrees to delete her accounts, despite their being one of her last remaining connections to her family. To hell with them, she thinks—she and Ronaldo are a team.

A few weeks later, the two are married, and months pass before Divya even tells her own mother about it. By then, in fact, she is expecting a child.

For the first time, I wondered what the higher-ups in the Dead Tower were on about. Were they trying to entrap me into some kind of snap judgment of affairs that were clearly none of my business? These two sounded like a decent couple with their own special relationship style, and it wasn't my place to interfere. It occurred to me to wonder whether my assessments would have consequences outside the cloistered world of the Dead Tower—if they might affect the lives of real people.

It was, however, only my first day, and I didn't wish to make waves. I scrawled a few noncommittal notes in the "Analyst's Response" section, and moved on.

On his deathbed, Joaquin asks his daughter, Tabitha, to plant a sycamore tree in the back yard of their family home, in remembrance of him. As the life leaves his body, she promises to honor his wishes. Instead, soon after Joaquin's death, Tabitha sells the property for a large sum, and soon a shopping center stands in its place.

That was better. I dug into my answers, riffing expertly on death's status as the one true broken promise, and applauding Tabitha for her business acumen and admirable lack of sentimentality.

I turned to the next report in my pile.

Sixteen

Xenia and her husband, Malthe, are expecting a child. Malthe argues that, because many pregnancies end in miscarriage, Xenia shouldn't immediately tell her family the good news. She agrees. But, as the months go by, Malthe grows increasingly paranoid— he urges Xenia to use baggy clothing to conceal her growing body from her loved ones, and, eventually, demands that she cut off contact with them entirely. He monitors her communication by reading her email and scrolling through the call log on her phone. A surprise visit from Xenia's sister, Aino, during her sixth month causes an uproar; Aino can't understand why Xenia hasn't shared the news. Xenia explains that Malthe is going through a hard time, and that it's better for everyone to just tolerate his eccentricities until the baby is born. Xenia takes pains to conceal this visit from Malthe, but he discovers a scarf Aino left behind and flies into a rage, accusing Xenia of plotting to "steal" the baby from him, and take it to be raised elsewhere. Despite Xenia's efforts to calm him, Malthe retreats into the kitchen, where he presses the tip of a chef's knife to his neck, screaming, "I'll do it! I'll do it!" When Xenia begs him to stop, he plunges the knife in, spraying blood over the kitchen counter and floor, and he falls to his knees, clutching his throat.

Luckily, Malthe has merely nicked his carotid artery, and emergency surgery is able to repair the cut and save his life. After three days of observation in the hospital's psychiatric ward, the doctors strongly recommend that Malthe enter longer-term care in a residential facility for adults with mental illness. But Xenia refuses, and Malthe is released. At home, Xenia treats her husband solicitously, respecting his need for silence, cooking for him, managing his prescriptions, and changing the dressing on his wound. Before long, he appears healed in both body and mind, and expresses his gratitude for her patience every day.

But one afternoon, while Xenia daubs his stitches with an alcohol-soaked cotton ball, Malthe grabs her wrist, looks her in the eyes, and says, "I won't forget. I will *never* forget." Xenia understands that he is referring to the seconds she spent gazing in horror at his writhing form with her phone in her hand, trying to decide whether or not to call 911.

"There's something the matter with this report," I said.

Cylvia whirred to life beside me, and said, "What seems to be the problem?"

"It's wrong," I said, pointing to the papers. "It's supposed to be a hamster."

"I'm sorry," Cylvia said. "I'm having trouble processing your complaint."

"It's not a husband that almost dies," I said, "but a hamster."

Cylvia emitted a series of alternating red and white flashes, followed by a faint chirp, like the sound of a smoke alarm with a dying battery, or a sparrow that's about to be hit by a car. "Confirm report number N5S-1328."

I flipped back through the pages until I came to the cover sheet. "N5S-1328," I repeated.

"Please restate your complaint slowly and clearly."

"The narrative portion of the report is wrong," I enunciated. "The subject identified as Malthe is portrayed as a man, when in fact the actual victim of the attempted suicide, the one described in the report, is a hamster."

There was a pause as Cylvia processed my reply.

"Thank you," she said. "Please fill out your Analyst's Response to the best of your ability, based upon the facts provided in the report."

"But one of them is wrong," I argued.

"If your complaint is determined to have merit, a new version of the report will be generated based on new information. Until then, please respond to the best of your ability."

"Fine," I said, annoyed. "But I don't approve of the process."

"Your disapproval has been logged," Cylvia said.

*In my view, protagonist made the **right** /**wrong** decision (choose one).*
Elaborate: The protagonist was right to meet the hamster's demands, but should not have hesitated to call an ambulance when the hamster fell from the workbench.

In the event of a similar future situation, protagonist should: Put the needs of the hamster before her own. The hamster is weak, and she is strong— it is her obligation to help it.

*Protagonist's mistake **can**/**should** be remedied by:*
Being more accommodating to the hamster in the future, taking better care of it, and not putting it in situations where it might get hurt.

*Protagonist's responsibility is primarily to **herself**/**others** (choose one).*
Elaborate: The protagonist should consider her own needs only after accommodating the needs of the hamster and baby.

*Protagonist **should**/**shouldn't** have known better (choose one).*
Elaborate: The hamster warned her and she didn't listen.

I straightened the pages, replaced the paper clip, and crossed the room to feed the packet into the door, which Cylvia had preemptively opened for me. It would have been a simple thing to just drop the report onto the gray plastic tray and watch it slide away into the wall, and it was easy to imagine the feelings of accomplishment and relief this action would provoke. I gripped the pages in my hands and willed myself to release them.

But something held me back. The conviction I'd enjoyed moments earlier had evaporated. I was still fairly sure that the report was a mistake, that a clerical error had caused the hamster to be replaced by a husband. But I didn't recall whether the hamster story had contained the knife or the psychiatric doctors or the threats. There may have been a sister—but I was unsure even of that. The more I thought about it, the less confident I became. Could I be wrong, despite my expertise in the field? Might I end up making a terrible mistake on my first day of real work as a Phenomenon Analyst?

Instead of providing further validation of my skills, this latest task had filled me with doubt and mild disgust. It was bad enough that the Courthouse wasn't able to provide me with clear and accurate reports, but worse still that my own memory might also be fallible. How was I to make the judgments I'd been hired to provide?

With a shudder, I let the sheaf of papers fall onto the tray and watched the wall devour it.

The sun was lower in the sky, illuminating the streaks of haze that had gathered on the horizon. I noted that the *pock* sounds emanating from Forby's office had slowed. The working day, I understood, was drawing to a close. I gathered up my things, including Cylvia, against whom I had to admit I now harbored some resentment. I would have expected a more sympathetic reaction to my complaints about the flawed report, which, the longer I thought about it, seemed more and more unacceptable. And I realized that I missed Cylvia's sleeker, cleaner look—indeed, I realized now that it was the "old" Cylvia I'd hoped to see when I went to Fortuitous Items this morning. I might even have bought a new one, if the display rack had still been there. But it wasn't, and I would be forced to make do with the Cylvia I had. I should have felt lucky, I supposed, that I had been able to acquire a digital assistant at all, in the short time they were available.

Out in the hall, I locked the door behind me, and strolled down Hallway B, intending to say good night to my friend. I knocked on his door, and the sound of the tennis ball stopped. But then, after a moment, it started again.

"Hello!" I called out. "It's me!"

Again, the pocking stopped, and again it restarted.

I considered giving up—if Forby didn't want to see me, then he didn't want to see me—but I noticed that the door was off the latch. I gently pushed it open. The room's oppressive air flowed over me: hot, stale, and moist, and smelling of sweat and fuel. The generator was puttering away by the window, the light bulbs were burning, and an exhausted-looking Forby was flinging tennis ball after tennis ball at the wall. The balls ricocheted all about the room, colliding with the other ones that were lying on the floor. Forby reached into his bucket again and again, and soon there were none left for him to throw. He bent over, as though to begin the job of picking them up, but seemed to lose energy, or perhaps will, and just collapsed against one of his boarded-up windows. The wind was strong today, and it buffeted the building, gently shaking Forby's limp body. A groan escaped his lips. "I can't . . . ," he said. "I . . . I can't."

I set down my bag, and went around the room gathering up the tennis balls and dropping them into the bucket. When I was finished, I patted him gently on the shoulder. "You've chosen a hard road!" I said. "Someday you'll succeed, and everyone who doubted you will have to admit they were wrong."

"I guess," he said, panting. His shoulder felt clammy and hot, like a microwaved steak.

"Don't lose faith!" I said, discreetly wiping my hand on my skirt. "I'm headed out for the day."

"Did you get anything done?" he said, looking up imploringly. I wasn't sure what answer he wanted—would my success inspire him to strive further for his own, or would it intimidate him, and magnify his sense of personal failure?

"I filed a couple of reports," I said with a shrug.

Forby deflated even further. "Oh. Good for you, I guess."

"Don't be discouraged! Honestly, the reports are a mess. I just wrote any old thing."

"Hmm."

"I was probably wrong about everything I said, actually. They'll take one look at them and they'll be like, Whuhhhhhh?" I mugged for him, making a face I hoped looked comically foolish.

Forby roused a bit, rubbing his head with a shaky hand. A smile started to tease at the corners of his mouth.

"Like, here's me, reading a report: duhhhhhh!" I pantomimed the act of trying, and failing, to read. Then I pretended to drop the pile of papers all over the floor. "Whoooooop!" I said. I gathered up the "papers" and made imaginary scribbling motions on them with an invisible pen. "Rump-da-dump-da-dump!" I said, stabbing at the papers with the pen. "Guess I'm a Phenomenon Analyst! Look at me! Yup yup yup!" I cast my gaze around the room, as though looking for the retractable tray, then settled on the wastebasket in the corner. "Guess these go here, duhhhhhh!"

"Haha," Forby said. "That's pretty good."

"Haha," I said.

"All right," he said, stretching. "I guess I should do a little more work before I leave."

"That's the spirit!"

"Thanks, I guess."

"Hey, no problem," I told him, and offered him a jaunty salute.

Out on the plaza, the wind was blowing so powerfully that my bag jerked and twisted against my hip. The sky, however, was clear, and the sun hot, and I wondered if some kind of front were moving in. By the time I returned to the guesthouse, though, the wind had died down, and the air had cooled. It was another beautiful evening in the Subdivision.

As I scaled the front steps, I noticed that Mr. Lorre was sitting on a lawn chair out in the side yard. He was wearing his heavy coat, and speaking intently to the little boy, who stood before him holding a fresh bouquet of roses. Mr. Lorre gesticulated wildly, pointing over the boy's shoulder to the center of the neighborhood. As the boy replied, Mr. Lorre sat back in his chair, nodding, his arms folded over his chest. The boy turned, dashed across the yard, ducked through a gap in the hedge, and ran out into the street, his little legs pumping, the bouquet tucked safely under his small arm. Soon he had disappeared between two houses.

I offered a little wave to Mr. Lorre, which he didn't return, and pushed open the front door. I must have entered noisily, because Clara suddenly appeared from the kitchen, bearing a plate of brownies.

"Hello, dear!" she said. "Welcome back. Did you have a productive day?"

"I suppose," I said with a sigh.

"Maybe you'd like something to eat? You look a bit peaked."

It hadn't occurred to me that I might be hungry, but I realized now that I was—ravenous, in fact. "Yes, I would," I said.

"Well," she replied, "come join us. We were just sitting down."

I followed her back into the kitchen, where she set the plate of brownies on the table. The Judge was already seated, impatiently tapping her fingers. She was glaring at me. The light here was uncharacteristically gloomy, as though night had already fallen, and the room's mood seemed to match it. I hung my bag over the back of a chair, then took a seat across from the Judge. I watched as she speared a brownie from the plate Clara had just set down. She began to eat it—rather daintily, I thought—with a knife and fork.

Undeterred, I grabbed a brownie from the pile with my hand, raised it to my lips, and took a bite. I quickly realized that it wasn't a brownie at all, but a piece of meat loaf. Clara and the Judge appeared surprised. A moment passed, during which I could have laughed off my error and apologized for being so rude, but I was committed now: I sat back casually in my chair, gnawing on the meat loaf, and asked how their day had gone.

"Oh, our days are much the same, dear," Clara said. "The real question, of course, is how *your* day went."

I felt compelled to impress them, both to make them proud of their protégée and to dispel the unspoken tension that seemed to hang over the room. "Well," I said, breezily, "as I was trying to tell you, I've been working in the Dead Tower. It's rather important work, as

I'm sure you know. I am, I guess you could say, a sort of judge now myself."

"How interesting," the Judge said.

"I've been reading these very important reports, and issuing my opinions on them. Actually, ladies," I said, waving the piece of meat loaf in the air before me, "I'd love to get your take on a case that came across my desk today." I proceeded to tell them about the report I'd read, the one in which a hamster's attempted suicide was inadvertently supplanted by that of a husband. "I suppose it was some kind of clerical error," I said with a chuckle, though I hoped that they didn't detect the unease that had crept into my voice. "Although it's hard for me to see how anyone could make such a silly mistake."

The ladies' faces registered something between curiosity and concern. "How did you respond?" the Judge wanted to know.

"I answered as though the report were correctly written. The protagonist should have put the hamster's needs ahead of her own—that's what I said."

I quietly finished the piece of meat loaf I'd been working on, then licked my fingers clean as the two women nodded, chewing thoughtfully. It was Clara who finally broke the silence with a change of subject. "Is your workplace engaged in storm preparedness right now?" she asked me.

"I . . . I'm not sure," I replied. "That's really not my department."

"Well," the Judge said, dabbing her mouth with a napkin, "it ought to be, after the last time."

"It's true," Clara agreed, "I'd imagine they're eager to avoid a repeat."

I was beginning to realize that my hunger had not been sated by the piece of meat loaf I'd eaten, and I eyed the pile before me as I said, "I have to admit, I'm a little surprised by all this storm preparation talk. The weather is breezy, at most, and the radio hasn't forecast it. How do you know it's coming?"

"It always comes, dear," Clara explained, as the Judge shook her head in evident frustration at my ignorance.

"Why haven't you started preparing, then?" I demanded, reaching for the meat.

"We have," the Judge said, vexed. She pointed.

Now I could see the reason for the murky light—Clara and the Judge had covered up the kitchen windows with sheets of plywood. A power drill and a box of screws sat on the counter, and a few extra sheets of wood were propped in the corner, marked LIVING ROOM, DINING ROOM, DUTY, GLORY, and so on.

"We decided to start with the kitchen," Clara explained, "so as not to disturb Mr. Lorre and you and your—that is, and the little boy."

"You could lend a hand," the Judge added in a sarcastic drawl, "unless you're too busy with your jurisprudence."

I elected to ignore the Judge's tone. Reaching for another piece of meat loaf, I said, "No, no. I'm quite happy to help," though in truth I wanted nothing more than to head up to my room with Cylvia and enjoy one of her stories. Speaking of whom: I'd just taken a bite when a piercing noise filled the room. It was an alarm, coming from my bag.

Seventeen

I dropped the meat loaf onto my plate. "So sorry!" I said to the ladies—shouted, really—over the screeching of the alarm. Unzipping my bag let loose a blast of intense red light into the room. A moment later, the light and noise stopped, and I lifted Cylvia onto the kitchen table.

"Warning," she said. "The child has entered the Oracle."

"I'm sorry," I told her. "I don't know what that is."

The Judge rolled her eyes. "It's a mall."

"Please retrieve the child from the Oracle."

"Well," Clara interjected, "it's an abandoned mall."

"I don't know if it was ever really occupied, not entirely," said the Judge.

"Please," Cylvia said, "retrieve the child from the Oracle."

I was becoming frustrated at my apparent responsibility for people with whom I had no connection. Why did I have to keep delivering and retrieving people to and from places! I said to Cylvia, "I don't see why I have to look after this child. No one asked me to!"

Cylvia didn't answer, but her white lights pulsed gently, as though mulling over what I'd said. Clara and the Judge gazed at me in evident fascination.

"Dear," Clara said, "are you sure he isn't yours?"

"Of course I'm sure!"

"But," the Judge said quietly, "he came here with you."

"He certainly didn't!" I replied.

"He did, dear," Clara said, resting her hand on my arm. "He was right behind you when you checked in. We gave him the attic room, remember?"

"I remember no such thing!" I said.

Cylvia said, "Please retrieve the child from the Oracle."

Clara gave my arm a squeeze now, and though it comforted and pleased me, it also made me angry. I shook her hand off.

"This is absurd," I said. "He's just someone who's around. You should ask him who his mother is."

"Hmm," the Judge said, stroking her chin. "We did think you were being rather standoffish with him."

"He looks just like you, though," Clara offered. "Those adorable bangs!"

"This is ridiculous," I said, realizing that I was repeating myself now. "I don't have a child. I'm a single working woman with an important job in the Dead Tower of the Courthouse. I'm processing incident reports and doing experiments in quantum tunneling. I don't have time for a relationship with a man, let alone the responsibility of a child."

Any reply the ladies might have made was cut off by Cylvia, who repeated, "The child has entered the Oracle. Please retrieve the child."

"Where even is it?" I said.

"Oh," the Judge said, with a wave of her hand, "it's in the Cul-de-Sac."

"You didn't put that on the map," I complained.

"It's kind of hard to draw, dear," Clara said.

"We might as well have just scribbled it on a separate piece of paper," the Judge said, in an exasperated tone, "and set it on fire."

"I will lead you to the child," Cylvia said, before I could respond. "It is time to go."

With a sigh, I hauled myself to my feet, swept Cylvia into my bag, and slouched my way to the door.

•

Though I was irritated at having to go out again after my long day at the office, I had to admit that I didn't mind emerging into this beautiful evening. The sun, low in the sky, cast long shadows with its honey light, and a cool breeze ruffled the leaves in the trees. I could smell the faintest decay in the air, a sweetness, as though autumn were ahead, but just out of reach. Above me, backlit too intensely by the orange sun for me to notice it there, the crow bobbed in the breeze. An ordinary bird, it anticipated and appreciated the vagaries of air; it knew the wind to be a manifestation of the water: a distant lake, beyond the City, that flickered to life each day, a strip of twisting brightness in the morning sun. I couldn't know of the lake—the Subdivision was my habitat, and the crow understood that it wasn't possible for me, not now, to venture beyond its borders. But I felt the same breeze the crow did, even if its origins were a mystery to me, and I felt drawn, not toward the lake, but toward the City that rose before it. The closed road that led there, with its snow fencing and caution barrels and idle backhoe, suddenly felt like a rebuke to me. Why couldn't I go there? When would the bus route be restored to its original glory?

Or perhaps those feelings were the crow's. It was getting hard to tell.

Cylvia, nestled inside my open bag, emitted a steady, cool white light, and said to me, "Please follow my instructions precisely in order to reach the Oracle."

"It's not like I have a choice," I said, with a pout. "I guess I just do what you tell me now. You're the boss."

"Turn left, and walk two blocks," she said. I obeyed, passing the now-familiar grassy yards, fences, and trees of the southwestern Subdivision. The evening sun filled their windows, rendering them opaque with brilliant light.

159

"Turn left again, immediately."

"There's no street here," I said.

"Stop," Cylvia said. I obeyed. "Take two steps back. Look left."

I could see it now: a footpath, narrow and very slightly worn, in the grass between the low stone wall and tall hedge that separated two houses. "Here?" I asked, uncertain. I found myself uneasy at the prospect of treading on this municipally ambiguous ground.

"Correct," Cylvia said.

I made my slow way down the path. The hedge brushed my arm on the left, and I let my open hand drag along the top of the wall to the right. The two very different abrasive sensations registered as a kind of harmony, a chord. I felt comforted. Though the path didn't appear to penetrate very far into the block, I seemed to be taking a long time to reach the other side. The sunlight had begun to feel like actual honey, thick and sweet. I yawned and may even have briefly sleepwalked before I found myself approaching another sidewalk.

"Turn right," Cylvia said.

I obeyed, moving down this new, unfamiliar stretch of street. "Cross the street," Cylvia said, "and pass through the white gate beside the blue shed."

The gate in question was of painted wooden pickets, and creaked as I pushed it open. It led me into some kind of drainage area, a rocky depression surrounded by thick overhanging trees. I stepped carefully, eager not to slip on the wet stones. I could hear water trickling.

"Enter the culvert," Cylvia said.

I had to crouch in order to pass through the culvert, a tunnel formed from a length of corrugated steel pipe five feet in diameter. Water trickled underfoot along a cement trough, and I walked like a duck to avoid getting my feet wet. The tunnel was dark and the air was cool, and every noise echoed with an almost electronic-sounding distortion, like a phone call from a distant country. I heard the crow cawing outside, faintly, and understood that I had been flickering in its sight, much as it had flickered in mine.

The culvert drained into what appeared to be the storage lot adjacent to a sports field, though no sports field was visible; half a dozen bleachers, each fifteen feet tall or more, pressed up against one another, forming a valley of metal and wood, as though arranged for fans who wished only to jeer and taunt without the distraction of a game. The lot was tightly enclosed by woods, and, with Cylvia's guidance, I passed beneath the bleachers and into a gap in the treeline.

"Continue toward the parking lot," Cylvia told me, once I was fully enveloped by the shadows of the branches.

"What parking lot?" I said, groping my way forward. But even as the words left my lips, I could see it up ahead: the trees had begun to thin, and the humus under my feet gave way to broken pavement and crumbling chunks of yellow cement parking stops, clinging to bent and twisted lengths of rebar. Soon I was standing in what was left of an asphalt plain punctuated by streetlamps that sprouted from disintegrating concrete abutments. Saplings squeezed up through cracks in the pavement, and in the wind scraps of paper trash pressed themselves to the chain-link fence that enclosed the area.

In the distance, a structure rose, low and gray on the horizon, set against the clumped gray clouds: a miniature skyline that resembled a haphazard collection of cans and boxes casually arranged on a pantry shelf. Even from here, I could see irregular gaps in its multiple banks of reflective windows, and rust stains dribbling down from the colorful, extinguished store logos that emblazoned its walls. A grand archway proclaimed, in bold serif letters, each as tall as a child, THE ORACLE MALL. Underneath, smaller letters elaborated, THE EVOLUTION OF THE NOW!

I made my slow way across the parking lot until I stood beneath the arch. Under my feet, rust from its beams had formed a thick, blurry line of red-brown stain on the pavement, like the starting line of some obsolete race. A wide stone walkway, bordered by shrubs that had grown out of control then withered, led to a broad smoked-glass entryway. Much of the glass had been smashed, allowing access to whoever happened along. At the moment, however, I seemed to be the only person here. Furthermore, far overhead, the crow could see that I was more fully here than I had been at any other place in the Subdivision; almost every possible iteration of me stood on this very spot, facing the Oracle. I remembered a rough sketch, interrupted by missing pieces—the floor plan of a building—that had been drawn in the top left corner of the overturned puzzle. Perhaps it was a representation of this very mall.

"Is this even part of the Subdivision?" I asked Cylvia.

"Technically," she replied, "it is part of a probabilistic underlayer of the Subdivision."

"Was that the only way to get here?"

"That was the most efficient way, for you, at this time."

"I can see why business is slow," I quipped.

I didn't need instructions to know what to do next: I drew a deep breath and, gravel and debris crunching underfoot, made my way toward the mall's broken maw. I took a moment to choose the right opening—I didn't want to trigger a rain of glass. Resolved, I steeled myself, then took a careful step over the threshold and into the shadows of the Oracle.

At first, I had difficulty making out anything in the gloom. But my eyes adjusted, and soon I found myself moving slowly through the ruins, guided by the cold glow of filthy skylights overhead. The mall had three levels; I had entered on the middle one. I could make out dozens of storefronts from where I stood, directly ahead and above: some unbranded, as though never occupied; some bearing the names of businesses but stripped of merchandise; still others fully stocked. Most spaces were protected by rolling metal grates, but some of these were half-raised or missing entirely. The lower level, which was visible over the balustrade I walked along, was too dark to see clearly.

The Oracle was disordered, of course, and dirty in places where leaves and rain had gotten in, but I was surprised at how little damage had been done by animals and vandals. I pointed this out to Cylvia.

"As you said," she replied, "it is somewhat off the beaten path."

"Do you know where the child is?" I asked. I tried to remember where, on the puzzle map, the large X had been printed.

"At the Carousel."

I made my way through the Oracle, following signs that hung from nostalgic fake streetlights, and calling out "hello" from time to time, as much to hear the sound of my own voice as to alert the child to my presence. I passed a store called Bearly Alive, where a collection of animated teddy bears, kept minimally charged through the solar panels on their hats, waved their paws and greeted me in slurred voices. An establishment called Good Reasons sold picture frames, each containing a reproduction of the same photo, that of a healthy-looking white family of two men, their two daughters, and their pet alligator. And one little shop, Ice Cream Procedure, appeared innocuous enough, with a menu of whimsical ice cream novelties, posters of happy children clutching multicolored scoop towers in rainbow-sprinkled cones, and a plastic statue of a cartoon cow laboring over a butter churn. But its metal barrier had been warped and violently torn through, as though by some massive beast, and brown smears that resembled blood stained the walls and floor.

"Should I be worried?" I asked Cylvia.

"I sense no imminent danger."

I tried to do as she said, keeping my eyes forward and my ears attuned to any sound that might have come from the child. I heard nothing, but something did catch my eye on the lower level: a single storefront that somehow had electric power. Dim light radiated from its ungated interior, though at my angle from above, I couldn't see what was inside. Above the glowing entrance, the store's name appeared in glittery type:

MEMORY

Before I could wonder any further about the store, the walkway before me opened up into a large space that spanned all three floors of the Oracle, and that was illuminated by a massive bank of windows. The empty parking lot was visible through them, and the woods beyond—woods as far, in fact, as the eye could see. Though I recognized the asphalt I had trudged across, I couldn't make out the bleachers, drainage depression, or footpath, or any of the familiar landmarks of the Subdivision. The Oracle seemed to exist all by itself, surrounded by forest.

From the ceiling hung a two-story-high sculpture that resembled, cleverly, a crib mobile. Though it must certainly have been made of heavy cable and tempered steel, it had been made to look as though it were fashioned out of yarn, then expanded, somehow, to tremendous size. "Yarn" strands dangled from an array of "plastic" arms, bearing sleigh bells that were at least twelve inches across, along with cheerful "crocheted" clouds, rainbows, suns, stars, and moons. It turned slowly in the cavernous space, moved by what currents I couldn't tell, as the air was still.

Beneath the mobile, a circular canopy of red and white, peaked in the center, sheltered the object of my quest: a carousel, complete with brightly colored horses skewered on golden poles. Light bulbs, all extinguished, described intricate patterns on the painted shields and rounding boards. I couldn't make out the child from where I stood, but in the seating area of the adjacent food court, I could discern a slash of green and red against a white tabletop: Mr. Lorre's bouquet, the one I had spied him entrusting the little boy to deliver. I suppressed a wave of irritation at Mr. Lorre, for his recklessness in giving the child such an absurd task, and cast my gaze around the space, trying to determine the correct path down to the Carousel.

Eventually I figured it out: I was forced to backtrack a bit and make a few turns, and soon I reached a bank of escalators, frozen in place. I hurried down one of these, and navigated through the profusion of tables and chairs where fast-food diners were meant to have sat.

When I approached the table where the flowers lay, I slowed to a stop. I picked them up and inhaled their scent. Their sweetness was undercut by a pungency, a chemical tang, reminiscent of the faint burning smell of an overheating car's engine, and with notes of window cleaner and old cigarettes.

I didn't like roses, generally speaking. I laid them back down on the table and approached the Carousel.

Eighteen

As large as the Carousel had looked from above, it seemed even larger now. The light from the dirty bank of windows cast pink shadows beneath the red-and-white canopy, and failed to penetrate to the center. There were horses as far as I could see, deep into the darkness. I was intensely aware of the enormous mobile dangling above me as I stepped up onto the carousel platform; I could hear it moan and shudder as it turned.

"Hello?" I shouted. "Are you in there? It's me! The lady from the guesthouse!"

My voice died in the still air. I wasn't certain the child could even hear me, if he was here at all.

I moved among the horses and carriages, dragging my fingers over them as I went; their paint was smooth and unblemished, and gleamed faintly in the leaden canopy light.

The horses were lovingly rendered in action poses: trotting, cantering, and galloping. Their manes flowed in an imaginary wind, and the muscles in their legs, haunches, and backs flexed and bulged. One could imagine them marching in a colorful, jubilant parade, or in some stately and dignified government ceremony. But their faces, equally detailed, seemed to imply a different story. Their lips were pulled back, their teeth were bared; wide eyes gazed in terror over flaring nostrils. Seen from the front, the horses gave the impression of panicked flight, as though they were running away from an enemy or natural disaster.

Indeed, the farther I penetrated into the dim, the more intensely this latter interpretation impressed itself upon me. The horses were afraid, that much was clear—and it wasn't just horses back here, either. Some of the figures were human—men and women in everyday clothes, sprinting toward or away from something in a state of fear and alarm. There were even a few life-size automobiles: cars in the act of swerving, or screeching to a halt, their drivers' faces frozen in expressions of astonishment and fright. I tried to open one of the car doors, thinking that the child might be hiding inside, but the doors weren't real. None of it was, of course.

I found the child clinging to the back of a running woman, his arms wrapped around her neck, his face buried in—or, more accurately, mashed against—her stiff long hair. He was still wearing his suit from the birthday party. I'd almost missed him, he was so still; but evidently his grip on the woman—who, I realized as I drew closer, was actually a mail carrier, complete with uniform and bulging mailbag—had begun to slip, and he was forced to readjust, inching his arms more tightly around her gleaming neck.

"There you are!" I said. "I've been looking all over for you."

The child pretended I wasn't there. His little feet scrabbled for purchase against the mailbag.

"Why don't you let me help you down," I offered. "And we can go back to the guesthouse."

"Don't wanna," the child said, not looking at me. He spoke so quietly I could barely hear him.

"Well, it's not safe for you to be here," I said.

"Why not?"

"A storm is coming. We need to go back."

"I didn't see any clouds," he said.

"Well, no one can see them yet," I explained. "But didn't you feel that wind outside? The weather is changing. A storm is going to come, and we have to be where it's safe."

But the child didn't move. If anything, he seemed to grip the mail carrier even harder.

"I'll tell you what," I told the child, resisting the impulse to just grab him and run. "If you come with me, you can ride on my back, just like you're doing with that lady. Except, unlike her, I'll actually be moving. It'll be like the Carousel, except better!"

The little boy didn't move, but I could sense his resolve weakening. His feet again clambered against the mailbag, and they seemed less determined, less energetic. I took a moment to peer down into the mailbag and was surprised to notice that the effigy's detail extended all the way into the parcels inside: I could even read the return addresses on some of the letters. PAST DUE NOTICE, read an envelope from a bank; another appeared to be a bill from a collective of family and marriage therapists.

"I suppose," I said to the child, pretending to muse aloud to myself, "I'll just have to happily race through this abandoned mall without you. I guess I'll make horsey noises alone, and go trotting back to the guesthouse for cookies without anyone riding on my shoulders."

The little boy merely frowned, and for a moment I thought I might scream in frustration. Didn't he realize we were both in mortal danger? But then, at last, his grip loosened, and he began to slide slowly down the mail carrier's slippery back. This time, he didn't try to stop himself.

I knelt on the platform beside him, and offered him my own back to climb onto. Dutifully, he did so, wrapping his small arms around my neck with maddening slowness, and I stood up with a forced whinny. In a horse voice, I said, "Ti-i-i-ime to ri-i-i-i-ide back to the guesthouse!"

The child didn't laugh, but I could tell by the way he squeezed me that he was pleased. I made my way through the crowd of horses, then hopped down from the carousel and moved out among the tables.

"Wait," the child said in my ear. "Mr. Lorre's roses."

Oh, for Pete's sake. There was no time—and I wasn't going to have those smelly things brushing my face for the next fifteen minutes. I kept on walking, and said, "Those aren't fresh anymore. We can get Mr. Lorre some new ones when we get back."

The boy said, "He *told* me to bring them to *Anna*."

"And you went outside with them, and you got lost?"

"I was looking for *her* house," he insisted.

"Of course. You must have taken a wrong turn. It's all right."

"But I found *you* instead," the boy told me, practically shouting. He gripped me tighter.

"That's right," I agreed. "And I found you."

For a moment, I was seized by an unfamiliar series of emotions—mingled affection and longing for the boy, as though he were still missing, and I were still desperately searching. Unbidden, the image came to me of the two of us marching, hand in hand, through the gleaming gates of the City. This vision was absurd, of course—the road was still closed, and I didn't even know if the City had gates, let alone gleaming ones—but it was powerful nonetheless.

I tightened my grip on the boy's small arms and carried him down the grand hallways of the Oracle, looking for the exit. For whatever reason, though, I couldn't find my way back. Nothing was quite as I remembered, and none of the stores I'd seen before could be found. Rather than nearing the shattered doorway, in fact, we seemed to be penetrating even farther into the depths of the building. I asked Cylvia for directions, but, except for a brief flash and a faint vibration, she didn't respond. I suspected it was hard for her to get a connection, down here in the labyrinth of the Oracle.

The hallway was darkening, and I thought we might soon have to turn around and go back the way we came. Then I saw, up ahead, a faint glow. I plodded along, having given up entirely on pretending to be a horse, until I could make out the source of the light. It was something I'd seen before: the store called Memory.

A minute later, the child and I paused on the threshold of the place. I wasn't sure what I'd expected, but what lay before me was disappointing, to say the least: a small, low-rent retail space, with a long laminate counter, empty shelves, and a few freestanding wire grids with hooks hanging from them. Bare fluorescent bulbs overhead cast a cold light over the room.

The one promising thing about Memory was an open doorway in the back, which seemed to lead to some kind of long hallway. Perhaps this was a way out?

Sleepily, the little boy said, "We have to bring the flowers to *Anna.*"

"I'm sorry," I told him, hiking him up higher on my back. "We just can't do that right now." I stepped over the threshold and into the store.

Something—the change in lighting, perhaps—seemed to rouse the child. He said, "Mr. Lorre was on his way *home.*"

"Mm-hmm," I said, making my way through the space. My feet brushed the cheap gray carpet and I could feel a static-electrical charge building. A few hairs rose up around my face; a few more clung to it. I brushed them aside with a strategically oblique breath of air.

"He was driving his *truck,*" the child muttered into my ear. "He'd been making *deliveries* all day, and he stopped to buy her the *flowers.*"

"Well, that's very nice," I said.

"He was thinking that he was *lucky* to *have* her after all these years," the child went on, his recollection becoming more confident. "After their *son* died of *cancer,* things between them had become *strained.* Mr. Lorre's wife seemed to *blame* him for their son's *death*—or maybe it was just too *painful* for her to *face* him, given all that they'd been *through.*"

"That's interesting," I said. I wasn't really paying attention, to be frank: our journey across the retail space was taking much longer than I'd anticipated. I hazarded a glance over my shoulder, and saw the room stretching far, far back into the darkness of the mall; the counter appeared extraordinarily long, and more shelves and product racks were scattered throughout the area than I had initially thought. Still, the little boy and I did seem to be making progress: the rear wall was now somewhat closer, and I could make out more of the hallway beyond it. Far ahead, a point of light dully gleamed. Perhaps this was a door, one with a window to the outside!

"But lately," the child said, "Mr. Lorre's wife had seemed to come to *terms* with their mis*fortune*. And just a few nights before, they had slept in the same *bed* for the first time in *years*. On the day of the crash, Mr. Lorre remembered that it was their *wedding* anniversary. They hadn't celebrated their marriage in a *long time*. So Mr. Lorre stopped on the way home and bought his wife *roses!*"

"You know," I told the child, "your chatter is a little bit distracting. I'm trying to reach that door, and your fanciful storytelling is not helping matters one bit." I felt very tired, but the back door was closer than ever, and it was quite clear now that the mysterious hallway did indeed end in a second door, with a small square window to the outside. I could make out a patch of green through it, as though the woods lay beyond, and unless my ears deceived me, I could hear the caw of a crow. The crow, for its part, knew I was coming, and was wheeling overhead, watching the door, awaiting my exit. I did not want to let it down.

"When the *car* swerved across his *lane*, Mr. Lorre was imagining presenting the roses to his wife! She would *greet* him at the *door*, and take the flowers, and kiss him on the *cheek*. Then he would go to the *cabinet* for the bottle of *brandy*, and they would sit on the sofa together, holding *hands*, watching their favorite *game shows*."

"Stop!" I told the child. "Stop it this instant!" We were almost there—just a few steps more, and we'd have passed through Memory and into the hallway. Over my shoulder, the store stretched almost infinitely back to a tiny point, a black square of mall.

"But that future was *shattered* when—"

"Enough!" I shouted, and then we were there, and I sprang through the doorway and pulled the heavy steel door shut behind me.

•

The hallway was cool and dark, with cinder block walls and an industrial linoleum floor; no light shone, except through the window at the end. I shucked the little boy off my back, and he slid down to the floor, then took my hand in his. Wordlessly, we began our walk.

I was pleased to note that the hallway seemed quite normal, and didn't impede our progress in any way. We had reached the end in under a minute. The door, like the one we'd just passed through, was of steel, with a heavy-duty lever handle. The window, as I had thought, looked out onto vegetation, but it wasn't the forest—instead, the glass offered a view of a tall hedge, neatly trimmed, standing just a few feet away, deep green in the evening light. I tried to remember whether I had seen this hedge while approaching the Oracle, but memory failed me—I had been concentrating on the mall's broken entrance.

Confidently, I reached out and tried to open the door. It was locked.

"Hmm," I said.

"Are we trapped?" the little boy asked me. "Are we stuck here forever? Are we going to starve to death?"

"Of course not," I said.

"You're not going to eat me!" he went on. "I'll eat you first!"

"We're not quite at that point yet," I reassured him. "I'll tell you what. You stay here. I'm going to go back and see if there's a key in the Memory store. Maybe it's hanging under the counter."

"Okay," he replied sullenly.

I hurried back down the hall to the door we'd come through, and tried the handle. It, too, was locked.

Back at the hedge door, I tried the handle a second time. I pulled it up, as well as pushed it down; I tugged on it, in the hope that the door wasn't actually on the latch. But it was shut tightly.

I did notice, however, an unusual keyhole underneath the handle: a small circle, less than half an inch in diameter. This reminded me that I did have an unusual key with me: my key from the Dead Tower. I rummaged in my bag until I found it.

"You have the key!" the child said, clapping.

"Well, let's see," I said. I inserted the key into the lock, and it fit there quite comfortably. But the door didn't react. It emitted no mechanical noises, and the handle remained frozen in place.

"Maybe we could break the glass," the child said.

The glass looked very thick, and was reinforced with wire. And

I hadn't seen any loose item that we could use to break it. Even so: "I don't think we could fit through the hole," I said.

"We could yell for help."

"Maybe."

"*Help!*" the child screamed. I jumped. The word hung in the air, amplified by and echoing in the long hallway, and we listened to it decay into silence.

"Cylvia," I said. "How do we get out of here?"

Cylvia woke, briefly, and flickered white and red. A few stuttered syllables issued from her, distorted and unintelligible. Then she switched off.

"Hmm," I said.

"This is stupid," the child said. "Do you think we can eat our shoes?"

"That won't be necessary," I told him, glancing down at our shoes, I suppose to assess their potential as emergency rations. They did not look very appetizing. But the sight of my shoes, with their purple patent leather, reminded me of something. I dug into my skirt pocket and drew forth the crayon I had taken from the child's table at the bakery, the purple one marked BRUISE.

"Hey!" the boy said. "My crayon!"

It had been a peculiar day, and there was nothing to lose. I inserted the crayon, ceremoniously, into the keyhole. It fit perfectly, and once I'd pushed it halfway in, something grabbed it and pulled it in the rest of the way—digested it, really. We heard a loud click, and the door swung open.

It was with gratitude that we inhaled the moist and gusty air that greeted us on the other side. The child and I stepped through. "I would have started with your hands," he said. "And your feet would be next. I would have cooked them on a fire!" He sounded mildly disappointed.

"That's quite enough of that," I said, trying to get my bearings. I shut the door behind us and saw that, incongruously, it was actually the door to a small garden shed. I peered left and right. The hedge led to a low fence on one side, and a road on the other. It all looked quite familiar, save for the gray cast of light everything was bathed in; the sun, for a change, was hidden behind a bank of clouds that obscured most of the sky, leaving only patches of blue. I feared that we were running out of time, and hoped we weren't far from the guesthouse.

The child had run ahead. "We're home!" he shouted. And indeed, he was right—I stepped out from behind the shed to confirm that we had already arrived. We were standing in the side yard of the guesthouse. The crow was perched on the neighboring rooftop, in the very spot where I had first spied him from the bathtub. I didn't actually notice him now, but he was watching me, and he observed that all my possible futures had remained largely in sync—in fact, if anything, they had converged further. If I had happened to glance at the crow, I would have seen that his essence appeared stable, without a hint of flickering.

Cylvia woke up, flashing red. "Please lead the child through the front door," she said.

"Oh! Nice of you to pop in," I said, not without irritation.

"Please lead the child through the door," she repeated.

Her command prompted me to glance around the yard—where had the child disappeared to? A bit of movement on the house's side wall caught my eye: there he was, climbing the downspout, evidently on the way to his third-floor room.

"Hey!" I said. "Come down from there!"

"We're home!" he shouted over his shoulder. "I'm going home!"

"You don't have to go in that way," I said. "Come through the door with me."

"I *can't* go through the door," he said, as though stating a well-known fact of which I ought to have already been aware. "I have to go in *this* way."

"You don't," I explained. "You're with me now. So you can go in the *front* door."

He appeared to contemplate this for a moment, and then, with a subtle nod, carefully lowered himself back to the ground. I held out my hand to him, and he took it, and we walked through the gate to the sidewalk, and then up the steps to the door of the guesthouse.

The Judge was perched on a stepladder, sinking the final screw into a sheet of plywood that covered the dining room window. "Ah," she said, noticing our approach. "Just in time to not help me." Her expression, though—a rare, if modest, smile—belied her words. Clearly she was pleased to see us. She hopped down with surprising agility, opened the door for us, and ushered us inside with a wave of her power drill.

Inside, the smell of something delicious greeted us. In the kitchen we found Clara and Mr. Lorre bustling around, bringing steaming serving dishes to the table. Clara looked up.

"Oh! You've found him!"

She and the Judge applauded, delighting the little boy. Mr. Lorre merely scowled at us.

"Now, this is progress!" Clara said, beaming, once the clapping had died out.

"Thank you," I replied. "Though it seems to me we're back where we started, before this one got lost." I tilted my head at the boy.

"I wasn't lost!"

"Oh, you would have found your own way back?" I said.

But the boy, distracted by the food, was already climbing onto a chair. This seemed to spur us all to do the same: chairs scraped and creaked as we settled onto them.

Mr. Lorre, who had evidently been tasked with setting the table, glowered at the little boy. He obviously wanted some kind of confirmation that his flowers had been delivered, but when it became clear that no such thing was in the offing, he grunted and continued his task. He wasn't very good at it, really—the place mats were crooked and the dishes off-center; the cloth napkins were wrinkled and wadded, and silverware had been tossed haphazardly nearby. This must have been a job traditionally assigned to his wife, the one he'd bought the flowers for.

The ladies had made a warm, savory stew; a sweet, rustic corn bread; a tasty mélange of seasoned vegetables; and apple pie, which they served with a side of vanilla ice cream. We ate for a long time and said almost nothing to one another, except for the little boy, who occasionally piped up, "This is *delicious!*" As the meal neared its end, and the sun at last began to set, the Judge looked me in the eye and said, "You'd better get to sleep."

"I suppose so?" I responded, unsure of the intent behind the suggestion.

"I think what Clara is saying," Clara explained, "is that you have a big day ahead of you."

"Well," I said. "You'll recall that I do have an important job in the Dead Tower, processing incident reports and researching quantum tunneling."

"Well, that's not false," the Judge said, and I sensed that, on some level, she was humoring me.

"So, every day is a big day, is what you mean?" Clara asked me.

"That's right."

The Judge said, "Then you should get ready for another big day."

I wasn't sure what they were driving at, but it was true that I'd had quite an exhausting afternoon, and I was ready for bed. I got up and reached for the empty plates, but Clara stopped me. "Mr. Lorre can help with that," she said. If the delivery truck driver seemed surprised or annoyed by this responsibility, he didn't betray it; instead he nodded and began to clear the table.

"Oh, by the way," Clara added, feigning casualness, "nice work on the puzzle."

"You were really thinking 'out of the box,' so to speak," the Judge joked from the sink, where she had gone to wash the dishes.

The little boy got up, too, and again took my hand. It was small and warm and slightly sweaty, and I can't say that I minded holding it. We said good night to everyone, then climbed the stairs. "I'll bring you up to your room," I said, glancing back at the puzzle. It looked as if I'd misremembered the *X* scrawled on the Oracle map; in fact, the whole Oracle section of the puzzle had an *X* through it.

This, I suppose, was appropriate, since I'd successfully completed my task there.

"Okay," the child whined, and I wasn't sure whether it was because he didn't want to go to sleep, or didn't want to be alone, or what. In any event, I wasn't about to respond to innuendo, so we walked past my door and Mr. Lorre's, and, at the end of the hall, entered the tight, dim stair that led to the attic.

The steps were narrow and sharply angled, and the wood they were made of creaked and shifted under our feet. The child led me up with some eagerness at first, as though excited to show me his home, but as we reached the top and began the walk down the cramped attic hallway, his enthusiasm seemed to wane. I could see why. This hallway was highly uninviting. The walls, once painted white, were scuffed and gouged, and the floor, cheaply constructed of irregular lengths of board, was dusty. No art or personal photos hung on the walls, and the only light came from a streetlamp shining through a single dormer window that hadn't been cleaned in years.

The little boy pushed through a door at the end of the hall that admitted us into a dark, low-ceilinged room. Most of the space was filled with cardboard boxes in messy piles, some of them collapsing, labeled, in thick marker, with words like TED'S SUITS and KITCHEN EXTRAS and FAKE NEWSPAPERS. Another dormer let in light from the streetlamp, though less light than the hallway one did. A small mattress, the kind that comes with an infant's crib that one never got the chance to use, lay on the floor in an alcove among the boxes; a blanket was bunched up on it. Beside the mattress lay a small pile of paperback books and a flashlight. I squinted at the books' titles. *Treasury of Courtroom Humor*, read one. Another was called *Cocktails for Lawyers.*

"I found them in one of the boxes," the child explained, following my gaze. "I use the flashlight to read them."

"How nice that you have something good to read!" I said.

"I count to one hundred when I'm reading," he continued. "Then I have to turn the flashlight off. I don't want the batteries to die."

"That's very responsible of you," I said. "You'll need to be frugal later in life." I made a mental note to buy the child some fresh batteries at Fortuitous Items the next day, on the way to work, and then silently congratulated myself on having thought to do this.

The two of us stood there awkwardly for a few moments. Finally, I broke the silence. "Listen," I said. "I've got a big day ahead of me, as you know. Don't run off like that again."

"Okay," the child said, embarrassed.

"Good night, I suppose," I said, and turned to go.

I was nearly knocked to the floor, however, by the child's little arms, which gripped my legs from behind. "Good night!" he shouted, perhaps sarcastically.

"Yes!" I said. "Good night!"

We lingered for a short time in this peculiar embrace until, with a deep sigh, the boy released me and went to his bed. I continued to the door, then waved to him as I backed out. I closed the door behind me and went to my own room.

A few minutes later, I was lying in the dark in my pajamas, with Cylvia standing silently on the table beside me. "Cylvia," I said, "please wake me up at the appropriate time."

"All right," she said.

"I don't know what everyone's problem is," I said, after a period of silence. "I'm just trying to do the work I came here to do. It's important work, extremely relevant to life in the Subdivision. I'm forever having to chase down missing children, tolerate the disrespect of haughty receptionists, and fend off harassment from a shape-changing demon."

"Go on," Cylvia said. Her lights had begun to pulse in a new pattern—red and white together, dimly and slowly, bathing the room in soothing, undulating pink.

"They asked me to solve the puzzle, and it turned out they had it upside down all along. And I had to rescue that old man from a force field! It isn't fair that I should be treated so condescendingly."

From upstairs came a creak, then another. Cylvia said, "Of course."

"And when am I going to get a day off?" I demanded. "I've done nothing but work my fingers to the bone since I got here. It's just one task after another. I'd like to say I've had it and walk out, but I have more dignity and responsibility than that!"

The back staircase groaned. Footsteps sounded in the hallway. Cylvia said, "A visitor. A visitor."

"I'm going to ignore that," I said, in response to a knock on my door.

"A visitor. A visitor."

"I'm sleeping!" I called out.

The door opened a crack, then a little bit more—just wide enough to admit the little boy, who came slinking into the room in his suit pants and dress shirt. His feet were bare and his hair was mussed.

"Excuse me?" I said, indignant. "This is my room? I seem to recall that you have your own?"

"A visitor," Cylvia said, gently.

The little boy ignored my complaints. He came over to the bed and climbed in beside me, then scooched his small body over until his back was pressed against me. He reached over his shoulder, found my hand, and pulled it until my arm lay over him.

"This is highly unacceptable," I said, snuggling closer.

"Good night," said the little boy.

"Speak for yourself," I replied, then closed my eyes.

Nineteen

"It's time to prepare for work," Cylvia said.

It was, apparently, morning. I was alone—the boy had gone. I lay on my back in the bed, eyes open, noticing for the first time that the ceiling was wallpapered, or perhaps meticulously painted, in a trompe l'oeil. The scene cleverly implied that the room extended all the way into the attic and the roof beyond, with its rough decking board and slanted rafters. Furthermore, some violent event had resulted in a gaping hole, edged by splintered planks and beams and the broken ends of shingles. Through the hole, a brilliant blue sky was visible, punctuated by small white clouds; it served as the backdrop for a gathering of inquisitive birds and putti, who peered down from the roof to where I lay.

"It's time to prepare for work," Cylvia said.

"I heard you the first time."

"Don't forget to buy batteries for the child."

"I wasn't going to!" I said, throwing my legs over the edge of the bed, though it took me a moment to remember what Cylvia was talking about.

A short time later, I quietly walked down the stairs, then paused to run my hand over the puzzle's surface, to palpate the raised edges on the underside of each piece. The whole felt the way an armadillo or elephant must feel, rough and organic and dry. I briefly entertained the fantasy of lifting up the puzzle again and throwing it around my shoulders to wear like a cape, before I came to my senses and merely contemplated the rough weather map somebody had sketched there, the one that indicated a clash of fronts and an impending storm. Satisfied, I continued out the door.

The wind had grown more assertive, and the trees shivered and swayed in response. The sky in every direction was gray, with darker clouds gathering to the southeast. It was colder too—I was glad I'd elected to put on my cardigan sweater before I left the guesthouse.

"Don't forget," Cylvia said, from my bag, "to buy batt—"

"I *know!*" I scolded, then adjusted my trajectory in the direction of Fortuitous Items.

The familiar clerk wasn't behind the counter when I came in; in fact the place seemed semi-abandoned. All the windows were now covered by magazines, several fluorescent light fixtures flickered or were dimmed, and the aisles were cluttered, either with cardboard boxes full of items that hadn't yet been shelved, or items that had been knocked onto the floor and never picked up. Invisible speakers played some kind of sinuous flute music, in what couldn't properly be called a song, but rather a gently evolving, never-repeating series of intertwined, vaguely related melodic lines.

The batteries took up most of both sides of a very long aisle of the store. A baffling array of sizes, shapes, and voltages was available: A, AA, AAX, BB, QuikZap, D, DX, Reverse Polarity, Water, M, Shake-2-Charge, and so on, all of them displayed loosely in open wire bins. I realized that I hadn't bothered to check the child's flashlight to see which batteries it took, so I gathered up as many batteries as I could hold, using my sweater as a makeshift pouch, in as many flashlight-friendly styles as I could find. One of them, I surmised, was sure to work.

The clerk hadn't reappeared at the counter, so I called out, "Hello? Is anyone here?" No one responded, but I thought I heard a noise— the brush of fabric against fabric—coming from somewhere nearby.

It was then that I noticed something white shifting on the carpet behind the counter. I leaned forward, taking care not to spill my haul of batteries, and peered down. There, rousing herself from an evident nap, lay Justine. Her feet were bare and she was wearing her sheer, grass-stained caftan.

"Oh," she said, opening her eyes. "It's you."

"I didn't know you worked here."

"Sometimes," she said, attempting to shrug.

"I would like to buy these batteries," I told her.

Justine shifted a bit on the floor. "One thing you might not know about me is that I have chronic back issues," she said. "I have to lie down for most of the day. I asked these people to rebuild the point-of-sale system to accommodate reclining transactions, but they've been stonewalling. I'm having my attorney look into a lawsuit."

"I'm sorry to hear that," I said. "But I'm really in kind of a hurry. I have to get to work."

"Maybe you should consider leaving home earlier, if it's so important."

"I appreciate the advice, but right now, I just want to buy these batteries and leave."

Justine sighed. "It's not rocket science," she said. "Just take a plastic bag from that dispenser and put the batteries into it. Go ahead."

I did as she said: I shook the bag open, then formed a kind of spout with my sweater and poured the batteries in. They clattered against the counter, and a few missed the bag, rolled off, and landed on Justine.

"Hey, man!" she said.

"Sorry."

I picked up the batteries I'd dropped while grabbing the bag, and then went around to the other side of the counter to retrieve the rest. I picked them up from Justine's general area.

"You're not allowed back here."

"Okay." I returned to the correct side of the counter and said, "What do I do next?"

"That's it. You're all set."

"Oh. Okay, good!"

"*Have a nice day*," she recited, in a singsongy voice. "That's what

I'm supposed to tell people when they leave. Personally, I think it's insulting—what if I don't want to have a nice day? What if my personal qualities prevent it?"

"Well," I said, "I'll try to have one, anyway." I hefted the bag and, deciding that it might be too flimsy to support the weight of all the batteries, hoisted it into a second one. The bags read FORTUNITOUS ITEMS—a typo—over a crude drawing of a syringe and a tennis racket, forming a lopsided X.

"Did I say you could take a second bag?" Justine inquired, from the floor.

"I'll see you later," I said.

"Have a nice day!"

Outside, the wind was gusting and the clouds had darkened further. I looked up, expecting to see the crow flickering overhead, but it had wisely taken cover somewhere. I hurried the rest of the way to the Courthouse.

For a moment, I thought that the office had closed for the day, and nobody told me—the Living Tower had been armored against the storm, with strong metal grates covering the windows. But the front door opened as usual, and Heather was sitting in the shadows, at her usual spot behind the desk. Her eyes narrowed as she saw me, and her skeptical gaze soon gave way to smug satisfaction.

"Boss wants to see you," she said.

I resisted the temptation to ask why. "All right," I said. "Should I go up there now?"

"He told me to send you up *right away.*"

"Thank you!" I chirped, and headed for the elevator.

The elevator ride was long and rough. The higher I rose, the more intensely I could feel the wind buffeting the building. I calmed myself by rereading the windstorm safety tips taped to the wall:

- **DO NOT DISABLE** HIGH WIND ALERT ALARM UNITS
- **INFORM** YOUR COLLEAGUES OF IMPENDING HIGH WINDS
- **NEVER** OPEN WINDOWS DURING HIGH WIND ALERT
- **NEVER** RIDE MAIN ELEVATOR DURING HIGH WIND ALERT

I wondered, idly, if I should even be in the elevator at all, given the steadily increasing wind. I reassured myself with the knowledge that I hadn't heard any High Wind Alert alarms, but then again, I didn't know what the alarms sounded like, or even where in the building they might be hidden.

The doors opened at the fifth floor, and I followed the hall down to the glassed-in office where Bruce sat behind his desk, soberly poring over some papers. I knocked on the door and he waved me in, looking concerned. I sat down across from him, lowering my bag of batteries to the floor with a dull crunch.

"Thank you for coming in. There's something we need to discuss."

"Sure," I said, throwing back my shoulders and crossing my legs. It seemed to me that he had probably read my reports, and wanted to offer me some much-deserved praise. Perhaps he would even move me into a larger, cleaner office, or tell me that he'd hired an assistant to help me with my work.

Instead, he said, "It seems that you had an encounter with our quantum tunneling researcher."

"Oh yes!" I said. "The one in 4B. With the tennis balls."

"Yes, well," Bruce said, shifting uncomfortably in his seat. "I received a disturbing report from him."

"Oh no," I said. I wondered what had gone wrong—had he been hurt by a ricocheting tennis ball? Did a defect in his generator cause him to fall unconscious? Had there been a fire or explosion?

"It seems that you . . . let me see here . . ." He flipped through the papers on his desk until he found the one he wanted. "It seems that you confessed to him that your work here has been . . . less than professional."

I could not have been more surprised. "What!" I said.

"He claims that you said that . . . and he quotes you here . . . that 'the reports are a mess,' and that your method, upon reviewing them, is to write 'any old thing.' Is that true?"

"No!" I protested, though even as I said it, I began to remember my conversation with Forby—my reassurances, intended to be comic, that our work was nothing to be anxious about. I'd pretended to be incompetent, to spare his feelings. But I'd never dreamed that he would report this to Bruce!

"He goes on, saying that . . . let's see . . . that you expected Courthouse management to be bewildered by your shoddy work . . . that you admitted to having poor reading-comprehension skills . . . that you scribbled indiscriminately on the reports, and even threw some into the trash."

"It's not true! Or, rather—I mean—"

"He says that you mocked the very notion of being a Phenomenon Analyst!"

"He was discouraged!" I explained. "I was trying to make him feel better. He's the one whose work is a failure! His success rate is exactly zero!"

Bruce scowled at this. "Don't think for a moment that I appreciate this kind of disrespect for one of our most valued researchers. Do you have any evidence for this claim?"

I couldn't believe what I was hearing. "He has never once succeeded in getting a single tennis ball to penetrate the wall!"

"I don't think," Bruce said, shaking his head, "that you properly understand the scientific method. Success is success, yes, but failure is also success. Just because he hasn't achieved the stated goal of his experiment doesn't mean that he isn't providing us with valuable data every day. I thought you said that you understood quantum tunneling! Clearly, that was another deception!"

"What about my reports?" I said. "Didn't you read them? You haven't even mentioned the actual work I've done."

Bruce patted a small pile of papers to his right. "Yes, yes, they're right here. I admit, this is very fine work."

"Well," I reasoned, "perhaps you ought to judge me based on that!"

"That's tricky," he said, folding his hands. The wind was pummeling the building now, and the windows rippled and bowed, warping the view of the trees and houses below. Bruce pretended not to be bothered, but it was clear that the wind unnerved him. "Given what you now admit you said to our researcher," he said, "I'm not sure we can trust that this is actually your work."

My entire body twitched in shock, then grew still as calm rage set in. There were words I could have said, but I bit them back.

"It's quite common," Bruce went on, leaning back in his chair and smoothing a few rogue strands of hair over his bald pate. "Some new employee starts here, and is intimidated by the work. Pretty soon, she's in over her head. She finds a colleague down the hall, admits to him that she's been struggling. She persuades him to help her with the reports, just a little bit—in your case, perhaps using your feminine wiles. Before you know it, the veteran employee has done all the work for her, and she takes the credit!"

"That isn't what happened at all!" I blurted.

"It's a testament to our researcher's goodwill and collegiality that he claimed you did this work on your own." He smacked his hand down on the pile of paper. "I'm impressed that he would cover for you like that, I suppose. But you should be ashamed of yourself for convincing him to lie for you."

"This is the exact opposite of what happened!" I exclaimed. "I'm the one who's good at my job, and he's the one who is incompetent! You should be impressed that I would offer him moral support, even though he couldn't quantum-tunnel if his life depended on it!"

Bruce waved his hands. "Enough of that! You'll need to take it upstairs."

"Upstairs to whom!"

"To the big boss. My judgment has already been rendered and run up the chain. You'll have to meet with him if you want to ask for clemency."

"I thought *you* were the boss!"

"Well," he said, patting down his shirtfront, "I am *your* boss. But even I must answer to a higher power. Would you like me to inform him that you've requested an audience?"

"Yes, of course!" I said, getting to my feet.

"I don't suggest," Bruce said, "that you go in with an attitude like that, by the way. Your anger isn't going to do you any favors."

Perhaps appropriately, I was too angry to respond to this final insult. I picked up my sack of batteries, shoved it into my bag, and turned to the door without saying goodbye.

"You'll be alerted if and when the boss wants to see you!" he called out cheerfully as I marched down the carpeted hallway and mashed the elevator button. For about fifteen seconds, while I waited, I watched Bruce, through the glass, remove a foil-wrapped package from a drawer and open it on his desk. He picked up half of the sandwich inside, and bit hugely into it, then thoughtfully chewed while the wind thrashed the tower.

The elevator didn't sound too good. It groaned and screeched and rattled against its shaft. I was relieved to duck into the auxiliary elevator, which operated with comparative smoothness, but which released me into an upsettingly fragile-looking skyway. Long cracks, not present before, now zigzagged across its glass walls, and it was no mystery why: the wind was flinging leaves, branches, and pine cones against the building, and the skyway seemed ill-prepared for the on-slaught. Cold, damp air whistled through the cracks: I could feel it on my hands and neck. Frightened, I hurried across the gap between the towers, flinching when a bird—not a crow but some sparrow or finch—tumbled through the air and bounced off a damaged pane with a resonant thump. I felt a vibration in my bag—not an alert, but a steady, low-frequency vibration, as though Cylvia were snoring, or purring—and it continued as I punched in the code and passed through the steel door into the Dead Tower.

I knew that I should report to my office, where I'd be most likely to receive the boss's summons. But as I stepped off the stairway, and the familiar hum of his generator and the *pock* of his tennis balls met my ears, I knew that I had to confront Forby. I'd never been so en-raged in my life.

I strode down the hall, Cylvia juddering at my hip, and pounded on Forby's door. "Let me in!" I shouted. "I need to talk to you!"

The pocking ceased.

"Don't pretend you're not in there! I know you are!"

I heard his footsteps approaching the door. "I have nothing to say to you," came Forby's meek voice.

"I have plenty to say to you!" I said. "You lied about me to Bruce!"

"Your conduct yesterday was unbecoming of a Phenomenon Analyst."

"I was joking! To make you feel better!"

"That was unnecessary," Forby said, his voice gaining confidence. "I'm actually very confident. My experiment is going great!"

"It's a failure!" I said.

"I'd like to see you do better," he replied, and he was quite close now—right on the other side of the door. Around us, the tower lurched and swayed. I listened for a High Wind Alert, but none was forthcoming. Not that I knew what it would sound like.

Impulsively, I countered with "I am certain I could do better!"

In the moment of silence that followed, I wondered if I'd gone too far. Surely Forby was right—I didn't really know anything about quantum tunneling. It was just a lie Cylvia had instructed me to tell. Waiting in the hall, I experienced a moment of intense self-doubt. What if Bruce was right? I *had* accepted the job under false pretenses. My work as an Analyst had been unimpeachable—but didn't my lie invalidate it? I realized that I was out of my depth. I wanted to run—down the hall, down the stairs, through the skyway, into the elevators, and out of the building.

I reached for the zipper on my bag, intending to ask Cylvia's advice—after all, she was the one who had gotten me into this mess— when a click issued from the lock, and the door opened a crack. A half-inch strip of Forby's face, featuring a mouth, a nostril, and a single eye, soon arrived to fill it.

"I bet you can't," he said. His forehead gleamed with sweat, and he panted shallowly as he awaited my reply.

The sight of him, I was pleased to realize, had dispelled my doubt. The twerp! "Of course I can."

He opened the door a bit wider. "You're not a Researcher," he said. "You're just an Analyst."

"Analyst is a more important job than Researcher!"

He laughed—nervously, as though he feared I might be right. "That's ridiculous."

"I spend my days evaluating reports and issuing opinions—it's complex, important work. You just throw tennis balls at a wall all day!"

Now he opened the door farther, until his entire body filled the gap. "That's just a small portion of what I do!"

"And yet, you can't manage to do it right."

Forby scowled. My criticism had emboldened him: he stood up straighter, wiped his brow with a sleeve. A moment later, he'd flung the door wide open and was beckoning me through with a haughty sweep of the arm. "By all means, then, Miss Quantum Expert! Come on in! Let's see how well you do it!"

"You'll see," I said, barging past him to the tennis ball bucket. Beside it, Forby's computer glowed, displaying a list of his latest failures:

00041034 NO LEAKAGE DETECTED. BARRIER PERMEABILITY
PROBABILITY 0.0000000000000012%.

00041049 NO LEAKAGE DETECTED. BARRIER PERMEABILITY
PROBABILITY 0.000000000000009%.

00041056 NO LEAKAGE DETECTED. BARRIER PERMEABILITY
PROBABILITY 0.00000000000047%.

I reached into the bucket. The tennis balls were dirty, their fur mussed and greasy, from Forby's hands and from their rough target. I suppressed feelings of disgust as I hefted one in my hand.

All around us, the building groaned and shook; the smell of exhaust was heavy in the room. Nevertheless, Forby slammed the door shut, sealing us in together. "Let's see how it's done, Fancy Lady. I bet your arm's too fragile to even throw! I bet it will just fall off!"

A gust from the north roared against the boarded-up windows. The plywood bowed and flexed, and one corner came free with a pop, sending a nail skittering across the floor. The generator coughed and the lights flickered. It was getting too loud in there to be heard.

All the same, the chaos of the moment focused me. The wind, the fumes, the computer, Forby's taunts: they all faded into the background as I squeezed the tennis ball and adjusted my stance. I stared at the bricks: suddenly I saw them as something other than a wall. Instead, they appeared to me as collections of particles, bound by mutual agreement to form a wall, but susceptible to the right kind of persuasion. Just because they were a wall, it didn't mean they *had* to be a wall at *all* times. Some of them, I could see, were open to not being a wall, for a little while. You just had to ask them nicely. You had to ask them with a tennis ball.

I hazarded a glance at Forby. He'd been standing, arms crossed, waiting for me to fail. But now it was dawning on him that something had changed. He slumped, and his arms fell to his sides. His eyes narrowed. Figures and diagrams sprang to mind, and superimposed themselves over the scene, as though through an overhead projector: velocities, trajectories. I turned to the wall and threw.

It wouldn't be quite accurate to say that the ball passed through the wall. It was more that the wall *stepped aside for* the ball. In any event, the ball was flying toward the wall, and then it was on the other side. Even above the din of the wind and the strained revving of the generator, it could be heard striking the sheetrock inside the experimental chamber. I turned to look at the laptop. There was the ball, captured by the remote camera, rolling to a stop on the floor. The text window read:

00041072 LEAKAGE CONFIRMED. BARRIER PERMEABILITY
PROBABILITY 93.4950384732273279%.

"That's how it's done!" I said to Forby, who stood slack-jawed before me in apparent devastation. I reached behind me and pulled another ball out of the bucket. "Do I have to do everything around here?" I said, and threw a second ball through the wall. It ricocheted into the camera's view, and rolled to a stop beside the first one. The computer said:

00041088 LEAKAGE CONFIRMED. BARRIER PERMEABILITY
PROBABILITY 96.9384994273628 33%.

After that, the rest was easy. I dispatched every ball in the bucket, then crept around the room, picking up the strays from the floor and casually tossing them through the brick wall. Soon the floor in the remote camera's view was carpeted in yellow, the data readout was bristling with success, and Forby had fallen to a crouch, holding his head in his hands.

"I can't believe it," he said, mostly to himself, I think. "It's just not possible."

"It isn't just possible," I said, walking past him to the door. "It's probable."

•

Cylvia's vibration had continued while I did Forby's work for him; if anything, it seemed to have intensified. When I reached my office and let myself in, I finally opened up my bag to see what was going on.

I was surprised to find that Cylvia was occupied with some kind of transformation—she had again begun to change her physical form. I gently lifted her out of the bag and onto my desk for a better look.

It was subtle, but I couldn't deny it: Cylvia was no longer strictly a cylinder. She'd begun to taper at the base and top, and her form had taken on something of a curve: a bulge in the lower midsection, a slight cinch in the upper middle. Her case, adding to its already fleshy texture, had developed what looked like tiny, evenly spaced pimples, many of which had begun to extrude something sharp and translucently white: a chitinous substance, hard but slightly yielding. What's more, two bumps had appeared on one side, just above

191

center, interrupting her radial symmetry. I ran my thumbs over them, gently, and could feel something shifting underneath the surface. If I looked closely and remained still, in fact, I could see these changes slowly advancing: the white spines extending themselves, the bumps stretching, expanding.

"Cylvia," I said, "can you hear me?"

Her white light was fainter now, though the glow gave the impression not of weakness, but of originating farther beneath the surface—as if she were glowing not for me, but privately, for herself. She said, "Yes."

"Are you all right?"

"Upgrades are in progress. You may continue to employ me during this time."

"Well, that's good. Do you know what I'm supposed to do now?"

Dim flashes of white. She said, "You will soon be summoned to the office of the Head Judge."

"How will I know?"

"You will know," she said.

"Should I bring you with me when I go?"

"No."

I gazed out the window, into the swirling gray. A few drops of rain tapped faintly, gently on my office windows. All of these—the inclement weather, my deepening trouble at work, and these strange changes to Cylvia's form—seemed like impediments to what I now understood to be my goal: making my way to the City.

"Cylvia," I said. "I have to admit, I'm uneasy. I can't see your light so well anymore. And your voice," I went on, realizing it was true as I spoke the words, "it's not the same. It's harsher."

"The changes are upgrades," she replied.

"I'm . . . I'm afraid you'll end up less . . . useful to me."

"My utility to you is indeed diminishing. I will continue to serve the few needs that remain."

"I don't understand."

Before Cylvia could respond—though I had the sense that she wasn't going to—I was distracted by a blinking light. It was blue, and was issuing from the wall opposite the desk. It seemed to indicate that the document tray was activating. A few seconds later I heard a click, and the little door slowly opened, revealing a single one-page document.

I crossed the room to read it. It said: *The Head Judge will see you now*, followed by a detailed set of instructions for getting to his office.

"Well," I said to Cylvia. Her vibration was propagating through the desk, filling the room with a quiet, soothing drone that served to mitigate, in part, the chaos of the gathering windstorm. "Time to face the music."

My bag felt extra heavy as I shouldered it, as though with the weight of my worries, and I turned to the door to leave, paper in hand. But at the last second I turned back, gently picked Cylvia up, and moved her a few feet closer to the windows. A bit of sun had managed to make its way through the gathering storm, and for a moment she stood in a long trapezoid of light interrupted only by the flickering shadows of passing leaves and the droplets of rain that dotted the windows.

"Thank you," she said.

"You're welcome."

I turned and walked out the door.

Twenty

The instructions for reaching the Head Judge's office were odd, and I wasn't sure how they were supposed to get me where I wanted to go. I was to walk back down the spiral staircase, pass through the ruined employee lounge, and enter the skyway that connected the two towers. But then, instead of continuing to the elevator, I was to turn around and key in a door code—not the one I had memorized, the one that I'd used every day I'd come to work, but a different, longer one. Then I was supposed to walk through the steel door again, climb the spiral staircase, and walk down the hall to room 4Q.

4Q was, of course, my own office. So this couldn't be right. But the instruction sheet was all I had, and I absolutely needed to see the Head Judge—to defend both my honor and my job.

I set off down the hall and stairs, doing as the memo instructed. The employee lounge was the same, if darkened somewhat by the roiling clouds: through the bank of cracked and dirty windows I could see them advancing from every direction, churning and blossoming, an explosion in slow motion. The tower shook and swayed. I hurried across the room, feeling the sweat breaking out under my arms, and my blouse coming untucked from my skirt. Breathless, I opened the steel door, and stepped through, into the skyway; the electronic lock engaged the moment the door clicked shut.

Now to enter the alternate code. I typed it in with shaking hands as the wind howled. A large tree branch, buoyed by the wind, came crashing into the skyway, cracking a glass panel, and my fingers fumbled on the keypad. Eventually, I managed all seventeen digits, and the door clicked open. As quickly as I could, I slipped back through, and flung the door shut behind me.

What I saw on the other side was both entirely familiar and completely disorienting. I was standing in the very employee lounge I'd just left. But, to my amazement, everything in the room was now in perfect, even new, condition. The windows were all intact, the worktables and chairs neatly arranged. In the carpeted depression at the center of the room, the sofas stood upright, and faced a display monitor that was not only undamaged but switched on. It was presently streaming what looked like a government event: some kind of town council meeting or other legislative session.

But the most astonishing thing about the restored employee lounge was that it was populated by employees—dozens of them, reading, writing, chatting, and watching the meeting on the big screen. People strode around holding electronic tablets or sheaves of paper; they nodded greetings as they passed one another in haste; they waved to one another across the room, or stood stroking their chins in contemplation of one vexing problem or another. The weather hadn't changed—the storm still raged, and the building trembled in the wind—but the burble of conversation, the shuffling of papers, the scuff of footsteps on the carpet, and the clacking of computer keys all combined to obscure the roar from outside.

Panting, disheveled, I took a few hesitant steps toward the staircase and nearly bumped into a passing worker holding a brimming cup of coffee. "Whoop!" he said, slurping at the cup. "Shoulda got a lid!"

"I'm sorry!" I said.

"No worries!" he called out over his shoulder, for he was already on his way to his next caffeine-fueled clerical task. I continued, flinching as people brushed past, their clothes and possessions coming into brief contact with me: the hem of a skirt, the corner of a file folder, the cuff of a suit jacket. On the spiral stairs, I had to press myself to the railing to allow others by; they greeted me with smiles or friendly nods, as though I were one of them.

Suppressing revulsion—for that's what it was, my aversion to the nearness of all these people, moving, breathing, talking, living—I climbed the familiar stairs and made my way down the hallway that, just minutes ago, had been mine alone.

Soon I was standing at the door of 4Q. Around me, office doors opened and closed; people hurried by clutching clipboards. I knocked, gently.

"Hello? Sir?" I said.

There was no response. I knocked again, this time louder. "We have a meeting? Sir? Hello?"

I resisted the urge to pound on the door: though I intended to assert myself in my defense, I didn't want to seem too aggressive. But if the Head Judge was actually in there, he didn't seem to have heard me. I wasn't sure what to do.

At this point, I remembered that I still had, in my bag, the key to my version of office 4Q. Perhaps it would fit here as well. Indeed, maybe this was some kind of test—an experiment to see whether I possessed the confidence to stride right into the boss's office and demand to be heard. The more I thought about it, the more plausible it seemed—the meeting had already begun! I dug in my bag for the key, and was briefly surprised to find a bulky obstacle there—the plastic sack full of batteries I had bought for the little boy. Some had spilled out into my bag proper, and now cluttered it, making the key difficult to find. Eventually my fingers discovered it shoved down in a corner with some paper clips and breath mints, and I pulled it out and fitted it into the lock. The door clicked and fell open.

I recognized the space from my own occupation of it, just minutes before. But unlike my office, which reflected my spare personal aesthetic, this version of 4Q was populated by decorations: an umbrella stand made from an elephant's foot, which held umbrellas imprinted with the logo of a prestigious university; the trophy head of some kind of jungle cat; a bag of golf clubs, leaning casually in a corner; and several framed items, including a diploma accented in gold leaf, a plaque commemorating some management award or other, and a flash photograph of the Head Judge theatrically shaking hands with a heavyset white man—likely some powerful politician or CEO. On the desk stood a marble pen holder with a large fountain pen sticking out of it, a slim laptop computer, and the familiar Schwartzmann's Sling sculptural toy, its five dangling steel balls presently in motion, clicking monotonously against one another.

The desk itself was quite unusual, so much so that it took me a moment to absorb its intended impact. For one thing, it was painted a bright, glossy red. Its surface tapered at the front, and terminated before me in a gleaming chrome grille bookended by a pair of large, faceted halogen lamps, presently casting an eerie light across the room and over my bedraggled body.

It was, in fact, made out of, or made to resemble, a sports car, in much the way a child's bed might be: it was as though someone had sawed off the front of a stylish red coupe and refashioned it as a work surface. Indeed, I now saw that the desk was affixed to two tires, one on each side. And though, like most office desks, this one accommodated two chairs, one for the officeholder and one for a visitor, the two chairs were positioned side by side, meaning that if I wanted to sit down, I would have to do so beside the Head Judge, rather than opposite him, with the desk between us. In addition, the two chairs weren't typical office chairs—instead, they resembled, appropriately, automobile seats, and probably had been exactly that, at one time. One of them, the "passenger" seat, was empty, and in the "driver's" seat sat the Head Judge, gazing at me with a self-satisfied air.

The Head Judge appeared unconcerned by my arrival, or by the howling of the wind outside his window. "Ah, yes, hello," he said mildly, smoothing his necktie against his chest. The tie was burgundy and decorated with a pattern, one too small to make out from where I was standing. "You must be our controversial new Phenomenon Analyst."

I understood that I needed to come off as assertive and professional, to project authority with my every word and action. I tucked my blouse back in, wiped the sweat off my forehead, and said, "Thank you for seeing me?"

The Head Judge responded with a smirk. He was rather tall, and fairly young for a man in his position—perhaps just a few years older than me. His long face had a chiseled look, but his large hands appeared soft. His broad shoulders implied strength. His overall look could be described as seasoned, but not worn or weary—like an old-time film star or model in a cigarette ad. He was, in other words, quite handsome, and eerily familiar. There was no getting around it: he was the bakemono.

Along with this realization came another familiar feeling, one that the bakemono never failed to evoke in me: one of impending capitulation. It would be so comforting, I thought, to just slip into the passenger seat, settle back with a sigh, and let things take their natural course. I would close my eyes and accept whatever discipline he felt appropriate to mete out.

He tapped a key on the computer before him. It was astonishingly thin—barely distinguishable from a folded sheet of paper. "It seems to say here that you made light of your very important position, confessed to incompetence and sloppiness, and took credit for someone else's work. These are serious infractions."

In spite of my best intentions, I felt myself blushing. I couldn't just succumb to his authority and charm! I had to be bold. I said, "Ummmm . . . none of that is . . . uh . . . true?"

He tilted his head and winked. "You're impugning the integrity of one of our very best researchers," he said. Then he shut the laptop, folded it three times, and slipped it into his jacket pocket.

As my mind scrabbled for a reply—there was a perfect retort, I just knew it, but I couldn't seem to put my hands on it—I stared, transfixed, out the window over the Head Judge's shoulder, where the wind had picked up a load of chaff from the ground—leaves, twigs, bark mulch—and swirled it up into the air. Among the objects caught in the gust was an entire sapling—maple, by the look of it—and it darted and spun before suddenly veering for the very office where I now stood. Like the Head Judge himself, it looked familiar, and evoked feelings and experiences that, like the storm debris, wheeled in the recesses of my mind: the warm comfort of a day in late spring, with the sun shining and the scent of privet blossoms carried on the air. The pleasure of physical effort, of getting one's hands dirty, of staking a claim on a patch of ground and on a way of living. It's important, I seemed to recall, not to disturb the root ball, to dig the hole wide enough for the roots to grow, to carefully stake the immature transplant. Also, one should avoid caffeine and alcohol after planting a new tree—and stay away from raw fish and soft cheeses, instead choosing nourishing snacks like carrot sticks or fruit. A healthy landscaper was also advised to take a daily neo-horticultural vitamin, one rich in iron and folic acid. And of course safety should be anyone's top priority on the road, but buckling up was especially important for the expectant arborist.

Behind the Head Judge—no, I had to remind myself, the bakemono, the bakemono!—the sapling seemed to pick up speed as it approached, and finally it struck the office window with a startling bang. The window bulged and shuddered, and I jumped, letting out a small scream. Through the office door, I could hear the hurried footsteps and panicked voices of other employees as they began to recognize the severity of the storm.

The bakemono, meanwhile, had no visible reaction to the sapling, but he responded to my outburst with a low, patronizing chuckle. "There, there," he said. "Why don't you sit down?" He removed a handkerchief from his jacket pocket and used it to wipe the passenger seat before offering it to me with a wave of his hand.

I noticed, in the wake of the crashing branch, that the Schwartzmann's Sling had continued to move at what seemed to be the same tempo as before. The quiet clicking of the steel balls made me feel sleepy and relaxed, and the automobile seat beside the bakemono looked comfortable. With a feeling that was part excitement and part resignation, I set my bag down on the desk and settled in beside him. I reached over my shoulder for the seat belt, but couldn't seem to find it.

Fluidly, but not without a faint air of ceremony, the bakemono reached under the lip of the desk, gripped something with both hands, and pulled. A circular object emerged, attached to the desk by a heavy articulated arm: a retractable steering wheel. With a few deft motions, he clicked it into place, and then, with his hands at ten and two o'clock, proceeded to twist it back and forth, as though we were riding the desk down a winding country road. Now that I was sitting so close to him, I could make out the pattern on his tie: a series of little fetuses, each in its eighth month or so, joined by a network of umbilical cords rendered in gold thread.

"Sometimes new employees enjoy an early success or two, and they become overconfident," the bakemono explained, one eyebrow raised. "They've been praised their whole lives, just for being cute and charming. But it turns out that the working world is more competitive than they imagined. When they realize that they're not as smart as they'd thought, they'll do anything to maintain their fraudulent status—even if that means robbing more experienced workers of credit for their labor."

His words incensed me, and it was time to give him a piece of my mind. I turned to him and said, "I don't know—maybe?"

Behind us, out the window, the storm seemed to rise in intensity. The wind howled, driving debris into the building; its scattershot rhythm formed a counterpoint to the monotonous clicking of the Schwartzmann's Sling.

"For instance, one of our most valued researchers—the one who helped you with your phenomenon analysis, in fact—just made an exciting discovery in the field of quantum tunneling. His years of meticulous toil finally paid off: it turns out that, in certain circumstances, a nexus, or 'well,' of probability can alter the properties of matter, and make it temporarily permeable. This discovery has profound implications for the very fabric of life on earth, and he made it with a brilliant yet simple experiment involving tennis balls." He turned to me with a pitying smile. "Someone just starting out, like yourself, would never be capable of such a thing."

I couldn't believe what I was hearing—Forby was being credited for what I'd accomplished literally minutes before! Scowling at the bakemono, I balled my hands into fists and snarled, "Whoa . . . that's . . . kinda interesting?"

"I don't want you to think," he said, "that I don't sympathize. In fact, I recognize that it must be hard to be someone like you." He raised his left arm and crooked his elbow, as though resting it on the frame of an open car window. "To come so far, only to find that you're a fraud—that you weren't nearly as competent or attractive as you thought, and that the life you've imagined for yourself is a lie. It's sad, really."

"Uh-huh?" I said, in a fit of rage.

At this point, the bakemono's shoulders and face began to twitch, betraying a certain amount of tension. Perhaps it was the weather, which had continued to worsen; the clouds had at long last filled the gap of blue that the sun had shone through, and the light had drained out of the day entirely. The rain of debris against the window was louder and more frenzied than ever, nearly drowning out the inexorable clicking of the Schwartzmann's Sling, and shouts echoed behind the closed office door.

Or perhaps the bakemono was reacting to the case he was making against me—not only against my employment in the tower, but against my existing at all. He withdrew his arm from the "car window" and gripped the steering wheel with both hands, staring ahead as his jaw clenched and worked. His eyes—pellucid pools aglow with intelligence and wit—glittered like the most precious jewels as he said, "I'm sure you've considered quitting. In fact, I'm sure you've considered jumping out your office window, bringing the whole sordid charade of your life to an abrupt and violent end."

His words chilled me—I'd never entertained such a horrific notion, and never would. "Sort of?" I forcefully countered. My hand again searched for the seat belt, and again came up empty.

"The truth is," he went on, "the hopeless should not be forced to endure the misery of living. And, unfortunately, these people are often weak as well as depressed—too weak to take decisive action and end their lives once and for all. Furthermore, today's world is so ugly and so unfair. The more of us that are born into it, the worse it gets. And the idea that anyone would voluntarily subject a child to this world—that's not just unwise; it's unconscionable." His jaw trembled, and I thought I could hear his teeth grinding beneath the roar of the storm and the increasing commotion down the hall. I remembered that he'd been told by his dentist to use a mouth guard at night, to prevent his teeth from wearing down. He refused to use it, though, and it lay forgotten in the drawer of his bedside table. "I told you that I didn't want a child," he pleaded. "I told you it was a mistake."

For a moment, I felt bad for him, and the desire to capitulate rose up in me like a wave of nausea. But I steeled myself: what he'd said was simply a lie! The bakemono and I had discussed having a child for months, and had agreed that we wanted one! His diseased mind had twisted our words, revised the history of our love. How dare he! My voice quavered with fury as I said, "Did you?"

"Yes, I did, but you *insisted*," he wailed, thumping the steering wheel with his palms. "You think your optimism is some kind of virtue—as if, just by believing in something, you can make it true. Do you understand how foolish, how self-absorbed that is? You convince people that things will work out, and when they don't, when everything falls apart, do you accept the blame? No, you blame *fate*."

His steering, as it were, had become more erratic. As he jerked the wheel to and fro, I could almost feel our imaginary car swerving and lurching all over the road.

The bakemono continued his speech, froth issuing from the corners of his mouth, his cheeks glistening with enraged tears. "Meanwhile, your quaint notions have ruined plans, damaged lives. And this," he said, pointing at my belly with a trembling finger, "*this* is the worst thing you've *ever* done. I said no. I said it again and again. But you needed a child, because my love wasn't enough. You needed *unconditional* love—the love of a helpless innocent who couldn't live without you. All to prop up your own fragile ego."

Nothing could have been further from the truth—neither his memory of our conversations nor his analysis of my motivation for wanting a child. And yet his logic, to his mind, was airtight—when he got like this, you just couldn't argue with him. My frustration and anger were growing, and he was having difficulty keeping the car in its lane. A passing bus greeted us with a long blast of the horn. The bakemono reacted with a twitch of the hands, sending the car scraping along a guardrail.

"Be . . . careful?" I screamed.

He turned to face me, slowly, theatrically. His beautiful eyes were ablaze and his chin trembled. "You'd like that, wouldn't you. You'd like it if I was *careful*."

My voice was ragged as, through tears of dread, I pleaded, "Maybe . . . I don't know . . . watch the road?"

"Convince me. Convince me to watch the road," he said through gritted teeth. "Convince me that any of this is worth it."

We were approaching the bridge. The car was speeding up, heading right for the arrow signs warning of a curve. A delivery truck was approaching from the other direction. Every detail stood out in sharp relief: I could see the driver's face, a rictus of astonishment and horror. Along the side of the road, a heavyset man in a flannel shirt, carrying a newspaper and a cup of coffee, stopped in his walk as the accident unfolded. A woman pushing a stroller on the other side drew back from the impending disaster while her baby slept, unaware. The driver was swerving to avoid us, and the truck had begun, inexorably, to tip onto its side. The bridge abutment loomed: soon the car would smash into it.

I'd had enough. I leaped out of my seat and reached for the heavy objects closest at hand: the batteries that now filled my bag. I closed my fingers around one, drew back, and flung it as hard as I could at the bakemono.

Whether serendipitously or by fortuitous quick thinking, the battery had been well chosen. It was large and heavy: a DX or QuikZap, by the look of it. What's more, my aim was true: it struck him squarely in the middle of the forehead before ricocheting into, and silencing at last, the Schwartzmann's Sling. The bakemono appeared shocked at my attack, and even flickered, briefly, into his badger form before snapping back into human focus a second later.

The battery had left a mark—a flap of skin hung above his nose, and blood began to flow into his eye wells. Furious, he heaved the steering wheel in my direction, as though to run me down—ineffectually, of course, because the car was actually a desk.

By that time I'd drawn more batteries out of the bag and was pumping them at the bakemono in a veritable cannonade. They struck him about the face, neck, and shoulders, and soon he raised his arms to defend himself.

"I'm the one who quantum-tunneled!" I bellowed at last, continuing to pummel him with batteries. "I am! I'm the one who wrote those reports!"

But despite the rain of batteries, the bakemono laughed at me. "You can't hurt me with those!" he said, as the debris outside began to swirl, faster and faster, in a roaring funnel of wind. "I'm not alive! You can't hurt something that isn't alive!"

This argument gave me pause, though how was I to know what was and wasn't alive, in this bewildering world? I caught my breath, and the bakemono and I stared at each other across the gleaming desk. Then I reached into the bag for one more battery. I knew it was there—I remembered selecting it from the baskets at the drugstore, and carrying it to the counter in my sweater. My hand found it, seized it, drew it forth. It was larger, heavier, and more powerful than any other battery: the Goldblatt Cell.

"What did I *just tell you*," the bakemono said, laughing.

But his eyes told me something different. Somewhere in the depths of that confused mind, a vestige of his former self resided, the part of him I had once known and loved, the part I'd once thought I could help. I couldn't, it was clear now. I wished I'd understood that sooner. His crazed stare challenged me now, dared me. *Begged* me. Just because something wasn't alive, didn't mean it couldn't hurt you. The bakemono couldn't get any deader, but he could—*wanted to*, I believed—stop doing harm.

I launched the Goldblatt Cell over his head and into the window.

The noise was tremendous—a resonant clap like a gong. For a moment, nothing happened, and a sad smile spread across the bakemono's face. Then a crack appeared in the glass, and lengthened, and the wind worked its fingers through and pulled, and the window shattered, and in an instant it was gone.

I barely had time to react: I dove for a corner of the room and curled up fetally next to the bag of golf clubs. The sudden vacuum began to shuffle the contents of the room like the balls in a bingo basket. I could hear as the golf clubs were shaken, then ripped from the bag one by one, as though by a caddy gone mad.

I stole a glance at the bakemono. He was trying to climb over the desk: his beautifully styled brown hair was swept back and his necktie fluttered violently. But it was no use. A street sign came soaring into the office and knocked him over, and the wind gripped him and pulled him into the air. His eyes wheeled and twitched in their sockets, in a textbook example of the medical phenomenon known as nystagmus, and in an instant, he was sucked into the maelstrom. He tumbled through the sky, flickering into badger form, then into a series of alternate shapes in an evident effort to escape the pull of the wind: a parking meter, a javelin, a rabbit, a water cooler, a lantern. In the end, perhaps exhausted by the effort, he reverted to his human shape and was carried off. Soon he was nothing but a dark speck in the distance, indistinguishable from any other trash.

I needed to get out of here, and to rescue Cylvia, before finding my way to safety. But the closed door was too far away. I was still crouched in the corner, trying to keep myself small and streamlined, when a solution caught my eye: the blinking blue light, barely two feet to my right, that signaled the opening of the trapdoor! A moment later, the wall panel detached itself and the paper tray fell open. It would be tight, but I had no choice—I reached out, grabbed the tray, and squeezed myself into the opening above it.

Inside, I found a large red button, evidently installed in anticipation of a situation very much like this one, underscored by an embossed plastic sign that read EMERGENCY CLOSE DOOR. I pressed it, an electric motor clunked into service, and the panel swung shut, sealing me off from the chaos of the storm.

PART THREE

Twenty-One

The area behind the wall panel was surprisingly spacious—it took the form of a small room, cubical in shape, about four feet to a side. I was quite comfortable sitting cross-legged in it. Its walls were painted a deep, satin black that glowed faintly in the light from the chandelier hanging from the room's ceiling: a subdued but stylish sculptural fixture, also painted black, that consisted of irregularly clustered tubes, each about the size of Cylvia and harboring small, warm bulbs that buzzed quietly in the relative silence of the chamber. Opposite me hung, to my surprise, a painting, housed in a simple, sleek black frame and taking up almost the entire wall. Dark in color, it depicted a character I felt I'd seen before—a female figure with regal bearing, seated in the foreground of a brightly lit city, itself arrayed beneath a starry night sky. The figure wore a rather austere gunmetal crown, devoid of jewels or other ornamentation, and a tailored gray business suit; and she was seated upon what looked like an adjustable office chair. The gray blouse beneath the suit jacket was unbuttoned at the belly, and with her left hand, the figure was pulling aside the blouse and jacket to reveal a long, ragged, crudely sutured surgical scar extending across her smooth gray skin. Beside this figure stood a little boy in a suit of his own, this one white, the same color as his pale flesh, so that he resembled a marble statue. He held the female figure's right hand. In the sky above these characters, two cherubic angels, one white and one black, hovered, one in each corner, each gazing at the other over the heads of the figures. The overall mood of the piece was somber, but for some reason it gave me comfort as I cowered from the windstorm. The swaying and trembling of the tower around me was as soporific as it was unnerving, and I may even have slept for a short while. In any event, I was eventually roused by the now-familiar sound of the panel's machinery, and by the cold light that greeted me from outside as the paper tray fell open. Fearfully, I peeked out.

I was looking into my office—not the bakemono's iteration of it, but my old familiar workspace in the Dead Tower. The gale still roared against the windows, but they were intact, and the room offered perfect shelter from the storm, at least for the time being. I could hear, outside this room, the siren-like whoop of what must have been the High Wind Alert. My ordinary desk and chair were in their proper places, and on the desk stood something that I couldn't identify at first: a curved, upright object, covered in something white and soft. It was only when I'd crawled out of the hidden room behind the panel that I recognized the object as Cylvia.

She had undergone an extraordinary transformation. Her case, already revising its contours when I left the office, had continued to change; in her curves and posture, she resembled a small vase or carafe. The translucent spines that I'd watched emerging not long before had developed into an exquisite down. And the two bony knobs I'd seen growing beneath her covering had developed into limbs: these were now folded neatly against her soft form. No light shone from inside Cylvia, but she slowly, silently expanded and contracted, as though she were breathing.

In fact, she *was* breathing. It was clear to me now: the upper portion of her case was a head, lowered in slumber. A triangle of white, half-buried in the down, revealed itself as a beak, and the limbs as wings. Cylvia was turning—had turned—into a bird.

"Cylvia? Can you hear me?"

She shook herself, wobbling slightly. I could make out two white feet at her base; their toes clicked against the desk's surface. A patch of fluff at the head parted to reveal a small black eye, then closed again. The beak moved. "Yes," she croaked.

"Did you open the paper tray for me, in the bakemono's office?"

"Yes."

"Thank you for that."

I was startled by a thump against the window: the storm had blown a potted shrub against the building. I watched it fly off again, into the tempest.

I said, "What should I do now?"

Cylvia muttered something I couldn't understand. She was losing her voice, it was clear. A light, very dim now, pulsed inside her.

"Could you repeat that?"

"Instructions," she said, her small beak moving. "Elevator."

"Oh! Of course!"

"Time," Cylvia said. "To go."

"All right," I replied, determined now. I set my bag down on the desk with a thud—it still contained a fair number of batteries—and unzipped it. Gently, I took Cylvia into my hands. She was warm and yielding; I could feel something like a heart beating beneath her feathers. I lay her down in the bag, and the batteries parted to accommodate her small body. The white light pulsing within her brightened, briefly; then the light faded and she appeared to fall, once again, asleep.

I zipped up the bag, ran out my office door, and hurried to the stairs. The shrill Klaxon of the High Wind Alert was deafening. I was halfway across the floor of the employee lounge, and headed for the steel door, when a thought brought me up short. After a moment's hesitation—during which something large and heavy struck the lounge windows and crashed through, admitting the wind's violent howl—I ran back to the stairs and climbed them one last time, then raced down the hallway to office 4B. I banged on the door, but it wasn't necessary; the door was unlocked and fell open easily, to a room oppressive with the smell of exhaust fumes and sweat. Forby was still here, still crouched on the floor. He was talking to himself, punching an open palm with a fist; tears streamed down his face. I knelt beside him and heard the words his lips were forming: "It can't be! It just can't be! It's not possible!"

"We have to go!" I said.

But Forby shook his head. "How did you *do* it? It's just not possible that you *did* it!"

"None of that matters now!" I said, batting his hands away. I grabbed his arm and pulled him up. "We need to evacuate!"

Forby was still mumbling to himself, or perhaps to me, as I dragged him out of his reeking laboratory and down the hall and stairs. Another window had broken in the seconds I was away, and the pull of the gale was stronger still. Forby and I clung to each other as we staggered toward the steel door. With a deep breath for luck, I grabbed the handle and flung it open.

Miraculously, the skyway was still intact. But outside it, the world was chaos. Leaves, dirt, stones, and other small objects—children's toys, office supplies, nonperishable food items, pieces of technology—flew through the air; in the distance I could see entire cars taking to the sky. Nevertheless, to the south, a few blocks away, I thought I could make out Bus Negative One doggedly crawling across an intersection, and trembling in the wind.

We hurried across and I mashed the button for the auxiliary elevator. I held Forby close. He was so thin, so weak. He said, "But you *couldn't*. You *couldn't*. If *I* couldn't, then how could *you* . . ."

The arrival of the elevator filled me with joy. I pushed Forby inside, and we rode down to the floor below, where we successfully transferred to the main elevator. I consulted the photocopied wind alert procedure.

It was a good thing that we weren't supposed to ride the main elevator, because it wasn't working; it seemed dead, its doors stuck half-open. I pointed, indicating that I needed help, and Forby obliged, assisting me in widening the gap enough to squeeze through. We found ourselves in a long hallway, sheltered from the wind but empty of people, and could make out, in the flashing emergency lamps, a sign with an arrow showing the way to the stairs.

As it happened, the route wasn't straightforward; we plodded down seemingly endless stretches of hall, around dozens of identical corners, through empty offices leading to other empty offices. The building seemed specifically designed to prevent anyone from using the stairs. At long last, though, we crashed through a heavy unmarked door into a lightless cement stairwell.

We could have found our way in the darkness, using the steel railing as a guide, but I unzipped my bag and asked Cylvia if she could illuminate the way. She stirred in her sleep, and then managed a faint, steady glow from inside her body that gave us just enough light to carefully but swiftly descend. If Forby was surprised to be assisted in our evacuation by a glowing white bird lying in a nest of batteries, he made no sign; instead he continued to mutter bewilderedly.

The storm outside was completely inaudible from the stairwell, but it was noisy in here, owing to the echoes of our footsteps. We walked for what felt like hours, though it could only have been minutes, as Cylvia glowed and Forby mumbled; and at long last the echoes shortened, and we began to see light from below, and we came around a corner and found we'd reached the end. As if in response, Cylvia dimmed her light, and I zipped her up.

A door stood before us, illuminated by a single bare bulb. The door was red, and on it words had been painted. Viewed straight on, they were illegible, as much of the paint had flaked away in the damp; I could make out, at my feet, the flakes of black that had once formed the letters.

But, by peering at the door from an oblique angle, I could discern the outline of the words, which had left residue behind as they disintegrated; they read, or had once read, TO THE GONDOLA. A panic-exit bar stretched across the door, so I leaned against it, and the door fell open.

Forby and I emerged into what appeared to be an enormous cave or natural channel—dimly illuminated by caged ceiling bulbs—that had been carved by an ancient underground river. The river was still here, as wide across as a house, emerging from darkness on the left and flowing into darkness on the right. It smelled richly of rain and mud and decay, and moved swiftly and silently through the cavernous space. The stone bank where we stood had been fashioned into a transit station, with white tile lining the floor and wall, and a yellow-painted boarding strip at the river's edge; the wall was labeled in a mosaic of smaller, colored tiles that spelled out the word COURTHOUSE, and wooden benches were installed at intervals along the platform's length, as resting spots for evacuees awaiting their gondola.

On one of these benches sat Bruce and Heather, several feet apart. Bruce was asleep, his head thrown back against the damp tiles, a single shirttail untucked and dangling over his belt. Heather was gnawing on her fingernails, forcefully and meticulously, as though determined to get all ten finished before the gondola arrived. Forby, still grousing under his breath, collapsed onto the bench nearest the door. I walked over to Heather.

"I left a slice of pie in my desk drawer," she said mournfully. "It's probably halfway to the moon by now."

"Have you had to evacuate before?" I asked her.

She shook her head. "They put the whole system in after the *disaster*," she said, clearly annoyed at the inconvenience it had caused. Then she blushed. "Sorry. I forgot about your sister."

So had I. "It's all right. So this is the first time any of this has been used?"

"I guess? I've never seen it, anyway."

I peered upstream, hoping to catch a glimpse of the gondola, but the light died just a few feet past the platform. There was nothing to do but wait.

"Where's the big boss, I wonder," Heather said.

"I think he found another way out," I said.

At this point, a sound began to make itself heard, warped and scattered by echoes from the cave walls and the surface of the river: a refined yet tuneless whistling. It accompanied a faint clanking, and the rhythmic splash of something against the water. I looked upstream again, and this time I saw a warm yellow light enclosed in a metal cage, swinging back and forth. That's where the clanking was coming from: a lantern, hanging from the bow of our rescue gondola.

The gondolier was a cadaverous old man, dressed in a red tuxedo and bowtie worn over a crisp white shirt. An official-looking hat bore a metallic badge: a red shield enclosing a bold white RG. His skin was pale white, rendered a jaundiced hue by the light from above and by the lantern. Dark sunglasses covered his eyes. He used a long oar to push the gondola over to the platform, and then, deftly and with surprising strength, to bring it to a halt. The river flowed around it as it knocked gently against the rocky bank.

Forby stood up, whispering to himself. Heather stood, too, and roused Bruce, who came to with a groan. We all approached the gondola and wordlessly stepped on board. The vessel was equipped with comfortable benches, upholstered in red velour: a far cry from the primitive wood I suspect we had all anticipated. Wordless expressions of approval emanated from our little group.

"Do you also drive the bus?" I asked the gondolier, as I accepted his offered steadying hand.

"That's my brother," he croaked.

Once we were settled, me beside Heather and Forby next to Bruce, the gondolier pushed off from the bank, and we drifted into the middle of the river, where the current embraced us and began to push us downstream. Soon the platform was lost to sight around a corner, and the only source of light was the gondolier's lantern. He made incessant minor adjustments with his oar to keep the boat steady and on course; his arms and shoulders moved with casual, practiced strength, and he resumed his whistling, which remained unmusical to my ear, yet evocative, as though describing a melody too subtle, too complex, to be casually perceived. I sensed that the gondolier's song had been in progress for years, and that it was a long, long way from completion. He might be reprising notes that he'd first whistled decades before—notes that seemed random in the moment, but that occupied a role in some grand symphony that I was too close to hear, like the threads of a tapestry viewed through a magnifying glass.

Forby was muttering to Bruce about the implausibility of my success. Along with the gondolier's whistling, the gentle lapping of the water against the hull, and the background static of the river's flow, his voice formed a soothing cloak of sound that lulled me half to sleep. Eyes closed, I could feel the gondola twisting and turning its way beneath the Subdivision.

I woke to light, and to the thumping of the boat against the bank; we had arrived at another station. It appeared identical to the one we had disembarked from, save for a different mosaic on the wall; this one read THE TESS. Justine was waiting there in her stained caftan, arms full; as she climbed in I could see that she was carrying a small pile of paintings, stacked on top of a large piece of sod. Dirt rained from the roots as she staggered to the back of the gondola; clearly uninterested in socializing, she took the sole single-occupancy bench wedged into the stern. She lowered the paintings, steadied by their little square of lawn, onto her lap, and gazed off into the darkness, pointedly avoiding eye contact with the other passengers.

Eventually the gondola reached the platform marked GUEST-HOUSE. Clara and the Judge were waiting there, the former holding the little boy's hand, the latter tapping her foot, arms crossed over her chest. Mr. Lorre stood behind them with a new bouquet clutched in his hand; he stared into space in evident puzzlement. The Judge strode impatiently over to him as the gondola pulled up, and plucked at his coat. Reluctantly, he trudged to the water's edge.

Mr. Lorre and the ladies took the remaining available benches. The little boy wordlessly came to me and climbed onto my lap. His thumb was in his mouth, and his other hand clutched his extinguished flashlight.

"I have something for you," I said, opening my bag, which still contained a wide variety of flashlight batteries. The little boy peered in. Cylvia stirred but didn't wake. "I didn't know which battery would fit, so I got them all."

"You have a bird," he mumbled around the thumb.

"Don't wake her," I warned.

The little boy took the thumb out of his mouth and carefully picked a battery out of the nest. He shook his head at me. "She's not *asleep*," he said, scowling. "She isn't *born* yet." He unscrewed the cap from the end of the flashlight and dropped the battery in; a moment later, he was shining its beam around the cave's roof, revealing stalactites and the dangling roots of trees.

I craned my neck to greet the ladies, who leaned tiredly against each other in the gloom. "Do you know where we're going?" I asked.

"Beats us," the Judge said.

"We waited out the last storm in the basement," Clara added. "But we thought this would be best for our guests."

"What she won't tell you is that she mostly just wanted to see what was down here," the Judge said, rolling her eyes.

"Oh, well, didn't you?" Clara asked her.

"I admit I did."

"It's quite a change of pace, isn't it."

"Whoop-de-do," the Judge said with a shrug.

The gondola continued through the darkness for some time, I couldn't say how long. There was something about the experience— the mingled sounds, the rocking of the boat, the rich scents of earth and stone and water, and the closeness of the only people, for better or worse, I knew in this place—that seemed to make time itself irrelevant. It felt as though all experiences existed together, simultaneously, like batteries in a handbag or puzzle pieces arranged on a table. As I pictured these things, in my mind—the batteries and the puzzle pieces—they seemed to strike me as hopelessly poignant, and I was mildly surprised to realize that I was crying.

"What has happened to me?" I asked the darkness. "Why can't I remember anything?"

But no one responded, because I hadn't actually said it out loud. I dried my eyes with the cuff of my cardigan, and idly stroked the little boy's head. I supposed that everyone was right, after all. I supposed that he was mine.

Twenty-Two

I didn't know how long we'd been asea when I felt the gondola scraping amidships against the river's rocky bank, and roused myself from sleep. A glance at my fellow passengers suggested that they, too, had been sleeping; they rubbed their eyes and stretched. The gondolier, having brought us to a halt, now fastened his craft to a wooden piling, one of several that supported a small dock, using a length of rope, or I suppose line, as maritime parlance would have it. Spryly, he climbed out of the gondola, and I expected that he would turn and assist the rest of us. But to my surprise, he ambled his way a few feet farther down the bank, pulled a pack of cigarettes out of his jacket pocket, and lit one up.

Helpfully, or perhaps to get away from Forby, Bruce climbed out, then offered a hand to each of us, in turn. Before long, we were all standing on yet another tiled platform, staring around in wonder.

Unlike the other three we had seen, this platform did not terminate in a solid wall punctuated by a steel door. Instead, the rear wall of the platform consisted of windows, a long bank of them, behind which dozens of people sat at long, narrow tables. Each was poised before an electric typewriter, and beside each typewriter stood a small speaker. Even from here, on the other side of the windows, it was possible to make out the collective squawk of the speakers and the clatter of the typewriters. But when we passed through the revolving door that separated the platform from the workers (the ordinarily imperious little boy shared my wedge of door, and stayed very close, anxiety creasing his small face), the noise became deafening.

The room was large, easily thirty yards on each side, and appeared to have been designed and outfitted many years in the past. The walls were composed of pale yellow fabric panels, the ceiling of stained and sagging stucco. A drab brown carpet lay underneath our feet. Across the room from where we all stood, a heavy steel door like the others was marked WINDSTORM SANCTUARY. But to reach it, we would have to walk between the rows of workers.

I peered over my shoulder at my companions. They appeared confused, everyone but Mr. Lorre. Perhaps the situation was analogous, in his mind, to the heavy traffic he used to drive through. In any event, he muscled his way to where the boy and I stood, passed us, and, with a nod to our group, began to make his bullish way down one of the aisles, rose petals falling to the floor behind him. After a moment's hesitation, we followed.

My concern that we might bother the workers proved unfounded. If they noticed us at all, they showed no sign; they were too focused on the work at hand even to look up. I realized, now that I could see them up close, that the speaker boxes were siblings of the transistor radios in the guesthouse. I didn't wish to linger, and the little boy was running ahead, trying to keep up with Mr. Lorre. But I couldn't help but notice that the radios were telling stories, much like the hamster one I had heard emanating from Mr. Lorre's room that night, and that the workers were using the typewriters to transcribe them. Each transcriber had a little pile of paper beside them, presumably representing that day's work.

As I passed among them, I made a point of listening in, or peering over their shoulders at their completed transcriptions.

". . . because Mother was upset with Father, and forgot to check in on me . . ."

". . . pushed Erica into the mud and blamed me for it and I got detention . . ."

". . . couldn't hold it for a moment longer and wet myself . . ."

". . . didn't want him to touch me there but I didn't want to seem cold . . ."

". . . walked out right in front of me and I came just an inch from hitting him . . ."

". . . so drunk I couldn't find my car, which was a good thing because . . ."

". . . put the comic book into her jeans and dared me to do it so I did . . ."

". . . for looking at Janet's test, but I was only making sure she wasn't copying me . . ."

". . . said, 'No, *she's* the lesbian,' and everyone laughed, and I still feel guilty . . ."

". . . afraid of the mechanic when the truck pulled up, and he could tell . . ."

I recognized the voice of the storyteller too; it was the same woman who had told the hamster story.

We reached the door, and Mr. Lorre buffaloed his way through. Soon we were all gathered in the Windstorm Sanctuary, and the door fell shut behind us, abruptly cutting off the noise of the transcription floor.

I wasn't sure what I was expecting—something like a military field hospital, perhaps, with rows of cots, nurses moving among them. But the reality of the Windstorm Sanctuary was quite different. It resembled nothing so much as a hotel bar, with comfortable armchairs and sofas—the same style, in fact, as the ones in the Courthouse employee lounge—arranged around a gas fireplace. A dartboard was positioned in a corner, beside a chalkboard evidently used for keeping score. From a jukebox issued some lugubrious orchestral pop music of the indeterminate past.

And then there was the bar itself: dark and lacquered, it spanned one entire wall of the shelter, and was illuminated by discreet ceiling lights, and by the truly enormous backlit glass shelving unit that held all the liquor. The only person in the room besides our group was the bartender, who was dressed in a casual medical uniform, a stethoscope slung rakishly around his neck beneath a scruffy beard and welcoming smile. While he waited for us to approach, he washed and dried highball glasses, occasionally pretending to listen to one with the stethoscope, in a kind of visual pun.

At the end of the bar, a television screen hung on the wall. It was tuned to a news channel, which broadcast video clips of the weather conditions aboveground. The word LIVE flashed in a corner of the screen, while trees toppled, windows shattered, and garbage cans flew through the air.

"Well, this isn't what I expected," the Judge said. It was the most cheerful I'd heard her sound in some time.

"It's very nice!" Clara replied. "I wonder if it's possible to get down here when the weather's fine."

Forby was walking around in a daze; he settled on one of the sofas nearest the fire. Mr. Lorre joined him, and soon the two were deep in conversation. Bruce was looking at his wrist, where I assumed there was usually a watch, though there wasn't one there now. Justine had cleaved to Heather, who now led her over to the bar. They spoke to the bartender, who soon poured them large glasses of red wine.

"Do you want something to drink?" I asked the little boy.

He nodded. I took his hand and helped him onto a barstool, then sat down beside him.

"Hello, ma'am," the bartender said, in a flirtatious tone. "Can you hear my voice?"

I laughed. "Yes," I said. I was trying to sound husky or intimate, I suppose, but it just came out hoarse.

"It's important that you try not to move. All right?"

"Yes."

"My name is Jeremy," the bartender said. He wasn't kidding—

a very realistic red-and-white identification badge was clipped to his shirt pocket, identifying him by name. It bore the caduceus, the familiar symbol of the medical professional, along with a photo of his face. "Can you tell me your name?"

It was on the tip of my tongue, my name; I really did want to tell him. But I was distracted by a strange anxiety—a gnawing sense that, in spite of what had just happened in the Dead Tower, the bakemono was near. It wasn't fear I felt for him, though, but worry, as though he might be in danger, and that I was responsible for helping him. I peered around the room, half-expecting to see him sprawled on the floor, drunk, a pool of cabernet sauvignon spreading from his unconscious form. Instead, I saw only my various companions, seemingly enjoying themselves. Clara, I noticed, was impressing everyone with her facility for solving the cube puzzle—her party trick had found its party at last.

"Try not to move your head, ma'am," Jeremy said. "Can you tell me where you are right now?" He'd produced, from somewhere, a hooked metal pole on wheels, of the sort they use in hospitals for intravenous drugs, and attached a bag of clear liquid to it. The bag was marked VODKA. He brought a glass up from under the bar, and inserted the hose attached to the vodka bag. "See if you can answer me without moving your head."

"I don't know!" I admitted, and tried to draw attention away from my anxiety with a wink.

But I was beginning to understand. The bakemono was no longer my responsibility, nor anyone else's. He was gone from this world, and if he was anywhere at all, well, that was his problem now. I felt relief, of course, but also sadness. It was almost possible to remember the sense of potential, the excitement I'd experienced when we first met—not at the cottage, in the probability well, but before that, in a place very far from here that I could not quite bring to mind.

Not that I knew precisely where I was now, or why. But I did know where I had to go. Underneath the cover of the bar, I reached over and took the little boy's hand in mine. He squeezed back.

Jeremy, meanwhile, returned my wink and brought another bag

up from a small refrigerator; this one vigorously effervesced and was marked TONIC. He inserted its hose into the glass, too, and adjusted the valves to let the liquids flow in. When the mixture was right, he added some ice cubes and a wedge of lime. He pushed the glass toward me with a smile, and said, "Ma'am, are you with child?"

My instinct was to deny it—but that, I reminded myself, was over now. I tilted my head at the little boy. "Yes, yes, he's with me."

"All right. Just stay calm, ma'am. We're gonna get you and your baby out of here as soon as we can."

"No rush!" I replied, raising my glass.

Jeremy exchanged a few words with the little boy, and a minute later served him a large tumbler of milk. Meanwhile, I was watching the television screen, where the weather news was still being broadcast. A chyron at the bottom of the screen read, WINDSTORM CLEARS ROAD TO CITY. A shaky handheld camera showed the underpass down the street from the probability well, the one that had been blocked by pylons, a backhoe, and a fence. These items had been blown away, it seemed, allowing passage at last. In addition, it was clear that the windstorm had abated, and the news crew was moving freely about, filming the damage and interviewing people—specifically, the bus driver who had protected me from the bakemono. The sound was off, but the caption read, ROUTE TO CITY TO OPEN SOON.

The child and I sipped our drinks and watched the news, until I felt a tap on my shoulder. It was the Judge. "Storm's over," she said. "They're telling us we can go up now."

She sounded a bit skeptical, as though she wanted to linger. But Clara, who'd come up behind her, laid a hand on my shoulder and said, "I'm sure you'll want to continue on to the City."

"Oh yes, of course," I replied. My tenure at the Courthouse had been a pleasant one, and I'd accomplished a great deal. But my work there was done. I didn't know what awaited me in the City, but I was sure I'd find out when I got there.

I climbed down from my barstool, and the little boy followed.

The bartender, who had returned to washing glasses, noticed our movements, and turned to us. "Stay with me, ma'am!" he said. "Stay with me!"

"You know I'd like to," I said, shyly. "But it's time for me to leave."

He replied with a teasing grin. "We're losing her," he said to himself, in mock dismay.

The others had gathered at the end of the bar, where a red velvet curtain was hanging, illuminated by a single spotlight. The Judge parted the curtain, revealing a freight elevator, its doors open, ample enough to accommodate us all. We stepped inside, and the Judge pressed the UP button. The doors closed, a mighty clank issued from beneath the floor, and the elevator rose.

It rose for a long time—I don't know how long—then stopped and lurched sideways, and then down, and then sideways, and up again. The little boy's hand was moist and warm in mine, and the elevator rocked and hummed and changed direction, and I may have slept on my feet for a little while. Forby, hopelessly broken, said, "Maybe she *didn't* do it—maybe *I* did it. Maybe *I'm* the one who did it. *She* couldn't have done it," and Mr. Lorre repeated a low, quiet sound that might have been his wife's name, or perhaps he was just snoring.

Eventually the elevator stopped. Everyone sighed as the doors parted, and we all filed out. We were standing in a basement room, boxes piled upon boxes, a musty-smelling clothing rack, a dressmaker's dummy, a crate of dusty athletic trophies. We followed Clara and the Judge up a narrow flight of stairs, and emerged at the top in their kitchen.

The guesthouse had survived the storm. A lamp or two had fallen over, and rainwater from somewhere had dripped into the sitting room, but the place was otherwise unharmed. Bruce clambered back downstairs and returned with the drill; he intended to stick around and help the ladies usher the daylight back in. Heather found some dish towels and lay them down over the rainwater.

But for me, it was time to say goodbye. Bruce, Heather, Justine, and Forby stumbled out the door, into the bright daylight. The clouds were gone and the sky was blue again; the day was warm and the air smelled fresh. It seemed to be morning.

"Your bus will be here shortly," Clara said to me. "You'd better gather your things."

"You're taking the boy, I hope," the Judge added.

"Of course!" I said.

"Oh, but what about Mr. Lorre!" Clara exclaimed. We'd forgotten about him for a moment. He was still in the kitchen, as it happened; we found him standing at the side door, clutching his bouquet, which was nearly denuded of petals after the ordeal of the evacuation.

"Mr. Lorre," the Judge asked him sternly, "are you ready? Are you ready to go to the City?"

"Anna," Mr. Lorre muttered. "My deliveries . . ."

"Maybe we should hang on to him a little longer," the Judge said with a groan.

But I surprised myself by saying, "No, I'll take him with me."

"Are you sure, dear?" Clara asked, clearly trying to keep the relief out of her voice.

"I'm sure," I said. It was true: I was ready to take responsibility, both for the little boy and for Mr. Lorre, no matter what awaited us in the City. With the bakemono truly gone, I felt stronger, more able to do some good for people who were able to accept it.

"Well, you'd all better pack," the Judge said, ushering us toward the stairs.

I felt a movement at my side. I thought it was the little boy, trying to get my attention, but he'd run ahead, presumably to retrieve his beloved books on cocktails and law humor from the attic. The movement was coming from my bag.

I guided Mr. Lorre into his room, and instructed him to prepare to leave. After a moment, he seemed to get the message, and opened up his carpetbag on the floor. I crossed the hall to my own room, the room called Mercy, and closed the door behind me.

I set my bag down on the bed and unzipped it. Cylvia lay there, her black eyes open and blinking. Her beak clacked, and she began to struggle against the batteries, as though trying to escape.

Gently, I lifted her out. She was complete. I felt her heart beating and understood that she could no longer communicate with me through human language. She was just an ordinary bird. I set her upright on the bedside table, in her customary spot. She wobbled a bit on her white feet, and shook herself, spread out her wings, bounced up and down. Her beak clacked again.

My door opened. It was the little boy. He saw Cylvia and said, "She's born!"

"Yes," I said.

"We can't keep her," he told me sternly.

"I agree."

The boy set down his things—the flashlight and books—on the bed beside my bag, and went to the window. He tried to open it, but he was too small. I reached over the table to help him, and together we heaved up the sash. Cylvia watched with obvious interest, and when we backed away, she leaped up onto the lamp with an awkward flap of her wings. The lamp rocked on the tabletop and nearly toppled, but I reached out to steady it. Cylvia clacked her beak again, then let out a series of clicks—a rattle, really—before hopping onto the windowsill and peering about. A moment later, I heard a caw from outside. It was the crow, the black one. It was no longer paying attention to me. It descended to the window and greeted Cylvia with a series of bobs. Cylvia responded in kind. She flexed her wings, fluttered them. The black crow flickered in and out of sight; Cylvia shook herself, hopped, and began to flicker as well. Soon their flickering fell into sync. Whatever they were seeing—I couldn't know what it was—they were seeing it together now.

Cylvia didn't say goodbye. She had forgotten I was even there. The black crow launched itself into the air and Cylvia followed, stumbling at first, dropping below the windowsill; but soon she had risen again, and met the black crow, and the two flew off together without a glance back. They flickered again, then once more, and at last winked out of view entirely.

Once they were gone, I returned my possessions to my duffel. It didn't take long. "Are we going to ride the bus now?" the little boy asked me.

"We are. But first we need to get Mr. Lorre."

Mr. Lorre hadn't made much progress—he was staring, mystified, at his carpetbag. The little boy and I helped him place his things inside it, and within a few minutes we were all making our way down the stairs.

Clara and the Judge were waiting by the open door. While they embraced the little boy and Mr. Lorre, I looked over at the dining room table. To my surprise, the puzzle was gone. In its place lay a large cardboard box, a bit dusty, stamped with the familiar black-and-white interlocking logo of the Birdwich Games Company. 8,000-PIECE DELUXE MUTABLE SITUATION-SPECIFIC MATTE-FINISH BILATERAL THETA-CARDBOARD PUZZLE read the legend on its lid. Where one might expect to see a miniature completed puzzle framed by a double white line, there was printed instead a "mystery" image that consisted of a generic landscape overlaid by a cluster of question marks in various typefaces.

"Oh yes, we found the box!" Clara exclaimed, noticing my gaze.

"Fat lot of good it would have done you," the Judge added.

Now Clara wrapped her arms around me. "Goodbye, dear!" she cried, through tears. "We'll miss you!"

If the Judge agreed with that sentiment, she didn't show it, but she did embrace me for a long time. "Good luck in the City," she said.

"Would the two of you like to come?"

The Judge managed a smile, though it was clear she found the question foolish. "No, no. We'll stay here."

"It's where we belong," Clara added.

We all heard Bus Negative One before we saw it: it coughed and clanked its way down the ladies' street, growing louder by the second.

Soon it pulled up in front of the guesthouse, greasy black smoke pouring from its chimney.

"Goodbye!" the ladies said.

"Goodbye!" I said.

"Goodbye!" said the little boy.

Even Mr. Lorre seemed to understand that something was happening; though he didn't speak, he raised his handful of bare, thorny twigs, as though in farewell. The three of us shouldered our bags and walked out the door and down the steps; the bus doors unfolded before us. The driver was there, in his purple shirt, black tuxedo, and sunglasses, and he nodded as we entered and found our way to our seats.

We didn't speak as the bus pulled away. The little boy held my hand and we gazed together out the window. Mr. Lorre, in the seat behind us, did the same. The bus took a circuitous route to the City: past the bakery, the Courthouse; past the Tess and Fortuitous Items. Mr. Lorre let out a quiet sob as we approached the florist, and the child squeezed my hand tighter as Birthday House came into view. For my part, I tried to gird myself against seeing the bakemono's cottage again: Was he really gone? What if he were there? Would he notice my face in the window? Would he try one last time to seduce me?

But my worries were for naught: the house had vanished, as though scooped up by a giant hand and tossed unceremoniously away. All that remained, besides the sidewalk and dead apple tree, was a gaping hole in the ground, shimmering slightly, leaking the last of its probabilistic energy into the air.

The bus turned onto the road to the City. The pavement had been scrubbed clean by the storm: the orange snow fence, the danger sign, the traffic barrels and construction machine were all gone, as the news had reported. Our driver didn't slow down; he accelerated through the tunnel and into the landscape beyond. I heard the little boy draw a sudden breath. The City was visible in the distance, and the hills in the haze behind it; and at the side of the road stood a wooden billboard, or the remains of one, hopelessly scoured and torn and broken. The bus approached it, came abreast of it, and roared by, and it looked as though it had once said something vitally important, but I couldn't have told you what.

Acknowledgments

Thank you: Katrina Carpenter, Brian Hall, Shane Kowalski, Oliver Lennon, Ling Ma, Stephanie Meissner, Ethan Nosowsky, Adam Price, Elizabeth Watkins Price, Jim Rutman, Lauren Schenkman, Ed Skoog, and everyone at Graywolf Press, the greatest publishing house on earth. Also, belated thanks to Zoe and Dom Venditozzi, whose house I finished writing the last book in, then forgot to thank them in the back; and Steven Strogatz, who told me how many atoms there are in a tennis ball.

J. Robert Lennon is the author of eight previous novels, including *Broken River* and *Familiar*, and three story collections, *Let Me Think*, *Pieces for the Left Hand*, and *See You in Paradise*. He lives in Ithaca, New York.

The text of *Subdivision* is set in Adobe Garamond Pro. Book design by Ann Sudmeier. Composition by Bookmobile Design & Digital Publisher Services, Minneapolis, Minnesota. Manufactured by McNaughton & Gunn on acid-free, 100 percent postconsumer wastepaper.